Peter and Paul Lalonde

▲

REVELATI⊕N
...the Book has been opened.

▲

▲

▲

Copyright ©1999 by Peter and Paul Lalonde
All rights reserved

Design: Peter Wing / Julia Blushak

Published by This Week In Bible Prophecy
P.O. Box 1440, Niagara Falls, New York 14302
P.O. Box 665, Niagara Falls, Ontario L2E 6V5

▲   ▲   ▲

Canadian Cataloguing in Publication Data

Lalonde, Peter
    Revelation: the Book has been opened

ISBN 0-9680758-6-X

I. Lalonde, Paul, 1961- II. Title.

PS3562.A5R49 1999   813'.54   C99-900053-5

Printed in Canada

To Mom and Dad...
for teaching us to believe.

▲

CHAPTER 1

▲

The Subversives

▲

▲

▲

▲

The man positioned himself behind some trees in a small wooded lot at the end of a recently developed cul de sac. It was the school bus' last stop, just three children living in the houses that had been built over the last couple of years. They were moderately sized but richly appointed—"Up Scale For The Average Family" the advertising proclaimed. And relatively speaking they were inexpensive, just not inexpensive enough for the residents to make ends meet without two jobs. The children getting off the bus each had a neck chain from which hung a house key. And inside each home, resting by the telephone, was a sheet of paper with their parents' telephone numbers at work, the emergency numbers for fire and police departments, the number for the poison control center, and the name and telephone numbers of their families' pediatricians. It would be another hour before any adults returned to the neighborhood, and by then he would be gone.

The man had a high-powered air rifle with telescopic sight. It was designed for shooting small game in relative silence, though the one he carried had been modified for greater velocity and penetration. It could kill a man at 25 feet, something he had proven for himself more than once. Today no one needed to die. This was the reason he had chosen a location without witnesses. Instead he planned to cripple the school bus long enough to examine the under carriage without arousing suspicion. The bus he had targeted was the same make and model, and though he had been able to learn about the construction from an engineer friend, he needed to know the exact spot where he could attach an explosive device. That required physically getting underneath the bus and that was why he had brought the rifle to the cul de sac.

Bracing himself against a tree, carefully aiming the rifle, he waited until the last of the children was heading towards his front door and the bus was pulling out of the development. The dart shot straight into his target, the side of the right rear tire, penetrating deeply. There would be a slow leak, the bus traveling a mile or more before the driver would experience handling difficulty that would cause him to stop to check. By then he should be able to catch up with him, posing as a Good Samaritan.

The man buried the rifle under a tree, covering it with leaves and rocks and dirt. He'd come back later for it, but this way he would not arouse suspicion as he cut through the woods to the other side of the development where his car was parked. He already knew the bus' route back to the holding area, knew that if he hurried, he should get to the bus before the driver could limp to the garage or call for a tow.

It took five minutes for the man to reach his car, five minutes more to find the bus whose tire was older and more worn than he had imagined. He had struck an area where the pressure of the dart caused the tire to explode only a couple of blocks from where he had fired the dart. The driver had been going slowly enough to remain in control, working the bus to the side of the road where he turned on his flashers and was standing, looking at the damage.

"Looks like you got a problem," the man said after stopping his car behind the bus. He got out of the car and walked to where the bus driver was surveying the damage.

"I kept asking them at the garage to check the tires," said the driver. "Check the tires. They buy us seconds to keep school costs down. Never think about what could happen if something like this occurred with a bus load of kids."

The man dropped to the ground, lay on his back, and looked at the tire damage, pretending that was his reason for stopping. He put his hand underneath, feeling the surface. The blast would tear into the undercarriage, lifting the bus, sending shards of metal through the interior. If he were lucky, the proper placement would mean none of the children inside would escape without being wounded. Every parent would be grief stricken, and the news media would have the lead story of carnage they so loved to show at the top of the hour.

He found the area he was looking for, feeling for heat and grease. There were only a couple of ways to quickly attach the device and he needed to assure himself one of them would work without the bomb falling off before it could be triggered. Then, having satisfied himself he could do the job he had been ordered to do, he sat back up and said, "The only problem's the tire. Lucky you weren't going very fast or you'd have broken an axle getting it stopped. You call for a tow yet?"

"Yeah. Guy came by with a car phone. Let me call the garage so they can send a tow truck.

"You know a lot about these things. You a mechanic?"

"Worked my way through school in a shop that took care of rigs like this. Been out of it for years, but you don't lose the touch. That's why I know you've just got a bad flat. Anyway, there's nothing more I can do. If you're okay, I'll be on my way."

"Thanks for stopping and checking," said the driver. "Most people wouldn't get themselves all dirty like that just to help a stranger."

"Hey, we're all in this world together, you know what I mean?" the man said, getting back into his car, then merging with the flow of traffic.

▲

Thorold Stone tried to pretend he was lost in

thought over the latest information memo from Overlord Parker. Not that he was fooling anyone as he passed through the O.N.E. agents' locker room. They had all received the same memo, the one discussing maintenance procedures and personal use regulations for assigned patrol cars. Still, if he was lucky, neither he nor his partner, David Smith, would have to endure the...

"Hey, Stone, heard about your big bust today."

The voice was Lloyd Jemison's, the biggest joker in the department. Stone ignored him.

"Overlord Parker should give you guys a medal for taking out all those Haters."

"We made the world a better place for the Messiah," murmured Smith, glancing at Jemison, then pretending to be interested in the same material Stone was finding so fascinating.

"How big a bust was it? Ten Haters? Twelve?"

"It was twelve and Crazy Annie," called Sam Goldfarb from across the room. "Lady Jesus and her disciples. I was there when they brought them in. Her 'congregation' smelled like they hadn't bathed in weeks. You could get drunk just inhaling the same air they were breathing. How long did it take you to fumigate the van, guys?"

"They were creating a public nuisance," mumbled Thorold. "Uniformed should have handled it like they've done with her in the past when she stops taking her medication. We got the call only because she had a Bible this time. That made it a felony. You got a problem, I'll tell dispatch to give it to you guys the next time the old lady leaves her pills at home and goes crazy."

"Touchy. Touchy. Not a nice attitude in these glorious times of the Messiah. You know what Overlord Parker says about our jobs. We're like the representatives of the big man himself when we help the people cleanse the streets in preparation for the Day of Wonders. We each have to pull our own weight. If you had to go arrest Crazy Annie this time…"

"She had a Bible, remember? She also had a few old religious tracts," said Smith, angrily. "Section 1411 of the Revised Code. You can check it if you guys ever learn how to read. Said she stumbled on them when she awakened in a Dumpster and decided she had a calling. She wandered the streets until she came on a bunch of guys who were crazier out of their minds than Annie ever gets, then began preaching to them. Probably never opened the book, but Parker's going to want us to go door to door in the area she described to see who was keeping such things instead of turning them in or burning them. Maybe Crazy Annie stumbled on a cache left by militant Haters and we'll find their hideout. You guys laugh now because then we'll come out smelling like heroes."

"Just so you don't smell like those glassy eyed drunks Crazy Annie thought were her spiritual followers," said Jemison.

"Face it, guys," called Goldfarb. "Any of us got the call instead of you two, you'd be teasing us unmercifully. You followed procedure and now you get to go to court to show why One Nation Earth is a better place for the Messiah's Day of Wonders because you two did your duty."

"They'll get a medal for sure," laughed Jemison. "Maybe they'll even be allowed to use Overlord Parker's parking space for a week."

Thorold felt like punching someone. He knew Overlord Parker would have Crazy Annie locked away someplace where she would be forced to take her anti-psychotic medication until she was stable again. The twelve drunks would be tossed in the holding tank until they dried out. Probably not a one of them ever thought of being a Hater. As for the Bible, he'd bet that when Annie was back on her pills, she wouldn't be able to remember in which Dumpster she'd found the thing, making it all an exercise in futility. And for that, he and Dave would have to write up thirteen separate arrest reports and spend at least a day in court telling the same story over and over again to the judge.

Stone and Smith hurriedly walked out the door to the police parking lot. It was late, after ten p.m., and they wanted to get home. Smith had a wife who was waiting. Stone had a six pack of beer, his VCR, and too many memories to try and forget. That was why they didn't pay attention to the two men in suits who were driving in to the back entrance of the One Nation Earth Headquarters Building. It was an area used only by maintenance, cleaning, and other support personnel. That was why he did not think about the fact that, at that hour, the only person who was authorized to be back there was Fiona Carsters, supervisor of the large laundry room which handled the cleaning of uniforms for janitors, bus maintenance workers, and similar personnel. Even if he had, he might have assumed that whoever was driving the car was picking her up at the end of her workday. He would not have realized that had he been less self-absorbed at the moment, he might have prevented the tragedy that would affect so many lives.

▲

"Did you see who it was?" asked one of the two men in the dark sedan as they pulled into the O.N.E. maintenance area parking lot, their headlights off. They had unscrewed the dome light in their car so they could open the door without being seen.

"Looked like Thorold Stone, I'm surprised he didn't swing back to take a closer look. Since he lost his family, he's tried to be Super Cop. Works long hours. Never lets himself be off duty. Sticks his nose into everything going on around him to keep his mind off what happened to his wife and kids."

"That type usually ends up eating his gun."

"Well, he hasn't yet, so count your blessings. We'd have to delay our mission if he spotted us and came to investigate. Or we'd have to kill him and that would draw too much attention to us. Just be thankful he's having an off day."

"I suppose. Still, that was a lot closer than I like."

"Couldn't be helped. Those guys are supposed to have their shift change earlier or later. Stone must have made a late bust and been swamped with the paperwork. Probably didn't even notice us."

The men left their car. One carried an attaché case. The other took a miniature camera, an old Minox, from a small leather case on his belt. He attached a tiny but powerful flash attachment to the top, then advanced the film so it was ready to take a picture.

The man with the attaché case stood by the hinged side of the employee exit door nearest the laundry. The man with the Minox positioned himself so that when the door opened, he could grab the person coming out. They had to grab the door and get inside before it closed and locked. Otherwise they'd need an identification card to re-enter. That would set off a surveillance signal to the building's central monitoring system, activating internal cameras. They dared not have that happen until they left.

Fiona Carsters saw the blinding flash of light exploding in her face, then felt the shock of hands grabbing her, one covering her mouth so tightly her teeth cut against her lip, the other wrapped around her arms, pushing her back inside the laundry area. There were two of them, she realized, as she was pushed roughly against the wall. Her arms were wrenched behind her back; her wrists tied with a rope. A thick cloth was looped over her head, pulled between her teeth, and bound behind her neck. A second cloth was secured over her eyes. Unable to speak or see, she was propelled back into the laundry area, placed on a chair, and more rope was used to bind her ankles.

"We won't be long," said one of the men, as he walked over to the rack of cleaned maintenance uniforms ready to be passed out to the morning shift. He pressed the button that turned the hundreds of uniforms, stopping it when he found his size. The one he removed was a jump suit with O.N.E. Bus Maintenance on the upper left pocket. Then he found another one, a size larger, for his partner.

"This has been starched," the other man complained. "I hate starch. I feel like a robot when I have to put one of these things on."

"Don't complain to me," said the first man. "You've got the person in charge sitting right there. Tell her about it."

"She's a little tied up right now. I don't know if she'll listen."

"Not my problem. Just put on the uniform. We've got work to do."

While the second man dressed, the first man, already in the uniform, his suit neatly folded, opened the attaché case and checked the contents. There were two pairs of gloves, a small bomb, a detonating device, receiver, magnets and duct tape for attaching the unit, a penlight, two remote controls, and spare batteries. They were leaving nothing to chance. "Everything's ready," he said, reaching into a file pocket and removing a Bible with several pages tabbed with Post-It Notes, and a handful of religious tracts discussing children and Jesus. "I'll leave the reading material with Fiona. That way she'll understand why we have to borrow these uniforms like this."

"Don't try to struggle, Fiona," said the second man. "The surveillance cameras will see you when we leave. Somebody will come by for you. In the meantime, relax. You're not going anywhere."

The men gathered their clothing and started to leave. As they reached for the door, the second man turned back and said, "And remember, next time no starch!"

▲

The restaurant was dimly lit, soft jazz enveloping the customers like a warm blanket. It was a place to begin a romance, celebrate the passing years of a committed couple still finding new joy in their relationship, or to mend a broken heart.

The food was like the ambience, prepared with subtle flavors that lingered after the last morsel had been eaten. And the service, though attentive and responsive, never intruded on the privacy needs of the diners.

Overlord Len Parker sat in a booth near the rear, a beautiful blond for his dining companion. She was wearing an expensive designer dress, her hair wrapped in a chignon, a diamond pendant on a gold chain around her neck. She had the elegance of a woman born into money, at home with luxury, the world's finest goods an expected part of her daily life.

"Do you realize I could have you killed if you don't please me," said Parker, holding the woman's hand and looking deeply into her blue eyes that seemed to dance with the flickering of the candle set at the corner of their table.

"Yes, Len, I do," she said, softly. She smiled tenderly at him.

"I could have you killed and no one, not even your father, would dare to question what happened to you."

"That's what I find so exciting about you. My father speaks and 10,000 employees in five countries of the world know their livelihood depends upon what he says. You speak and whole nations tremble at your words." She shivered involuntarily. She felt like a lamb frolicking near a lion, knowing that the moment the lion gets hungry, she could be devoured. To be with such a man brought with it an excitement, a danger, like a moth flitting in and out of a candle flame that at any moment might ignite its wings.

"Do I please you, Overlord Parker?" she asked, teasingly.

"For the moment," he laughed, delighting in this woman who was as amoral as himself. He dated very little any more, saw little reason for it. But that night, with the preparations for the Day of Wonders almost complete, he wanted to relax with someone whose thinking and desires closely matched his own. "You're really very beautiful."

"And you are..." She paused for a moment, trying to think of just the right word. He wasn't handsome exactly, not in the manner of a movie star. Yet he radiated something, a subtle violence barely under control which she found immensely exciting. "...you are the man I've dreamed about all my life."

"You must have very boring dreams."

"On the contrary. It's just that all the other men I know are like Daddy. They have money, but I have money. They have influence, but my name has influence. What they don't have is...forgive me for saying this...a certain ruthless, cold-blooded attitude towards others. Not in a bad way. It is a trait so important that those rare individuals who possess it have been known to change the world."

"It's the nature of my job, I'm afraid," said Parker.

"It's the nature of the man, you, Len Parker. The job exists because of who you are, not the other way around."

Parker shrugged.

"Have you ever personally killed a Hater?" she asked.

"Yes," he whispered, softly.

"In jail or on the street during an arrest?"

"Both."

"Was it self-defense? Did you have to kill them?"

"Sometimes it was self-defense. Most times it wasn't. Does that trouble you?"

"No. I find it delicious. So tell me about this Day of Wonders. If you and I decide to keep seeing each other, will we still be together after the Messiah reveals his plan?"

"I have no idea. Let's just enjoy the moment."

"After dinner will you take me back to your office building and show me where you keep the Haters?"

"It's not a pretty sight," he replied.

"That's what excites me. To have people so deluded, so despicable that whatever is done to hurt them doesn't seem quite enough. Isn't this a wonderful time in which we're living?" she said happily as the server brought their food.

▲

They left their car outside the fence, then stepped across the padlocked chain that served to protect the buses. The storage area was low security. There were no cameras, no alarms. Just a high chain link fence open at the driveway, the entrance chained and padlocked at night so the buses could not be driven off the grounds. No one thought about someone coming in to attach a bomb. No one thought someone would ever endanger the lives of children.

The uniforms the men had stolen were a precaution. O.N.E. personnel would have no interest in anything taking place around the garage, but the security service that covered the maintenance yards might have someone patrolling nearby. More likely the person was making rounds and thinking about where to take a nap. Nothing ever happened in most of the maintenance yards except an occasional vandal with a can of spray paint. Still, if the men looked right they knew they would not be hassled.

The bomb was attached near the rear axle. "Got to make certain it's high enough so it clears the ground," said the smaller of the two men. He had slid underneath the bus while his partner stooped down, holding the flashlight so he could see to work. He was using a combination of a powerful magnet and the tape to secure the explosive, detonator, and electronic receiver. "Otherwise they're liable to roll over a rock or curb and knock it off."

"You're sure it can't go off accidentally? I don't like the way you're banging around under there."

"I'm using a variation of plastique. You could bake it in bread the way the French resistance did during World War II without it exploding. You could roll it into a ball and play catch with it. Even though this is a new formula, the stability's the same. That's why it's always been popular with terrorists."

"You sure you've got enough with all this?"

"You wouldn't want to be sitting within ten feet of this when it goes off. As heavy as a school bus is, this stuff is stronger."

"And you're sure it will work?"

"Yes. I used it enough times when I was trained in the military. But don't worry. If it doesn't, no one's going to find this baby until somebody has to work on the undercarriage. If it doesn't go off, we'll take it off tomorrow night and try something else. Remember that it doesn't matter when we kill the children. We just have to make certain they die."

▲

The maitre d' was apologetic as he approached the table where Len Parker was dining. "Mr. Parker, we have a telephone message for you. Apparently your cell phone wasn't working. I was told it is important." He handed Parker the paper with a number written on it.

"I have to have a cell phone for my work," he said to his companion. "But that doesn't mean I have to leave on the ringer when I'm dining with a beautiful woman." He glanced at the message, then said, "Would you mind if I made this one call. I'm afraid it might be important."

"Far be it for me to interfere with the man helping to determine the fate of the world."

"It's probably not that dire," he said, smiling as

he punched in the number.

"Parker, here. What is it?" he said into the phone, listening for several moments.

"Yes, it is curious that they'd go to all that trouble to steal two bus maintenance uniforms. But you're right. What they left with the woman must mean they're haters. Ask the day shift commander to have the patrols check for vandalism wherever the workers wear those jumpsuits. But I wouldn't get overly concerned. It sounds like the Carsters woman got the worst of it. Let her know I'll arrange for her to get a couple of days off with pay if she feels the need."

"Something serious?" asked the woman when he had again turned off his cell phone.

"More curious. At least two men broke into the O.N.E. laundry area and stole two maintenance worker jump suits."

"A prank?"

"Maybe, but they tied up the woman who works there at night and that seems more serious than a prank. Still, it wasn't much of a theft."

"And for that they had to interrupt your dinner?"

"Whoever did it left a Bible with marked pages. That makes it a Hater crime and that means I have to be alerted the moment the problem is discovered."

"Haters. That's all you hear about on television anymore. Why anyone would want to be a Hater is beyond me. They're such righteous fools. I think they're too poor to really enjoy life, and I guess that makes it kind of sad. I just wish they'd shut up and go away."

"We're trying to handle them. That's why we

have the re-education camps to help the ones who can be saved for the Messiah."

"And that's why we still have capital punishment," she said, wetting her lips and smiling. "Remember, you promised to take me to see the cells where they're kept when we get through with dinner."

▲

CHAPTER 2

▲

The Round-ups

▲

▲

▲

▲

They moved as they had been trained to do, quietly entering the neighborhood from different streets. The mini-van that served as the mobile command post looked like just another vehicle for a large family. The sophisticated communication equipment was hidden in back by tinted windows, the specialized antennas built into the roof in a manner that made them impossible for a casual observer to spot. The specialized weapons they would need if there was unexpected resistance were concealed in a picnic cooler and in shopping bags from the neighborhood supermarket.

The other vehicles were likewise unremarkable

—an older sedan with bumper stickers from various vacation spots, a small station wagon, and a rather battered four wheel drive vehicle. There was nothing to identify them as part of the One Nation Earth Division Four Tactical Strike Force.

The men and women of Division Four had been selected for the tactical unit based both on their skills and on their ability to blend in to the neighborhoods where they operated. The Tactical Unit was diverse enough to have two members in their fifties, two no more than thirty, blacks, whites, a Hispanic woman and an Asian: the type of people you might see in a neighborhood coffee shop on any given morning. Their vehicles moved as though they lived in the area, not hurrying, each so carefully briefed that their actions seemed random, not carefully choreographed.

The oldest couple, a man in his mid-fifties, wearing a rumpled suit and carrying a battered briefcase, and a white haired woman two or three years younger and wearing a simple house dress, walked up the driveway first. If the tenant, one Jack Braxton according to the computer printout, spotted them, they would be taken for harmless salespeople or perhaps someone looking for an address in the neighborhood. But Braxton didn't spot them. Not when they paused in front of a window. Not when the man dropped to one knee, opened his case, took out what looked like a longer version of a flare gun, loaded a shell, and fired at the glass.

As the window exploded inward, shards of glass filled the living room, sending a sleeping German Shepherd yelping into the kitchen, his legs and head bleeding slightly from several tiny cuts. A man, presumably Jack Braxton, emerged from the kitchen just as the shell struck the floor, then exploded with a deafening roar. It was a concussion grenade. The sound was meant to stun and momentarily disable anyone not prepared for it.

The noise was the signal for the others to make their move. Donning bright orange and black O.N.E. caps for easy identification, they raced up the driveway, taking positions in front and back, then kicking in the doors, grabbing the man inside, and throwing him to the ground. He was made to lay face down, his hands stretched out to his sides, his legs crossed at the ankles. As one officer kept his knee in the small of the man's back, a high voltage stun gun was held against the man's shoulder.

The strike force team moved from room to room, weapons drawn, checking for other residents. The dog, which had gone into the kitchen, had recovered enough from his fright to come looking for his master. Seeing the man on the floor, he bared his teeth, growled, and slowly advanced towards the strangers.

In a corner of the room, Agent Jane Kilman was opening drawers to a desk, which held a computer, a small stereo unit, and a book filled hutch. When she heard the dog, she turned, swiftly aiming her handgun at the animal and firing a single round to its head. The dog dropped instantly. The man on the floor screamed and started to rise until the officer holding him down squeezed the trigger of his electronic device. The man convulsed wildly, his body shaking, his pants suddenly wet from his inability to control himself.

Finding no one else, the team began a methodical search of the house. Desk drawers were emptied, then removed, to see if anything had been hidden behind or beneath them. The lid of the toilet tank was removed, heater vents were opened, and bed mattresses were pulled off and ripped apart to see if anything had been sewn inside. When they were through, the team members found the contraband they had been seeking. It was what Jack Braxton had advertised on the Internet, thinking he was safe from detection. He did not know about the sting operation. He did not know about the "lock back" program O.N.E. internal security technicians had installed to instantly trace the source of anyone making contact with the web site created as a false front for the task force's "Operation Mop-Up."

"There are five, just like he offered," said Agent LeMar Douglas. "Three King James and a couple of New International Versions. Unless he has something on disk, he must not have found any takers for this Hater trash."

"Whatever was on the computer is gone now," said Agent Leonna Debke, laughing. While the others searched, she had set up a powerful electromagnet on the desk by the computer. When she was through running the special wand across every inch of the equipment, all files on the hard drive and disks had been erased.

The five books were placed on the floor of the living room, doused with a flammable liquid, then set on fire. As the team prepared to leave, the agent who had been guarding the man still convulsing on the floor asked, "What about this Braxton? Should we take him in?"

"Leave him," said the unit commander. "If he recovers before the smoke gets too thick in here, his story will be a warning to other Haters."

"And if he doesn't...?" asked the woman who had shot the dog.

"One less Hater," said the unit commander. "One less threat to the Messiah."

▲

They had gone out to cover the story as though it was just another day. The camcorder operator, sound tech, and reporter shot the video, rushed it to the studio and sent it by satellite up-link. The story was edited for airing at six, then updated for the eleven o'clock news. It was just routine....

Except that this time it wasn't routine. That day they knew there would be no six o'clock news. There would be no six o'clock anything. They were acting as trained observers of the last minutes of a world gone mad as they worked on the streets of New York, Los Angeles, Chicago, Toronto, London, Rome, Paris, Tokyo, Moscow, Baghdad, Tel Aviv.... They had assigned themselves the last project they would ever undertake – giving the viewers at home live coverage of their own deaths.

Long and intermediate range ballistic missiles armed with thermonuclear warheads were minutes from vaporizing the wealthiest, most powerful cities in the history of the world. Shorter range missiles armed with deadly nerve gas and biological agents such as anthrax would shortly eliminate the populations of the Middle East, Africa, and much of Asia. The lucky ones would die instantly. The unfortunate few would linger a day, two days, three at the most, their bodies in agonizing pain.

Resistance was futile, yet thousands of heavily armed soldiers moved through Megiddo. Fighter planes swarmed high above the Jezreel Valley. Battle ships and aircraft carriers flew the flags of dozens of nations postured off the coasts of Europe, Africa, Asia, Australia, South America, North America…. It was a show of force the like of which had never before been assembled. Yet with the weapons that had been launched, the armies and navies were as harmless as plastic toys in a child's game of soldiers.

The reporters who had taken to the streets knew all this. They knew that what they were doing would ultimately be meaningless. Yet on that day when death was near, when the future was a nightmare so beyond comprehension that they dared not speak of it, it was the routine to which they turned for comfort. They used their cameras to record the anguish of parents whose children would never grow old, the last stolen kisses of lovers who would never say the holy vows their hearts had made, and the serene faces of the silent ones who, having found reality too horrible to contemplate, had retreated into the false peace of madness.

They did not let themselves think of their own loved ones. They did not let themselves think that in the images they recorded, they were looking into a mirror of the last minutes of the lives closest to their own.

That had been three months ago. Those moments, captured for eternity, had been edited for Franco Macalusso to watch in his private screening room in WNN's corporate headquarters. First came the street interviews, the close-ups of the faces glancing at the reporter, glancing at the sky, looking here and there like rabbits cornered by wolves, desperate for a way to escape, knowing there was none. Then came the larger than life projected image of Macalusso himself emerging from the helicopter transport on the Mount of Olives near the Western Wall of the city of Jerusalem. Even on the screen Macalusso could still feel the heat of that day, remember the sensation of the dry earth being whipped about by the helicopter blades, striking his face like tiny darts until he could move clear of the rotor.

The technical crew had edited the footage to show the missiles bearing down and the faces of fear so intense they seemed to radiate a sour odor that filled the viewing room. Macalusso used a remote control to momentarily freeze the image of an almost toothless old man, his flesh wrinkled like cured cowhide left in the desert sun. Tears swelled his yellow eyes. His mouth was open as if to speak, yet only a cawing sound emerged from his parched throat. His dread seemed almost contagious. As his image filled the screen, Franco Macalusso, now sitting comfortably in the air conditioned building, looked closely at the face and smiled.

It was the fear he had come to treasure when he relived that awesome day, heart-stopping fear so terrible even the strongest of men lost all control. Give them fear and a sense of hopelessness, then remove it ever so slightly and they will give you unwavering loyalty Macalusso had suspected. And that was what he had proven.

Macalusso released the pause button, then watched the image of himself look up at the sky, then at the rapidly approaching missiles. The people of Jerusalem would be able to see the missiles explode before the slower moving sound waves reached what would by then be dead ears. He saw himself once again on the screen, raised his hands above his head and shouted,

"ENOUGH!

"WE WILL HAVE PEACE!"

And then, in what should have been an interlude no greater than the blinking of an eye between life and unimaginable tragedy, there was silence. Air traffic controllers were shown staring at screens where the rapidly moving blips of the unstoppable missiles had vanished. The voices of pilots could be heard stating that the bombs they had been carrying had vanished from their bombers' bays. Soldiers were seen staring in shock as their weapons seemed to vaporize. Political leaders whose desire for power had led them past the point of no return dropped to their knees, weeping like babies.

He stopped the tape then, not needing to see the rest of a story he had scripted himself. Smiling, his spirit refreshed, Macalusso left the room.

▲

They had come together hesitantly that first time. Aunt Naomi and Uncle Ralph were the first to arrive at Jimmy's house. He hadn't been with them for six months or more, not since his vacation when he got to play with their children, his cousins. They had all gone to a county fair, daring each other to go on rides they would have been too afraid to try without such prodding. And they all had fun, so much fun that Jimmy could not understand why they saw so little of each other. "It's just that way in some families," his mother had said, sighing.

The next time they came together, Jimmy knew much had changed. Grandma... Grandma had disappeared. That was the term the kids were told. That was the word his schoolteacher had used when classes began again after what she called the "day of miracles." Everyone was solemn, and when he asked Aunt Naomi if she had brought his cousins, she quietly told him, "Maybe later. This is for grown-ups."

Aunt Naomi's eyes were puffy and red. He knew she had been crying. There was tension in her voice

Aunt Peggy was the next to arrive that day, along with her daughter, his cousin, Jessica. He had rarely seen Aunt Peggy, and he had only vague memories of Jessica taking care of him once when they were all together a long time ago. Now Jessica was eighteen. Having just graduated from high school, she was planning a career as a commercial artist. She had a job as an assistant to an assistant at the local newspaper, and her talk was as boring as that of other adults.

Even Uncle David, usually so willing to get down on the floor to wrestle or go into the family room to play video games, was unusually subdued. "Not today, Jimmy. We grown-ups need to talk," was all he had said that first night.

And talk they did. Jimmy couldn't remember a

time when they had all been together and talked so long. They talked through dinner. They talked in the living room. Long after Jimmy went to bed, they were still going on and on. He knew something was happening, but he could not then understand how that gathering, so different from the last time they had been together, would change his life.

Sometime in the night they stopped talking and made up makeshift beds on sofas and even the floor. His dad made an early morning run to the grocery store for breakfast supplies. Then all of them laughed and joked through a hearty breakfast before going their separate ways.

A "miracle" his mother had called it. "We never got together like this before Grandma...before Grandma disappeared. There were too many quarrels. Grandma was always frustrated with Uncle David who went through too many girlfriends. She didn't understand Aunt Peggy's need to live with men, rather than date them. Sure George had been a big mistake. But did Peggy have to live with all those men to be sure she didn't make the same mistake again!

It was still hard for his mother to discuss the day Grandma disappeared. One minute the older woman had been berating her daughter for refusing to take Jimmy to church on a regular basis. The next minute she was gone, her clothing left in a neat pile on the floor.

"We all thought she was wrong to push her morals on us," Jimmy's mother tried to explain to him. "The Bible was for a different time, for different people, but Grandma couldn't see that. Morality has to change with the times, something she could not understand. She just kept talking about Jesus as a living presence,

29

much like some of the Haters do. I just thank the Messiah for his wonderful lesson showing us that we have progressed too much to even want to have a Bible in our homes. Grandma couldn't understand that all her talk about the false prophet was causing dissension.

"We all miss Grandma, Jimmy, but if the Messiah saw fit to take her, we should learn from that example. There's a New World Order and Grandma…. Well, I'm sure Franco Macalusso would want us to remember her with kindness and compassion. She was influenced by the Haters, would have been one of them if she were still here today. It's no wonder the Messiah removed her from our lives, and I'm sure he's treating her with love wherever…."

His mom had grown silent then, filled with memories of her last argument with Grandma. That one hadn't seemed so bad. The old woman could not understand that her children and grandchildren were of a different time, a different generation. "You lived in a simpler time, Mom," Jimmy's mother had told the old woman. "Daddy worked for the dairy and you stayed home to raise us kids. You made our clothes. You cooked our food. There was Sunday morning church and Sunday afternoon brunch where you made fried chicken for all the relatives. You had a rhythm to your life, rituals that were unchanging because there were no challenges to them. You didn't even answer the telephone when we were eating, and now we're all tied to our cell phones and pagers. There are different demands. We all have fond memories of those days, but the world has moved beyond what you knew, beyond that outdated relic of a book you keep quoting."

His grandmother had been shocked by his mom's comments, especially her flippancy towards the Bible. She had cried, something Jimmy had never seen her do before, and it made him feel badly about his mom's anger. But his mom refused to back down.

"We're slaves to our jobs because we have to be. We've got this big house, and Larry and I each need a car. Jimmy's in Little League and Karate class. He's got his activities fees for school, and the cost of the clothes he has to have...."

"Mom, kids today have to buy what all the other kids are wearing. If their clothing doesn't have the right designer name on it, everyone makes fun of them. It's expensive today. There are so many pressures, so many necessities. That's why Larry and I both have to work. That's why we need Sunday to sleep in, that is until we have to get ready for the Little League game, or Pee-Wee Football, or Junior Soccer, or whatever else is scheduled for that week. Church is just one more appointment I would have to put into my weekly planner, one more stress in an over-crowded week. Frankly it's the one event we can miss.

"You always tell us we need time to rest, and Sunday's the only day I get to sleep in a little longer. We go at Christmas. We go at Easter. We go on those days when we all get up early and there's nothing scheduled."

Then, trying to appease her mother, she added, "I know you'd like us to go more often than we do. Maybe we will when Jimmy's older; maybe when we have more time. It's just not what my generation is all about."

It was an argument her siblings had all had with Grandma. It was an argument they expected would continue for years. Then, suddenly, their mother was gone. Ruth Davis Malone, 72 years old, was a woman who was by all accounts gentle, loving, hard working, caring, a good neighbor, and a good friend. Yet she was also rigid and unyielding when it came to "the word of God." And she had disappeared along with so many others on that awful, yet ultimately glorious day.

After all their talking, well into the night, her children had come together in her absence as they had never done in her life. All the petty jealousies and arguments which had smoldered just beneath the surface of civility for too many years were suddenly meaningless. The world had been on the brink of war. The world had flirted with total annihilation. One minute there was no future. The next minute there was the start of what seemed to be heaven on earth thanks to Franco Macalusso, the Messiah. Yes, many had vanished, but many more had been saved. And because of that glorious day, when the missiles vanished in mid-flight, poison gases were neutralized, and weapons of every kind turned to molten metal, the sons and daughters of Ruth Davis Malone found their common bond. The family was reunited. Love was reborn. Life began anew for them all, or so they truly believed.

None of the family members could remember just who made the suggestion that they ritualize their now regular gatherings. Jimmy thought it was his mom, but his cousin, Linda, said she thought it was Aunt Kate who had been unable to attend the gathering that first night when the talk had been almost solely about Grandma and the others who had disappeared. Whatever the case, they began coming together every Friday night after work, alternating among the homes, letting the children take turns telling the story over a meal whose preparation they all shared in.

That night the gathering was at Jimmy's house. It was his turn to speak during the ceremony. He was ready and proudly answered the questions his Uncle David asked him or the other children each week.

"Why is tonight different from all other nights?" Uncle David would ask. In the middle of the softly glowing candles on the dining room table was a picture of the Messiah, his arms upraised on the Mount of Olives, at the moment he stopped the war. It was a photograph that now hung on the walls of many family homes throughout the world, a photograph that adorned billboards and the sides of buildings. But other than the picture and the new ritual, Jimmy's home had changed little from before. What was different was what his mother called "our own Macalusso Miracle." What was different was the way they all were inside their hearts. No one spoke of adultery, alcoholism, or sin. No one condemned the choices they had made as adults. They respected and accepted one another.

"Why is tonight different from all other nights?" repeated Jimmy. "Tonight we remember the coming of Franco Macalusso."

"Praise his holy name," responded his parents, his cousins, his aunts and uncles.

"Tonight we remember his arrival on the Mount

of Olives," Jimmy continued. "Tonight we remember the soldiers massed for war on the planes of Megiddo, the missiles just moments from their designated targets, the world on the edge of…" Jimmy always stumbled over the next word, even though Uncle David had written out what he called the family liturgy, giving a copy to each of the children so they could practice their turns before they had to speak.

"Oblivion," whispered his dad.

"Oblivion," Jimmy repeated, loudly.

"And who do we remember with sadness?" asked Uncle David.

"Grandma," said Jimmy. "And all the others who disappeared."

"Oh, Messiah, change their immortal souls," the others chanted. "Let them know the truth about your coming. Let them understand how they went astray, and reunite them with us in the New World Order, the time of peace and love."

"We ask this of you, Franco Macalusso, the one who was promised," said Jimmy.

"In your holy name," said the others.

"Now let's eat!" said Uncle David, breaking the solemnity and reaching for a big bowl of mashed potatoes.

▲

They moved about the streets as though they still belonged. One young woman raced on roller blades, as though enjoying a casual morning of exercise in Franco Macalusso Park. A young man dressed for tennis, his racket and balls casually at his side, came from another direction, seemingly oblivious to the woman scooting by him. An elderly man in tattered clothes shuffled as though on a walk to nowhere. A janitor in uniform moved about. A nightclub employee still dressed in low cut blouse, high cut shorts, and thigh high boots, moved rhythmically to some musical beat only she could hear. Each was seemingly unconnected. Each moved as though there was no urgency, no appointed gathering place.

A passer-by might have heard a few words spoken barely above a whisper by these passing "strangers" —"St. Mark's Cathedral." "First Baptist Church." "Community Church of God In Christ."

A close observer would have seen one of them shudder for a moment, a tear coming to the eye. Another structure was to be destroyed. Another house of the Lord was soon to be but a memory.

Privately, they would remind themselves that a church is not God. Buildings were for the gathering of the faithful. Buildings were dedicated to the Lord. Buildings became holy because of the worshippers, the love of the community, the Christ centeredness. The church was ultimately only in the hearts and minds of the believers. It was their souls, which had a firm foundation, not the bricks and mortar which could be destroyed by the whim of humans. They understood that their bodies might be fragile compared to the structures they had loved for so many years without appreciating them for anything other than their architecture. Now, too late for the rapture, they had come to understand to understand the sacred nature of the buildings. They had come to understand the strength of their souls, that their recent knowledge of Jesus would give them eternal life.

That's why they had read the forbidden books, and continued to read them when they could find a copy that had not been destroyed. More importantly, they knew that wherever two or three gathered in His name, there He was in the midst of them.

Certainly their children, if they had children, would come to know joy in furtiveness, to hear the Word in basements, picnic pavilions at highway rest areas, and wherever else they could find where they would not attract attention. The churches would be a glorious part of the past, but they were past. For now their lot was to be called "Haters," the despised ones, the psychological lepers of a world gone mad.

And so they moved about the streets, trying to look indifferent to what was happening, trying to blend in, trying to seem as one with those who proclaimed the Messiah. They dared not publicly speak the truth as they knew it, that the so-called savior was not a deliverer but the harbinger of Hell.

▲

Carlton Filmore was late. Not that it mattered, he supposed. Not that everyone gathered together would think him any less faithful for having had to change a tire on the way. Even the Messiah could not make long over-used radials immortal, and Carlton had been told repeatedly that his tires were growing as bald as his own head.

The gathering was larger than usual this week

so he had to park more than a block from the old church. There was something haunting about the building, as though the Haters were still inside, chanting their insidious propaganda. Even boarded up as it was, the walls covered with graffiti and posters declaring the forthcoming Day of Wonders, he knew he would not be fully comfortable until the bulldozer and wrecking crane now sitting idle in the lot, were put into use. Nervously, he quickened his pace. He was anxious to get past this artifact of the world. He was ashamed even to remember the name of the one the Messiah called He Who Came Before Me.

Then he heard the music, and the voices lifted in song:

> *Amazing Grace, how sweet the sound,*
> *that saved a wretch like me.*
> *I once was lost, but now I'm found.*
> *The Messiah's come for me.*

It was a variation of the song he remembered from his troubled childhood, a song his mother had sung so many times when he was a boy. It had sounded so beautiful coming from her lips, so joyous. Until the day when he was nine years old and his father, his face ashen and tear stained, had come for him at school. His mother had been struck by a car on her way home from the church where she worked as the pastor's secretary.

He never said anything then, never talked about his true feelings. Jesus was a myth, a nice story people told each other. He had to be. Otherwise it was true what people had told him, that Jesus had come for his mother, a good woman whose death had left him inwardly grieving to this day. And if Jesus had taken his mother, then he didn't want anything to do with Him. Jesus wasn't his friend. Jesus was his enemy; the man who talked of love then took the person he had loved above all others away.

But that was before the Messiah came. That was before he knew the truth, knew that Franco Macalusso was not the one responsible for his mother's death, knew in his heart that she would be reunited with him through the Amazing Grace of the true savior. That was before he became a regular member of the Messiah's holy gathering, once more hearing the joyous music of his childhood, fully understanding its message for the first time with the new lyrics:

> *The power of mind has been released,*
> *but for now it's just begun.*
> *The real powers won't be ours,*
> *Until we're truly one.*

The people singing were standing in the parking lot next to the old church, but in this company, Carlton felt at ease. They were united in purpose. They were gathered in triumph, about to destroy the former gathering place of the Haters.

Loudspeakers had been set up around the parking lot so that everyone could hear the one who was talking, an uniformed member of Macalusso's regional leadership circle. Such men and women had taken the roles once held by local Mayors and City Managers. Not that such officials had lost their jobs. It was just that increasingly there was a spiritual side to the work that had to be done, the reason someone close to the Messiah was needed at such gatherings.

"Three months ago, millions of people vanished from the face of the earth," the leader said. His voice echoed throughout the parking lot. "They were removed because of their unbelief. And because they only knew the ways of hatred and division."

There were cheers from the crowd and Carlton, normally a quiet man who once experienced life as a passive observer, found himself excitedly joining the shouts of "Praise the Messiah. Praise Franco Macalusso's holy name!"

"On that glorious day, when the Lord himself returned and removed the chaff from the wheat, some feared that we were seeing the end of the world. But today, thanks to our Messiah, Franco Macalusso, we all know that we were really seeing the beginning."

To his amazement, Carlton found himself crying tears of joy. All the questions of the past had been answered on that glorious day. All the pain of his youth had been put into a perspective he could at last understand. To think that he would have lived to gain not only understanding but also the joy of peace in his heart…. "Thank you, Franco, my savior," he said in silent prayer. "Thank you."

"But not until we rid the world of the rest of those whose unbelief is still holding us back will we be able to embrace the future and say goodbye to the past," continued the spokesperson.

The crowd cheered as the speaker signaled to two overall clad men in hard hats who had been standing, waiting, beside the construction equipment. One climbed into the cab of the bulldozer and started the mighty engine. The other climbed onto the crane, and raised a giant wrecking ball that would soon batter the tower of the boarded up cathedral.

▲

Later, when discussing the incident with friends, Carlton would not be able to remember from where the stranger had appeared. The stranger was well dressed in a suit and tie. There had been nothing about him to draw attention during the earlier part of the ceremony. All that was certain was that one moment the man was a part of the crowd, and the next he was standing in front of the wrecking ball.

"Stop!" the stranger shouted. "Stop. Don't do this terrible act. You're making a mistake. You don't understand."

There was murmuring from the crowd, the man was a curiosity they were trying to understand. But no one moved until one young woman screamed, "Look out! He's got a Bible!"

"A Hater!" shouted another. "He's one of the Haters."

"Franco Macalusso is an imposter. It says so, here, in the Bible!" he shouted. He raised a copy of the forbidden book above his head, his appearance that of a warrior brandishing a sword of righteousness. There was no fear, though he was surrounded by people who would hear his message as treachery, people who believed in death for those who spoke as he was doing.

The crane operator slowly raised the wrecking

ball over the Hater, not as a threat, but out of compassion for a deranged individual who might otherwise throw himself between the ball and the wall of the building. The other construction worker leaped down from his bulldozer, determined to physically remove what he perceived to be the evil in their midst. For a moment the gathering hesitated. Then, in clusters of twos and threes, others came forward, moving in on the Hater, their faces registering the disgust they felt for so pathetic a fool.

"I'm not a Hater," shouted the man, his face covered with sweat, his body suddenly foul with the odor of fear. He had come to warn them, to stop them. He had not come as a martyr, yet like Peter after the resurrection, he knew there was no turning back. He was committed to bringing the truth even if bringing it meant death.

"I come in love in the name of our Lord and Savior Jesus Chr..."

The first blow struck with such force, that it broke his jaw. The second blow struck him in the stomach, doubling him over. He fought to catch his breath. He fought to stay conscious; fought to speak.

Someone shouted for the uniformed members of the O.N.E. special forces. They knew how to handle such matters.

"Get back," someone else shouted to the mob. "We are the chosen people. We do not need the blood of a Hater on our hands. Leave him for the courts."

But the anger of the gatherers knew no bounds. They had been freed from the past; freed from the guilt created in their minds by hearing the falsehoods spoken in the name of Jesus. As far as they were concerned, this man was a demon in their midst, a demon they would exorcise with blood.

The leader signaled at the shaken choir to continue the rest of the hymn. Perhaps it would soothe the crowd. Perhaps it would give the O.N.E. officers the chance to rescue the Hater from the angry mob and throw him in jail where he could be re-educated.

He stopped the bombs, he froze our guns.
He united soul and mind.
The chaff has vanished. The Earth is clean.
The wheat has been left behind.

Carlton could not see all that was taking place, other than that people were moving back from where The Hater had stood. He then spotted a van that was slowly moving forward. It was an emergency vehicle from the local headquarters of O.N.E.–One Nation Earth. On its side was the pyramid and eye symbol with the One Nation Earth banner beneath it, the logo of Franco Macalusso's elite forces. Several men and women in O.N.E. uniforms stepped out, moving the mob back. They checked the fallen Hater, now lying on the ground, blood dribbling from his mouth and nose. They routinely brought out a stretcher and emergency equipment, but it was obvious only a miracle would save him, and the Messiah did not work his wonders on unrepentant Haters.

As the Hater was loaded into the van, the choir finished its song:

For those who still are not on our side,
you cannot hide or run.

There'll be no time to change your mind,
when the Day of Wonders comes.

As the last voice lapsed into silence, the wrecking ball rammed the bell tower. The sound was explosive. Bricks shattered. Shingles flew in all directions. The giant church bell fell onto the staircase with the muted sound of a dying past.

The people watched first in awe, then in delight. A cheer arose spontaneously. For the spectator/ participants, it was a glorious Sunday morning!

▲

CHAPTER 3

▲

The Search For Haters

▲

▲

▲

▲

Thorold Stone sat as he had almost every night since the disappearance of his wife Wendy, and his daughters Maggie and Molly. Too tired to stay awake, too lonely to go into the bedroom, he sat on the recliner chair in the family room, staring at the television set. On the end table next to him was a half-empty can of beer he had set down...when was it? Three days ago? Four? A week? Wendy would have been annoyed with him for leaving it, instead of pouring the remaining beer down the drain and putting the empty can in the recycling bag.

She would have been angrier with him for drinking again, remembering the way he had started to drink with his dinner and, if truth were told, his breakfast as well. But he had gotten through that crisis. The photograph of Wendy, Maggie, and Molly had reminded him of what he valued most; the people he would be hurting by his actions if they....

If they what?

Ten years ago, when Thorold Stone was new to the force, he had a captain whose family was murdered by some madman. The killer had gotten out of jail on one of those technicalities that make everyone cringe when talking about the justice system. The man had nurtured a hatred for the captain who had had the nerve to put him in jail for being a serial rapist and killer. The madman swore vengeance at his trial. He never denied what he did. If anything, he was proud. But he felt that his victims deserved their punishment, and that he was an avenging angel. He promised to destroy the lives of everyone who had challenged his right to commit the crimes that had made him infamous.

The captain had thought nothing about the threats. He assumed that the man would be locked away behind bars for the rest of his life. He did not know about the appeals, about a parole board looking at the man's behavior in jail instead of the actions that placed him there, of a governor who owed a high-powered defense counsel a political favor. He did not know that the routine notification of everyone once threatened by a felon being released from jail had gone astray in a computer mix-up. What he knew was the shock that greeted him when he returned from work and learned the horrors of the damned had been visited upon the people he loved most.

The captain had experienced a cop's loss. It was the type of crime every officer fears because every officer, if he does his job long enough and well enough, will experience the same kind of threat. Yet if truth be told, and Thorold was ashamed of his thoughts, he felt the captain had an easier experience than his. The captain had closure. He had buried his wife, buried his children. He knew where they were. He could visit their graves, and he could have the solace of whatever healing was possible under such circumstances.

Wendy and the girls had just.... That was the problem. He knew what the Messiah said about those who disappeared. He knew the words of such a great and powerful man must be the truth. Yet he also knew Wendy, his beloved Wendy, the woman he had loved since they were kids in junior high school together. She was a good woman who cared deeply for others, and if she followed a false prophet, she did so with a heart so pure there was no reason to condemn her to....

And the girls....

He looked up at the television screen. He was playing one of the home videotapes they had been making since Wendy was first pregnant.

Once they had wondered if it was a foolish expense. He was a patrol officer and she was a registered nurse working for a free clinic serving the poor in the inner city. The several hundred dollars they spent on the camera seemed a needless extravagance. And yet something compelled them to buy it.

They told each other the tapes would be shown to their grandchildren. They said the tapes would be a joy in their old age. They said it would be a part of a Stone family history. They said....

"Daddy! Daddy! Take my picture," Molly called from the television set. She was sitting in the bathtub, surrounded by a mound of soap bubbles, mischievously holding something under the water.

Suddenly there was a splash, and Maggie emerged from under the water where she had been half hiding, half held down by her older sister. "No, take mine, Daddy!" called Maggie, giggling as she pushed Molly away from her.

"Will you girls stop splashing," came a voice from off screen.

"Smile Wendy," Thorold heard himself say as the camera swung to the left and zoomed in for a close-up of his beautiful wife with soap bubbles on her nose and in her hair.

"Oh, Thorold, turn that thing off. I look terrible," said Wendy.

And again, his own voice, "Far from it, sweetie. You look fantastic. In fact, maybe when the kids are done in the bathtub...."

"Thorold...."

The image then shook as Thorold had set the video camera down and moved into the picture with his family.

Thorold watched himself kissing Wendy with a passion that had been a part of their relationship, a relationship that didn't last long enough. He watched as he and Wendy snuggled together, delightfully watching the play of their small daughters. He watched until his eyes filled with tears. He used the remote to turn off the VCR and tune into some mindless television show.

Reluctantly, Thorold rose from his chair and went over to a bookshelf on one wall. There were pictures there of the kids on swings, and at a county fair. There was a picture of his mother in her wheelchair a few weeks before she died from the cancer that had been eating away at her body for more years than he cared to remember. He stared at his Police Academy training manuals, Wendy's medical books, and the collection of novels they had amassed. There was also her Bible, dust covered, unused since her disappearance, a book now forbidden as subversive.

For a moment he thought he should get his gun and arrest himself for being sympathetic to the Haters. After all, how many people had he arrested for owning just such a book? How many times had he heard someone say that the Bible wasn't his or her own, it belonged to a spouse, a child, a parent, or a friend? It was there as a reminder of happy times, of friendship, of love. It eased the sadness, he was told. He hadn't believed them.

He told himself he was different, that the reason he held on to Wendy's Bible was different. The dust that had gathered on the book his wife once read each day was certainly proof that he wasn't a Hater. Yet he was an officer of the law, sworn to follow the orders of the Messiah, and in his private life he had failed to do so. There were those who would consider his sin of omission cause for being fired, jailed, or worse. He knew he would one day have to do the right thing by burning the book. But not now. Not while he was hurting so badly. Not while the book seemed his one link with a part of Wendy's character he had always admired, even though he had never wanted to share it.

Finally, drifting off to sleep, he had the same dream that had been haunting him of late, a dream both joyful and terrifying. First there were the girls, sitting on the swing set in their backyard. They had learned to swing themselves but they still loved the idea of their father pushing them to get started. "Faster, Daddy!" "Higher, Daddy!" giggled the girls one after the other until they began pumping with their legs, taking themselves to the limits of the chains. Then he would sit on the ground with Wendy, watching happily.

The dream would then change. Thorold would find himself in a heated discussion with Wendy. It was always the same, always about her wanting him to believe in God, to read the story of Jesus, to understand why it was so much a part of her life. "I don't want to hear it," he would tell her. And then Wendy would tell him he didn't have to read it as believer. He just had to look at the words with an open mind and an open heart.

Thorold began to move on his chair. He was still in a deep sleep, yet it seemed almost as though his body was trying to avoid what would come next, what always came next.

"Daddy, Daddy, come and push us right up to the sky!" the girls would shout.

And in the dream he turns, and sees his daughters vanish in a blinding flash of light. The swings are still in the air, but the seats are empty. Shocked, he turns to Wendy, only to find she is gone, too. A scream starts to form in his throat....

Thorold jerked himself awake as he had for so many nights. His body was covered with sweat, and his heart pounded rapidly. He bolted from the chair, forcing himself to become fully awake, forcing himself to...

He clutched the table, fighting for breath. A cry like a wounded bird escaped from his lips. Why couldn't he rid himself of the nightmare? Why must he be so tortured night after night after night? Why?

The telephone rang, forcing him to get control. In the background he could hear the television set still playing. The daily news was reporting on a speech in Jerusalem where Franco Macalusso was speaking about the upcoming and much anticipated Day of Wonders. The story had been the focus of most news shows for the past several days, and Thorold gave it only a moment's attention before using the remote to silence the set as he answered the telephone.

"Thorold Stone."

"It's David, Thor. There's been another bombing. I'll be by to pick you up in a few minutes."

Thorold turned off the television, took one last look at the photograph of his wife and daughters, and went to the bathroom to quickly shave before going out to meet his partner.

▲

The crowd that gathered on the fringes of the schoolyard was a somber one. They stood, mostly silent, watching, trying not to interfere with the police, the ambulances, and the grieving parents whose anguished sobs chilled the morning air. The Messiah had come. The world was supposed to be at peace.

It was difficult to realize such violence was still taking place. A school bus, filled with happy children anxious to begin the morning's classes, had suddenly exploded just as they were preparing to walk down the aisle and out the door. The ground was littered with book bags, lunches, the dead, the dying, and the wounded. Rescue workers had established a triage to treat the children who would live, and give comfort to the dying from wounds so severe there was no hope of surviving more than a few minutes. Ambulances were rushing the wounded to area hospitals. Police had sealed off the area so the scientific unit could analyze what had happened. Even though the crowd was asked to go home, observers clustered just outside the taped off crime sight, watching, trying to make sense of what just occurred.

Overhead, several helicopters, with the call letters from various radio and television stations on their side, hovered as best they could. Reporters described the carnage, while videographers brought the images to life with their cameras.

▲

Thorold Stone and his partner, David Smith, arrived as the last of the injured were being loaded onto gurneys. The bomb had been located in the right rear of the school bus, the head of the bomb squad told them. It lifted the bus up and over on its side, causing additional injuries as the children were thrown about. Bodies were piled on bodies. Some of those on the bottom had been wedged so tightly their chests had been compressed and suffocation occurred before rescuers could reach them. Others were more fortunate. They were protected from flying shards of glass and twisted pieces of metal that took the lives of the children who landed on top of them. It was a matter of chance as to who died and who lived. Everything depended upon where a child had been standing or sitting when the blast occurred.

Smith parked just outside the crime scene, and the two partners hurried past the tape barrier. Their badge cases were placed open over their belts for instant identification, although most of the officers knew the detectives. Emergency services had been consolidated in recent weeks so that everyone carried the same type of One Nation Earth identification papers. The cars, including the one Smith had driven to pick up Stone, bore the O.N.E. pyramid and eye symbol.

Even as the partners listened to a quick briefing, Thorold noticed one little girl, resting on a gurney, with an I.V. going into her arm. She was so covered with blood and soot that he could not tell her age. For an instant he thought the child could be Maggie or Molly. Then he realized he was still emotionally overwrought from his dream. This was real, not a dream. This child was alive. She was someone else's daughter.

Thorold walked over to the little girl as the

paramedics prepared to load her on the ambulance. Her parents were not around. They probably had not yet been located. The child seemed a little afraid. Thorold stroked her forehead and told her everything would be okay, that the paramedics would take great care of her.

The child looked up at one of the rescue workers and smiled weakly. Then, as the gurney was being lifted, she turned to Thorold and asked, "Why do they hate us so much?"

"I don't know, honey," he answered. "But we'll find them and put them in jail where they can't harm anyone else. I promise you that."

Thorold watched as the ambulance took the child from the parking lot. David Smith walked over, put his hand on his partner's shoulder, and said, "That child someone you know?"

"She reminded me of..."

"Yeah. I understand," said Smith. "You okay to do some work?"

"I have to. I promised her," said Thorold, forcing his attention back on the situation at hand.

"The bomb squad guys think they have a handle on the device that was used," said Smith, as the two men walked over to the burned out remains of the bus. A short, lean, muscular man wearing a jacket that read "Bomb Squad" was carefully examining an electronic device in a sealed clear plastic evidence bag.

"Miniature high frequency receiver," said the Bomb Squad investigator. "It was what we suspected when witnesses told us the bus exploded just as the doors opened and the first child started to get off. It had to be either a device connected with the door mechanism, or one of these remotes. We ruled out the door connection because that might have gone off anywhere along the driver's route. This is a line of sight receiver."

"You mean someone stood in the parking lot and activated it?" asked Smith.

"That would be too dangerous. I figure they might have been on an upper floor of the school building, in a car on the street, or in one of those buildings just outside the campus. Most of these have a range of between one and two miles when used on completely open land. They're assigned a frequency response that will not be duplicated by radio waves from portable phones and similar devices. But the power's deliberately kept low so they won't interfere with one another. They're used a lot by contractors doing demolition or excavation. Safer than the old fuse and blasting cap devices. But out here, with the school, the homes, and the businesses, the signal can't go as far. No more than a mile in any direction is my guess, and if it wasn't line of sight, they must have had a spotter watching for when the bus started to unload. We should be able to pinpoint it directly when we compare the frequency with the satellite sweep data."

"You have the frequency?" asked Stone.

"These devices are coded. If you find enough of the transmitter, you can get everything else you need with a telephone call to the people who track these things.

"We got lucky with this one. Whoever wired it was concerned with killing kids, not with whether or not trace evidence would be left behind. The bomb squad investigator placed the receiver on an outside corner of the bumper, and ran an antenna wire along the edge. Two more wires led under the bus to the area near the tire well where the explosive device had been placed. The angle of the blast and the thickness of the steel between the bumper and where the bomb was located meant it was blown back. You can see the receiver's almost whole. With other bombs we've had like this the receiver was bundled with the explosives, leaving us with a jigsaw puzzle from hell. This time...."

The bomb squad investigator was interrupted by a well dressed youth wearing polished black shoes, dark, creased slacks, a white shirt, and a uniform blazer jacket with the O.N.E. logo on the upper left pocket. "Which one of you is Agent Stone?"

"I am," said Thorold.

"We got the source of the frequency transmission from the satellite review," said the youth. "I was told to bring it to you."

"And...?"

"It's a warehouse, sir," said the young man. "The one that used to house the food cooperative before they built a larger facility a couple of blocks from here. It's maybe a mile down the road on Front Street."

"I know the place. Come on, David, let's check it out," said Thorold.

That there were Haters at all was a difficult concept for many of the law enforcement officers to understand. That the Haters could be committing terrorist actions after the day of miracles was even more difficult to understand. How many there were, their motivation, and how big a threat the Haters posed were all unknowns.

"It just doesn't make any sense," said Thorold as he and his partner drove to the warehouse. An undercover response squad had been dispatched earlier to secure the perimeter of the building. Stone and Smith had been told they were on Alert 7. Any Haters located at the warehouse were to be considered armed and so extremely dangerous that they were to be terminated on sight.

"All of these bombs, all of these killings, and what have they accomplished? They are only proving what the Messiah says about the Haters. Now the whole world hates them for their actions and wants to see them die. And for what? To be martyrs for a fraud like Jesus Christ who they believe is their savior?" grumbled Smith.

"It's what I've always said about the human mind. You can show ten people the same event and you'll get ten different reactions," he continued. "We've all seen the start of the war at Megiddo. We've all seen the miracle that occurred that day, the peace, the harmony, the changes the Messiah has brought us. How can someone see all that and not believe. How can they see that and still have hearts so hardened they'd kill children to get attention?"

"Maybe that's the problem, David. Maybe we've all seen too much," noted Thorold.

"What do you mean?"

"Think about what this world's been through in the last thee months. One minute we're about to all go up in a giant nuclear mushroom cloud and the next minute millions of people just vanish into thin air. Suddenly the world was turned upside down.

"I mean, it's like we were all in some nightmare. The only thing we can truly understand is the loss, and we're so busy grieving, so busy trying to comprehend how we got into this situation, that we're really not thinking clearly."

"What are you getting at, Thor?"

"I don't know. I guess it's just that things aren't always what they seem to be when you're trying to look at life through an emotional filter.

"I saw it happen with Wendy when her mother died a horrible death from cancer. They had the poor woman so doped up with painkillers she should have been off in space somewhere, yet she still suffered greatly. Wendy couldn't understand why such a good woman, and she really was—the way Wendy responded to the needs of others you could see she got from her mother—had suffered so much.

"As for me, well, all the years on the job we've both had, I just said life isn't always fair. Bad things happen to good people. I don't know why. They just do.

"But Wendy couldn't accept that. She felt there had to be a reason. Not that her mother was being punished for some dreadful sin or anything like that. Rather it was like the woman was a vehicle from whom others might learn, from whom others might be touched. I think she was really reaching, but I went along with her. That's when she started talking about God's will and God's mysterious ways. That's when she got the kids really involved with the church, and next thing I know, Wendy's praying it won't rain when we have a family picnic and the kids were praying for me when I came home grouchy after a particularly bad day. It was her way of coping."

"And you're saying that calling Franco Macalusso the Messiah is our way of coping with all that's happened?" asked David.

"Yes. No. I don't know.

"Look at the facts, David. This guy stands up right when the world is in the biggest mess we've ever been dumb enough to get ourselves into. He claims he's God himself. He claims that he's the one responsible for all the miracles, and we're so relieved that we're still alive, we buy into it. You know what they say. A drowning man will even grasp at the point of a sword if that's all that's offered to him."

"The point of a sword? The world was creating a real-life horror movie that was going to destroy every member of the audience and this guy stopped it. And you call his actions the point of a sword?

"I'm as cynical as the next guy, maybe more. My father died when I was three. He was working two jobs, one as a janitor at a car parts plant and the other as third shift clerk at a convenience store. He didn't have much education, but when we kids started arriving he wanted to make certain we got out of the ghetto mom and him were living in. He wanted to have the money to help us make something of our lives. Then some hopped up fool who couldn't see beyond his next fix came in, killed my daddy, and ran off with the $27 in the cash register. $27 and he changed the lives of a family forever.

"The preacher came by to see my mother, and a couple of the church women took care of us kids through the funeral. But then it was, 'trust in God, Sister Cecelia. He'll provide.' And this from a man with the largest church in the inner city, a man who bought himself an expensive new car every year. Paid cash, too, because, he said, the Lord provided as it would for my family."

"And did He?"

"Not through that church. You know how we kids got to college? The people at my dad's plant took up a collection. And some of the customers at the convenience store came through with more money and gifts of food than Mama knew how to handle. She still cries when she thinks about how their kindness let us keep our home. Not that it was all that much, but between Mama's job and the jobs we kids took in high school, we got through. And you know what that preacher did when the paper ran a story about the trust fund established at the local bank? He came and told Mama God wanted her to tithe to his church.

"I learned one thing from all that. It's what people show me that counts, not what they say they are or what they say they believe. And when the Messiah stopped the missiles, stopped the war, stopped everything that was destroying us, he made me a believer," conceded Smith. "You notice he hasn't established his own house of worship. He hasn't asked us to give him money. He did what he did because it was the right thing to do to save us from our foolish self-destruction. He was just like those people at Dad's plant."

"He made you a believer in what? Macalusso vaporized my family. He took them as swiftly as that robber killed your father," Thorold argued in return.

"They wouldn't open their minds, Thorold. You know that. He's explained it to us."

"And your dad wouldn't open the cash register. What kind of savior vaporizes someone sweet and gentle just because he disagrees with them?"

"Maybe we're not ready to understand, Thor. Maybe...."

"Wendy I can handle. I don't believe it, but I can handle it. The same with all the other adults who disappeared. Maybe they had some festering evil inside, some spiritual cancer ready to explode. I'll grant him that possibility. But the kids...? My daughters weren't some subversives threatening One Nation Earth. They were just...children. You say you only trust what you were shown and I was shown that a jerk like me who's never really believed in anything can get left behind while innocent kids are..."

"They were holding the rest of us back," David responded. "That's what Macalusso said. "We don't know where they've gone. Maybe they're not dead the way we think. Maybe they're getting re-educated somewhere. Heaven's a pretty big place, after all. Maybe that's what this Day of Wonders he's talking about is going to be. A time of reuniting with loved ones who have been changed."

"And maybe we should be considering alternatives, David."

"Such as?"

"I don't know. Maybe he's just a really good magician. Like when David Copperfield made the Statue of Liberty disappear, only on some sort of cosmic scale. Or maybe he's just a guy who saw what happened and jumped up and took credit before anyone came to his or her senses. For all we know Macalusso and his cronies are just aliens from another planet."

"Give it a rest, Thor. If the guy was an alien, he wouldn't be the only one doing miracles."

"Look, all I'm saying is that someone should be asking some questions. Why am I the only one?"

"Because you're a cynic. You've always been a cynic. And this hell you're going through over Wendy and the kids isn't helping.

"How long have we known each other? Since fourth grade? Fifth?" David asked.

"Longer than that. We started school together."

"So, make it first grade. The point is, I've known you almost forever and you're always questioning. I'll bet when everyone still believed in Santa Claus you were trying to find some way to get up on the roof to check for reindeer footprints. I know you couldn't watch a puppet show without looking for the strings or sneaking behind the curtain to see the people working their hands. Even at the training academy, you were forever challenging the instructors with your 'but what if…?' questions. What Macalusso did in Israel was all the proof I needed. Yet the whole world has changed, and that's still not good enough for you," chided Smith.

"Maybe that's because I'm not looking for God, David. I'm just looking for my family."

The friends were silent as they approached the warehouse. There was a time when law enforcement officers dreaded domestic violence calls. They knew that an angry husband or wife was more impulsive than a professional criminal, or even a killer was. A knock at the door of a home where screaming and hollering was disturbing the neighbors could lead to a bullet flying at you. Try to arrest a man beating his wife, and the woman, her face battered, might jump the officer to make him release her husband. Men and women had died trying to help a couple resolve a crisis point in their marriage.

Domestic violence calls still existed, but the uniformed division always handled them. For David and Thorold, the new danger came from violent Haters. Someone who had blown up a school bus might have booby-trapped the entrance to his or her hideout. The Hater might be armed, desiring to die a martyr with the blood of the O.N.E. on his hands.

Most of their work was peaceful. Most Haters were surprisingly gentle people. They did not resist arrest. They were not armed. But the ones who had turned to violence, like the Hater who had bombed the children, were unpredictable. Smith and Stone slowly circled the block, checking to see what security was in place. Their orders were to be as discrete as possible given the potential violence they were facing. Macalusso's assistant, Len Parker, had made clear that what he called "terminal Hater operations" were to be conducted as much as possible so that the general public was not aware they were taking place. At the warehouse, plain-clothes officers were scattered about all the escape routes. Two were "working" in a gas station across the street from a rear driveway to the building. Another was cleaning the parking area of a convenience store. Another was "napping" in a van. Still another was "drinking" from a brown paper bag containing a two-way radio rather than the bottle of liquor a passer-by would suspect.

Smith and Stone parked their marked car around a corner and out of sight of the empty building. There they were met by Officer Jeanne Hutton, the handler of a large dog trained for such assignments.

"Everyone's in place," said Officer Hutton.

"Then I guess it doesn't matter if any Haters see us," said Smith, as he and Thorold put on their O.N.E. jackets. The logo would make for fast identification of the "good guys" if there were an altercation with any Haters hiding in the warehouse. Thorold also took a shotgun from the car, chambering a shell so it would be ready to fire. Smith took out a small electronic device that had been provided to some of the key department personnel.

"What's that thing?" asked Officer Hutton.

"Willy Holmes' new toy. A few of us are trying it out," Smith responded.

"Willy Holmes?"

"The guy in the wheelchair who works in the electronics lab. Real genius. Always experimenting with things to make our work easier."

"I don't know why he works for the department when he could be making a fortune in private industry," said Thorold.

"He once told me his one dream in life, other than the chance to walk again, was to be a police officer," said Smith. "The guy tried everything. Learned some modified martial arts for the upper body. Sued for equal access. But there was no way he'd ever be able to go on patrol, so they made him a cop, but kept him in electronics. Seems to make him happy, and we've benefited in ways that otherwise would have been impossible."

"So what is that thing?" Officer Hutton repeated.

"According to Willy, it can read human DNA through solid concrete."

"I don't get it," Hutton commented.

"It's to help us stay alive. The dog's great, and if we get into trouble, we've got another weapon to help us get control. But a dog's nose can't warn us of danger until we're almost right on top of it.

"The old heat sensors are still pretty good, although they can mistake a large animal or even a space heater for a human being. Willy says this will only register a living, breathing person. We can know if someone's waiting behind a closed door or down a dark corridor before the person can blow us away."

"<u>If</u> it works," said Thorold.

"There you go up on the roof looking for reindeer, partner."

"Pardon?" asked Hutton.

"Private joke," said David. "You two ready to go in?"

The three officers and the dog walked swiftly to the side, then started down an alley leading to a side entrance and fire escape for the abandoned building. Smith slowly moved the electronic device from side to side, watching a series of light-emitting diodes glow with varying intensity. There was also a meter whose needle Smith watched intensely.

Suddenly the dog whimpered and tugged on his handler's leash. She gave him slack as he moved to the door, sniffing. Smith walked up and pointed the meter in the area where the dog was now alert. It showed nothing.

"No one in there, boy. Whoever it was must have left," he said.

"I guess they can improve on Mother Nature," said Officer Hutton.

"Or someone's going to shoot us through the door and the dog's going to say, 'I told you so,'" joked Thorold.

Suddenly the lights grew bright. Smith stopped, holding the meter steady, and pressed a button to stabilize the reading. Then he moved slowly from side to side, watching the instrument closely. He reached up to his lapel and activated the radio clipped to his jacket. "This is Smith. Stone, Hutton, and I are at the South End. We've got eighteen of them inside."

"Roger," said the voice on the radio. "Will dispatch."

Within seconds the armored van used by the O.N.E. SWAT Team rolled into view, and the O.N.E. team members jumped out, ready for action. The undercover officers abandoned their pretense and moved into position to assure no one escaped.

Lt. Harrison Braxton was the SWAT team leader for the terminal hater operation. His job was to work with the O.N.E. agents like Smith and Stone to assure they had whatever firepower and security they needed. He laid out a floor plan of the building so they could see what possible interior hiding places of the Haters they were facing. With the location pinpointed, the men were briefed on the safest point of entry.

"Our orders are to shoot the Haters on sight," Thorold explained to the members of the O.N.E. SWAT unit. "Tell your men they're to kill anyone who resists the moment they think they're in danger. Otherwise, I'll give the order when to fire."

"Why is this a terminal operation?" asked Lt. Braxton. "Is there something we need to know about? Will we need special equipment?"

"They bombed a school bus. They're obviously armed and dangerous. There are probably other explosives hidden in the building," said Thorold. "If there's anything that might endanger the men, I haven't been told about it. I just know that headquarters has ordered us to shoot to kill."

"Are they all in the one room?" asked one of the men.

"That's what's indicated now," said Smith. "But I don't know the range of this thing. We'll know more when we get inside."

"Are we smashing in the door?" asked another team member.

"It shouldn't be necessary. The homeless and vandals have been using this place since it was closed. The locks have already been broken a number of times according to one of the uniforms who patrols the area. We should be able to get inside quietly. David and I will go in first," instructed Thorold.

"That's not the way we usually do things," said Lt. Braxton "I know we're supposed to follow your orders, but...."

"These are not the normal times. And if I'm wrong, then David and I are the ones who get hurt."

"The idea of O.N.E. SWAT is to protect the officers so only bad guys get hurt," argued Braxton.

"We're still doing it my way, Lieutenant," Thorold said, sternly.

"I want your men to hold their fire until Smith has a chance to check the immediate area after we're inside," Thorold continued, repeating his warning. "They should only shoot if their lives are threatened. Otherwise I'll give the signal. Is that clear?"

"Yes, sir," said the O.N.E. SWAT Team officers. "Then let's do it."

Inside what had once been a corporate meeting room, eighteen men and women, young and old, black, white, Hispanic, and Asian, were on their feet, swaying, and waving their arms, as they joyfully sang:

> He has made me glad.
> He has made me glad, I will rejoice for
> He has made me glad. I will say this is
> the day that the Lord has made.
> I will rejoice for He has made me glad.

A half dozen people held Bibles as they sang with their eyes closed. Others held their hands in the air in joyous supplication. Except for the small number of people and the unusual surroundings, it might have been an old-fashioned revival meeting.

Smith and Stone were able to force open the door before the singing stopped. They moved quietly inside, followed by the O.N.E. SWAT Team members. They could tell which room sound was coming from and took their positions. No one heard them. No one saw them.

For a moment Thorold felt uncomfortable. He felt as though even if the people were aware of their presence, there would be no attempt to resist arrest. It was not something he could understand. These were killers. He had seen the proof of their carnage. There was no one else in the building so he knew they were the guilty ones. Yet praying to Jesus…? It reminded him of Wendy, a woman who would never hurt anyone. Then he remembered the aftermath of the bus bomb. That was when his heart hardened to the emotions his memory had evoked when he heard the songs familiar from earlier, much happier times.

Victor Davis, a former member and occasional attendee at Mt. Olive Baptist Church, a 500-member inner city congregation, was leading the celebration. He found it ironic that his missing mother had once wept bitterly in despair over his cavalier attitude towards God and the church. Now here he was, heading a gathering of believers who regularly risked their lives to sing the songs and tell the story he had so often avoided hearing on Sunday mornings.

"Are you glad?" asked the man they all secretly

called Elder Davis.

"Yes!" shouted the others.

"Are you really glad?" His voice became more fervent.

"Yes!!!" they shouted, delightedly.

"Why?" he asked, his voice rising dramatically. "Why are you glad?"

"JESUS!" they roared.

"It's blasphemy," whispered the Lieutenant as he positioned himself in the shadows.

"They're talking of Jesus and they've just killed or injured a bus load of school children?" said David, derisively.

"They're true believers, David," whispered Thorold. "They think that anything they do in the name of God is somehow blessed. They probably have rationalized that, since the children will go to Heaven, killing them is giving them a better life."

"That's sick," said the Lieutenant. "People like that have no business being in our New World."

"That's why we've been given the shoot to kill order," said Thorold. "Fanatics are too dangerous to have around."

Yet, even as he said these words, Thorold thought of Wendy, and of what she would be doing in his place. He knew she would join Davis and his group, embrace them, and stand with them to die if necessary. She just would not understand....

In the gathering place, Elder Davis continued

preaching. "I'm telling you tonight that there are those who don't agree. And why? Why don't they believe? Because they're looking with their eyes and not with their hearts.

"Well, I'm here to tell you my friends that seeing is **not** believing in God's world. No, sir. In God's world you won't see it <u>UNTIL</u> you believe it!"

The congregation responded with "Amen" and "Praise the Lord."

They were a gentle people, their faces filled with the ecstasy that comes from knowing the truth with such certainty it could not be challenged by anyone. Their churches had been destroyed, boarded up, or converted for other uses by order of the representatives of Franco Macalusso. They had suffered losses; suffered with the knowledge that they were despised, yet they had found solace in unlikely gathering places.

"Remember that our Lord and Savior said that wherever two or three are gathered in His name, He is in the midst of them," Elder Davis had said when he began organizing the like-minded friends and acquaintances who formed the backbone of the floating congregation. The times are like those the early Christians faced after the Temple was destroyed in 70 A.D. Families were divided because of the hostile actions of the Romans. Christians were no longer welcome in the Jewish services in which many of them had been raised. Families wrote off converted children as being dead. There was much pain, much stress, much loneliness. They truly knew what it was to pick up their cross and follow Jesus. And that is where we find ourselves, carrying on the tradition in a world where the occupying force is not the Roman Government but the fraudulent embodiment of evil."

Elder Davis' words scared many people who did not agree with the adoration of Franco Macalusso, but who were unwilling to stand apart. They were more comfortable going through the motions of praising the man people were calling the Messiah. The eighteen now gathered in the warehouse represented the largest gathering of Christians the O.N.E. agents had encountered when raiding worship services. Usually there were two or three gathered quietly in homes, seldom-used office meeting rooms, and other private places.

The Davis congregation came together because of their longing for the type of service they remembered from childhood or from the times their spouses made them attend Sunday worship. They had not appreciated the community of the faithful when such gatherings were normal, not a felony potentially punishable by death. Now, when they were called Haters and seemingly the whole world was against them, they felt the need to stand together, to try and reproduce the type of worship service once considered a normal part of society. Yet all of them knew the risks, knew that the gathering meant imprisonment, torture, or death.

"We've all got to walk by faith and not by sight. We are living in an age of deception, in an age of delusion, in an age of trickery. And believe you me, whatever this imposter is going to offer the world, it's going to be every bit as tempting as the forbidden fruit was to Eve," preached Davis.

"Amen, brother! Praise the Lord."

"That's why we have to look at the world through our hearts. That's why we have to let the love of God lead us every step of the way. And that's why the Bible says that <u>only as a child</u> shall we pass through the gates of Heaven. Do you know what that means?"

Suddenly Thorold could tolerate no more. He had arrived late at the scene of the bombing, and had missed the sight of most of the carnage. Still, he had seen innocent children crying in pain, helpless, and scared. There was no greater evil in his mind than a Hater who dared talk of loving children, yet could comfortably kill and maim such innocents. Elder Davis' words made him physically ill. He stepped forward, holding his pump action shotgun. He knew he should be alert to everyone, knew he should be watching for hidden weapons, or for someone trying to flee. Yet despite this, he found himself riveted on the face of the preacher.

"Let me guess what that means," said Thorold. "That we should all try to kill as many innocent children as we can? Is that why you had your people bomb the school bus? So they could get to your Heaven?"

Elder Davis stared uncomprehending. The rest of the congregation stared in shock and confusion. Smith, holding his nine-millimeter handgun, was standing at his partner's side. The remaining O.N.E. agents were in position. The Haters could see heavily armed men and women wherever they looked.

"You're all under arrest," said Smith, his finger kept to the side of the trigger guard so he would not accidentally fire. There seemed no danger for the moment, and if there was, he could shoot before anyone but a Hater would get hurt. Still, he was wary. These people lurked in the dark, planting bombs that killed innocent children. "Kneel on the floor and place your hands on your heads!" he shouted. "Now!"

The members of the assault team moved towards the kneeling men and women. One by one they were pulled to their feet, pushed against the wall, and carefully searched. Then they were handcuffed. The O.N.E. SWAT team waited for instructions to escort them from the building. Most were silent; cooperating with the inevitable, wondering only why the officers seemed so surprised at not finding any hidden weapons. Only one, Mrs. Anna Davis, the pastor's wife, seemed on the verge of saying something. She was a short, slightly heavyset woman in her early forties. She looked at Thorold angrily.

One of the members of the SWAT Team who was now handcuffing Mrs. Davis, commented, "Hey, lady, you should thank him. If it wasn't for him, you'd all be lying here full of bullets right now."

"What do you mean?" she asked, startled by the comment.

"You know the law. What you people did to that school bus…"

"You keep saying something about a school bus," said a handcuffed Elder Davis moving to stand by his wife's side. "I don't understand. We're just Christians holding a worship service. We're not armed. We don't hurt people. You wouldn't be here if the world hadn't gone so insane that it's now a crime to worship the true God."

"A school bus was bombed not far from here," said Thorold. "School children...little children like you say this Jesus of yours is supposed to love...were killed and wounded. There was blood everywhere."

"The Lord Jesus bless their souls," whispered Mrs. Davis, genuinely shocked. "But who would do such a terrible thing?"

"Have you looked in a mirror this morning?" said David, angrily.

"We don't blow up things," she said, her shock changing to defiance. Her lilting soprano voice had a firmness to it that reflected years of fighting to find joy in the midst of sorrow. She had married too young, dropping out of high school for "happily ever after" only to discover abuse, alcoholism, and a series of dead-end jobs. There had been no need for divorce, her husband skidding out of control on a bridge during the first heavy snow of the season after they had been married less than three years. His blood alcohol level was twice the legal limit. The only good thing he did was not go driving when others were on the road.

For a while Mrs. Davis had been a singer in a rock band that was noisier than they were competent. She had cleaned rooms in a local hotel, eventually returning to get her high school equivalency. From there she had worked nights and gone to college days. She was active in Alcoholics Anonymous where she met her husband, a man with an equally troubled past. Together they had found love, had a daughter, and in recent weeks discovered the truth about the rapture, Macalusso, and Jesus, their Lord and Savior. As she joked with her husband, "Just when we finally get it right, it seems like the whole world is getting it wrong."

"We didn't blow up anything," said Mrs. Davis. "If you think we did this terrible thing, you must have reason. But we're Christians. You must have heard the Bible when you were young. You don't have to be a believer to know a Christian can't do such a thing. Not to children. Not to anyone. We're being set up."

"Shut up, lady!" said Smith, angrily. "The signal for the detonator that blew up the bus was traced to this building. We didn't see anyone else in here, did you?"

A teenaged girl, no more than sixteen, stepped away from the group of Haters now waiting to be taken to jail. "Leave my mother alone!" she said, angrily. One of the O.N.E. SWAT Team members started to grab her by the arm but Thorold signaled him to let her alone. Clearly none of them were now in a position to cause any harm. What harm could they cause by speaking? "My mother's not causing you any trouble," the young girl continued.

"The truth causes these men trouble. The truth has been in very short supply since everyone started buying this Macalusso's story," said Mrs. Davis.

"What is the truth?" Thorold asked, moving close to her. His voice was harsh, his size menacing. He realized he was needlessly frightening this woman and put his weapon back in his holster. There was no risk of attack. Not from these people. Not now.

"They probably think the Messiah's the devil in disguise," said Smith. "Come on, Thor, let's get them out of here so we can look for the triggering device.

Remember the reason we came here. Remember the kids."

"Your idea of the devil is probably someone in a red suit with horns and a pitchfork," rebuked Mrs. Davis. "If Macalusso is so good, why is everyone afraid to open a Bible? Why are you people destroying Bibles? If the word speaks the truth and Macalusso is the truth, then why is he afraid of people reading the word? We're going to jail for loving the Lord and you call the man who orders this abomination the Messiah?"

"The Bible has been nothing but trouble for the world since the day it was written. My wife read the Bible every day. She tried to get me to read it, to pray with her. Look where it got her," said Thorold.

Mrs. Davis, beginning to understand, softly asked, "She was one of the disappeared?"

"And my children," he said, suddenly uncertain why he was having this conversation, when he should be loading them on the van to take to the holding facility for processing.

"They're in Heaven, young man," said Mrs. Davis. "I believe that with all my heart. It's no comfort. I lost my mother and sister on that day and there isn't a week goes by when I don't cry myself to sleep over the loss. But we'd have been with them if we had listened. We'd still all be together if some of us hadn't been such stubborn, self-deluding fools.

"I'll tell you this, young man. My husband, my daughter, all of us you see here today are guilty of the same thing as your wife. We believe what she believed. We think as she thought. Do you think she'd be blowing up school buses if she were still here?"

Thorold was shaken by the question, but realized some of the officers were listening to the conversation. It was inappropriate and he knew it. This kind of talk could result in his being removed from the streets and placed on administrative duty while being evaluated for fitness on the job. He was on the edge of a dangerous precipice and knew he had better back away.

"Save it, lady!" he said, more harshly than he felt. "You'll be able to tell it to the judge."

It was a lie and he knew it. He had no idea what would happen to these people, but he knew they would not be going into a court of law. Macalusso's word provided justice now, and all Haters were condemned to…to a fate Thorold neither knew nor wanted to know. Justice would be…whatever justice would be. He looked away for a moment, then turned back towards Mrs. Smith. To his surprise she had moved close to him, staring defiantly at him despite her helplessness.

"If you'd just open your mind a little," she said, quietly. "You seem like a good man. You seem like someone who…"

"I said, SAVE IT!" he responded harshly.

Mrs. Davis was silent, yet she continued to look at him. He felt like a small child having a temper tantrum when he knows he's wrong and his schoolteacher is just waiting for him to come to his senses. It wasn't a comfortable feeling. Defiantly he kept his eyes on the woman, realizing that though she was much shorter than he was, he felt like she was the one in charge.

Then, so softly only Thorold could hear, the

woman asked, "Why didn't you shoot us? If I've been hearing correctly, that was what you were supposed to do to us dangerous subversives."

"You just didn't look all that dangerous to me," responded Thorold.

"If we're not dangerous, then why do they say we did a terrible thing? Why do you think they want all of us dead?" she asked.

"This is where the bomb was triggered from. You're the only ones here. You're…" He paused, looking again at the woman, then her daughter. "I…I don't know."

"Can you get something out of my purse without these other men becoming suspicious?" the woman asked quietly, deliberately looking away from where it was resting in a corner of the room.

Thorold stood looking at her for a moment, saying nothing. She was probably going to have him take her Bible, then turn him in as a Hater. They were all devious like that. He had let his guard down, talking to her the way he did. Confiding anything in such a person was going too far. He had had such truths drilled into him in training. It was only his emotions over Wendy….

"It's not a Bible, if that's what you're thinking. It's just an old romance novel even your Messiah hasn't banned, but it's important that no one else gets their hands on it. Not until you've looked at it." She paused, staring intensely at him, then said, "Not until you've really looked at it."

"I can get it. It's got to be bagged, searched,

and checked into the property room. I can take it with me instead of it going with the uniformed men who will be transporting you in the van."

"Then do it," she whispered firmly. "Take the book. Take it home with you. It has the reason they think we're so dangerous."

"Is this a…"

"There's a CD in the cover. I slit it and slipped it inside. I worked for O.N.E., like you, up until a couple of days ago when I got the CD. I…You don't need to know any more. Take a look at it. You'll…"

"I'm not interested in Hater propaganda. I don't need conversion," stated Thorold.

"I understand. This isn't about converting you. Take it. Look at it. Do it for your wife," pleaded Mrs. Davis.

"Time to board the vans for the station," said one of the SWAT Team members walking over to the handcuffed Mrs. Davis and taking her by the arm. "Any problem, Thor?"

"No. Take her and the rest of them."

Unresisting, Mrs. Davis let herself be led towards the door. She stumbled for a moment, barely keeping her balance with her arms restrained behind her. No one noticed that she deliberately bumped a nearly invisible signal button on the way out.

One of the uniformed officers, a plastic evidence bag in hand, started to go to Mrs. Davis' purse.

"Leave it," said Thorold. "You guys have enough problems with a group of Haters who blew up a school bus. Give me the bag and I'll bring it in."

"Be careful of booby traps," he said.

"What? An exploding lipstick? These Haters are too clever to keep any weapons where we can find them." Thorold opened the purse, taking out the novel, then picking up car keys, a wallet, some photos, make-up, and other innocuous items. He put everything but the romance novel back in the purse, then placed the purse in the evidence bag.

"I'll read this before I turn it in. Always wondered what they were like. Probably better than a sleeping pill."

The officer laughed, taking the book from Thorold's hand, opening it, and looking randomly at the pages within. "You're right, Thor. I'll bet you don't get past the first twenty-five pages before falling asleep." He handed it back to Thorold, then left with the others. Only David remained, looking quizzically at his partner, saying nothing.

Peter & Paul Lalonde

▲

CHAPTER 4

▲

The Haters' Hideout

▲

▲

▲

▲

The more Helen Hannah read the books and papers her grandmother, Edna Williams, left behind, the more she thought of herself connected with the earliest Christians. She remembered John's story of the disciples hiding in a room. She remembered Paul's letters to the early churches. They were usually no more than someone's home where the newly saved gathered for worship. She remembered the stories of Roman persecution, of Christians whose faith was tested by forcing them to face certain death.

The difference was that from these early gatherings came forth the prophets that were called to preach, to teach, to lead. They were often unlikely vessels of God: former persecutors and individuals of weakness and indecision, until that moment when the Lord's hand touched their hearts forever.

Not that Helen thought of herself as one of the unlikely vessels. She was not standing up to Macalusso and his myriad of followers, speaking the word of God for all to hear. She had not been thrown into a pit of lions, her tormentors demanding that she renounce her love for Jesus or face certain death. Instead she was in what had once been a shelter meant to protect WNN employees from an attack by the former Soviet Union. The shelter was part of the sprawling WNN world headquarters complex, physically located in an area where few people bothered to go anymore. The stockpiles of food, medicine, and water had long since been removed. Only the wiring, some chemical toilets, and a few portable generators, too old for the corporation's present needs, remained from the past. Most of the rooms were now used for long-term storage of materials no one at the network used any more but didn't want to throw out. There was plenty of room to add shelving, sleeping bags, and notebook computers, whose low voltage drain would not be noticed by anyone checking the electric bills in accounting.

It was John Goss, a former videographer for WNN's news department, who suggested to Helen and the other "Haters" to use the shelter as a hideout. "I once did a story on some old Mafia Don who had avoided arrest warrants for ten years. None of the Feds could find him, even though they knew he was living somewhere in New York City. He was finally caught when some rookie cop happened to see his name on an apartment building's resident list while answering a domestic violence call. Seems the building was directly across the street from the police station. He told the embarrassed Feds that he had long ago learned to live in plain sight. So what better place for us to be than in one of the buildings owned by Macalusso?" asked Goss.

Helen had been wary at first, yet she had no better alternative. She couldn't return to her apartment. She couldn't go to the building where her grandmother had been living. And though she had been able to dye her newly cut hair, change the type of clothes she normally wore, and walk with a false limp to disguise her appearance, she did not know how long her charade would protect her. She lived now in the shelter, going out only during shift changes when so many people were moving about that it was easy to blend in with the crowd... If there was a chance to stay free, she had to admit they had found it.

It had taken weeks to build the safe houses for the other followers of Jesus, the people denounced in the media as The Haters. Abandoned buildings and secret rooms in the homes of people who disapproved of the violent actions of Macalusso and his followers, served as hiding places for men, women, and children. John Goss had used his skills with electronics to develop a system of wireless communication devices between some of the hideouts to alert everyone when something was happening. They were also linked by computers and fax machines, tapping into telephone lines to be certain they were never directly traced.

Helen Hannah was the first person to get to the computer when she heard the alarm signal coming from one of the hideouts, thanks to Goss' communication system.

"They got the Davises and their congregation," said Helen, sadly. This was worse than she had anticipated. Anna Davis had promised to meet her that day to pass along "something of great importance."

"What about the CD?" asked John Goss, excitedly. He hurried over to the screen, as though staring at the computer would somehow give him the information he needed.

"There's no way of knowing. I think we have to assume they got that as well."

"And if they did... That CD was our only chance of trying to crack the coded plans for the O.N.E. Day of Wonders.

"John!" said Helen, angrily. "The Davises and their group would no more miss a scheduled time to praise the Lord than they would stop breathing.

"If it's gone, there will be another opportunity, a different opportunity. You'll see," said Helen.

Suddenly there was a loud bang as Cindy Bolton slammed shut the book she was reading. "Another opportunity?" shouted Cindy Bolton, her voice shrill. "<u>Another</u> opportunity?" She turned her head in the direction of Helen and John, cocking it slightly to hear better. The dark glasses, the thick Braille edition of the

New Testament that had been on her lap, all were outward signs of the blindness she had known since early childhood. What did not show, however, was how different life had become for Cindy since she had been denounced as one of the Haters.

"I have been trapped in this dump for three months. You people can change your appearance, sneak outside, see daylight. I can't disguise my blindness. I can't throw away my cane and pretend to walk the streets like everyone else.

"It was all right at first. This was exciting, like being an Old Testament prophet chased by a king whose leadership he had denounced in the name of the Lord. I felt like I was a leader in a battle against good and evil, right and wrong. Me. Cindy Bolton, the blind kid who all her life had to sit on the sidelines and listen to other kids running races, playing tag, playing baseball. For the first time in my life I felt fully alive, fully a part of something special.

"And then the walls started closing in. I know every inch of these rooms. I know where the computers are, and how to work the voice program so I can communicate with the others. I can tell you how many supplies we have left. I can tell you...

"That CD represented freedom for me. That CD meant that maybe we could prove Macalusso was a fraud. The CD meant that maybe we could turn the people against him, show him as the false Messiah, show him as...."

"Cindy, I'm sorry this has been so much rougher on you, but the CD wasn't a ticket to freedom. The CD was another possible weapon in preventing some people from getting caught up in Macalusso's strangle hold on the world. No one ever said we'd be able to get out of hiding."

"And no one ever said we wouldn't!" said Cindy, her voice echoing her inner rage.

"You people don't know what it's like to be handicapped. You talk of sunrises and sunsets, of the beauty of God's world, of the smile on a child's face, the frolicking antics of a puppy at play, and I nod my head and say, Praise the Lord, as though I know what you're talking about. All my life I've lived in two worlds, one of pain for my loss and the other of hope for the future. Each time there is a new development in eye research, I think that at last there will be some miracle surgery that can restore my sight. Each time I hear about new communication technology, I think that this time I will have another way out of my loneliness. And when I learned that the CD may help us learn the secret of the Day of Wonders, I had hope that this was finally an answer. This was a chance to rid the world of Macalusso and bring forth a world of miracle healings. I only want what the blind beggar got from Jesus, and if we've lost the CD, all I can think about is another day, another week, another lifetime in this...this hole...."

"Cindy, I'm sorry. We sometimes forget how much harder this is for you. Perhaps we can sneak you out of here. Perhaps we can disguise you in some way. Perhaps we can...."

"Perhaps we can get ourselves killed because poor blind Cindy wants a field trip," she replied, bitterly.

"There's not a soul out there who wouldn't happily blow us to pieces if they got the chance. Every time you go outside I keep waiting to hear the signal that you've been arrested. How do you think you'd fare with me being along?"

"I know. But you can't blame them, Cindy. They don't know that we're all being set up for something. They don't know that Macalusso is having everyone who disagrees with him tortured or killed. All they see are the miracles. All they see is the show he has so carefully orchestrated. The tragedy is that it's working so well."

Cindy looked in Helen's direction for a moment, then picked up her Bible and began running her fingers over the patterns of raised dots that enabled her to read. She again had control. She was through talking.

Helen watched the young woman sadly. How much she had taken for granted. She felt as she had when she realized how right the words of her grandmother had been. That had been after the rapture, of course. That had been when it was too late to avoid this time of trial. And now she was misreading the heart of a fellow believer...

Helen rose from her chair and walked over to the command center. There were several computers, a pair of fax machines, a television set, a short wave radio, and other equipment. Voltage stabilizers had been installed on the telephone lines used by the modems and other equipment so that a monitor in the Telephone Company could not trace their location based on power consumption. As John Goss had explained, every device used on your telephone line requires a tiny but measurable amount of electricity. For the last several years, engineers within the telephone company's technical centers could tell how many devices were connected to your phone by measuring the voltage drop. The machine he installed boosted the line power so the equipment could not be detected.

The generators reduced other forms of power consumption, though they did have to tap into the existing lines for some of their needs. They only hoped their use was so insignificant as to not be noticed by WNN auditors.

The wall above the electronic equipment was covered with maps, papers, and scrawled notes or short Bible verses meant to help them sustain their vigil in such turbulence. A number of charts detailed elements of Bible prophecy and other Bible research meant to help them through the troubled times. Cindy normally handled radio research and the tasks she could do with the voice program installed on one of the machines. Ron Wolfman, a former military intelligence specialist before becoming a civilian computer consultant for a number of multi-national corporations, was their technical wizard. It was he who was going to help them learn what was on the CD; what was to happen on the Day of Wonders that Macalusso was promoting throughout the world.

"How are you doing, Ronny?" asked Helen, walking over to where he had been working when news of the Davis arrest had reached them.

"I'm all set to access the O.N.E. personnel file. I'll be able to get in there tonight disguised as a security agent. I've inserted some memos in their monitoring system so they'll clear me right through. Once inside…well…without the CD I don't really know what I'm looking for."

"Anything, Ronny. We need to know anything that will give us a clue as to what's being planned for the Day of Wonders. Even if we know just the key personnel assigned to the project we might have something. We can use our knowledge of their skills to anticipate what Macalusso is likely planning for us Christians."

"Are you sure it's going to be that bad, Helen?" asked Ron. "The man basically controls the entire planet. Every Christian is either in jail, nervously moving about the streets, or in hiding. No one can admit his or her faith without the risk of mob violence. What more does he want? What more can he do to us?"

"Plenty," responded Helen. "From reading all the books my grandmother left me and watching all her videos, I know that worse is yet to come."

"If they persecuted me, Jesus said, they will persecute you. In fact, Jesus said in John 16:2 'the time will come that whosoever kills you will think that he is doing God a service,'" noted Helen.

"And they call us 'The Haters'…" said Ron.

"Yes," said Helen. "And good is bad. Bad is good. Black is white. White is black.…But Jesus also said in John 15:18 that if the world hates us, remember that it hated Him first, and not to worry because He has chosen us out of this world. Does that help you any, Cindy?"

But Cindy did not respond. She had set aside her reading, put on earphones, and was listening to music on a cassette player.

Ron laughed, noticing the frustration on Helen's face when she realized the young woman had missed what she had tried to share with her as well. "John and I understand, Helen. And I'm sure Cindy's heart is in the right place. Right now she's hurting. Let her have her little escape. You can tell her again later."

▲

"So much for the big shoot-out at the O.K. Corral, huh, David?" asked Thorold as he and his partner watched the Davises and their congregation being quietly loaded into the vans that would take them to Jail. They removed their flack jackets and handed them to a uniformed officer. "We sure won't need these. Put them with the others, will you, please?

"You know we're going to get in trouble for disobeying our orders, Thor."

"What trouble? I know what headquarters said. Haters who kill are Haters who die. No mercy. No trial. But that's assuming the Haters are armed and offering resistance. That's not what we found. For all we know, they really did have nothing to do with the bombing."

"Thor, get real. Just because they had Bibles instead of guns and bombs doesn't make them any less dangerous. We both know that when a thorough search is made, we're going to find the remote device and those people will be executed."

"At which time I'll say they deserve it. Don't tell me the Messiah wants us to act on emotion and not knowledge. We're supposed to be a government of laws divinely led. Isn't that what has been drilled into us these past few weeks? If these people are guilty..."

"If they're guilty. Thor..."

"I'm sorry, David. I looked into the face of Mrs. Davis and all I could see was my Wendy arguing with me in the living room. She was wrong, okay? I'll grant you that, though I still have doubts I know will never be resolved. She followed a false god. Macalusso's made that very clear and I suppose I have to accept that. But Wendy would never hurt anyone. She had a love for others that..." Thorold wiped a tear from his eye. He looked past his partner as he tried to get his emotions under control.

"I just find it difficult to believe those people, so much like Wendy, could be the ones responsible for killing all those innocent kids."

"We both know that appearances can be deceiving. When I was a detective a few years ago, I had a series of unsolved murders of construction workers. The deaths were violent and these guys were big, powerful men who wouldn't have been easy to kill. We looked at everything in their lives, trying to find some connection. It took us months before we found the killer. It was a sweet little old lady in her seventies who lived in a wretched old apartment building slated for demolition. All the men were connected with the crew scheduled to handle the eventual demolition of the place so that a new building could be erected. To look at her, you'd never have thought she was capable. But we proved the case and she eventually confessed to the series of murders."

"I know. It's just that..."

"I checked the electronic satellite surveillance information myself, Thor. The signal that detonated this bomb came from this building. And you saw the DNA scanner. There's no one else in there."

"What if the detonator was on a timer? It could have been hidden in the building by someone who knew it was abandoned. Or it could have been hidden by someone who knew the Haters would be there; someone who wanted us to think the Haters were responsible. The real bad guys might have been gone long before these people showed up," argued Thorold.

"No way. That bomb went off exactly when the first kid was about to leave the bus. It was perfectly timed to maximize the death toll. Whoever set it off was watching, their finger on the remote button," David argued back.

"So they'd at least have binoculars and a sophisticated radio control. I didn't see any of those things when we made the arrests," Thorold persisted.

"And what sort of search did we make. The guys from the bomb squad will be going through the place a lot more thoroughly than we did. They'll find whatever was used and then those people…"

"I know. But then there will be evidence that one of them was involved. I'm okay with that. I just don't think this was some big conspiracy. If one of those people did it, and I mean if <u>one</u> of them did it, I can't see all of them being punished."

"Okay. So maybe it was one of them. Maybe it was none of them. Maybe this is some giant extra-terrestrial conspiracy with a bomb being detonated from a space ship.

"Look, Thor, I grant you they seem like nice people. I'll grant you that Mrs. Davis talked like Wendy when she was riled. They're still Haters. They still can't accept what they saw with their own eyes. They were witnesses to a miracle, just like us, and they still persist in following someone who even the Bible doesn't credit with the type of miracle the Messiah pulled off in the Middle East." David Smith looked at his partner, realizing the depth of pain he was still feeling from the sudden loss of his family. He realized that Thorold was still trying to sort out what had happened, what had gone wrong with so wonderful a woman like Wendy. More quietly he said, "Thor, I know how rough this has been for you. I know what that woman said in there must be eating away at you. It's only been three months and none of us know how to deal with what's been happening. That's why this job has been so good. It's like being kids again, playing cops and robbers. There are laws and we enforce them.

"You're shaken because our orders were shoot to kill, yet why not? Maybe you made the right judgement call in having them taken in to the station. Certainly we didn't encounter any weapons. But these people still can be fanatics. They can still kill for their sick beliefs. Frankly I think the stress of being alone the way you've been has made you unsure of yourself. You don't want to believe the truth if it isn't pleasant, and we both know how fanatical these Haters can be. I can't stop you from working so hard, but at least try to…"

"To what? Keep an open mind?"

Smith looked at his partner, started to say

something, then thought better of it. They began walking, studying the building as they went.

It was around the side, near an area partially overgrown with bushes, where they saw the door. It was small, with rusty hinges that come from weathering. A closer look revealed that flecks of oxidized metal had chipped from the hinges and fallen to the ground. The only way there would have been such a change in the rust would be if the door had been used recently. Otherwise the wind and rain would have washed away the evidence.

Thorold studied the handle, then touched it, holding it firmly so it would make no sound. He gently tried to turn it, but it was locked. "Do you think we should ask for the dog back?" he asked David.

Then he said, "No. Give me that people detector thing instead, David. It's supposed to be better than a dog's nose for finding people, right?"

"You think someone's inside there?" David asked.

"This door has obviously been used. Maybe it's the entrance the Haters used. It's a lot harder to spot if someone's going down the street."

"Just push this button on the device and watch the light grid. Careful, though, it's a lot heavier than it looks," David warned.

Thorold was startled by the weight. He was expecting something that felt more like one of those handheld video games. This felt like a barbell he might use for working out.

"What's it made of? I thought these electronic gizmos

were supposed to be so light you could keep it in a shirt pocket."

"It's a prototype, Thor. And it does fit in your shirt pocket. I've carried it there. I mean, it's not <u>that</u> heavy."

"Miracles. That's what your buddy Macalusso keeps promising."

"Come on, Thor. The Messiah's not a friend. I met him once with Overlord Parker just like you did. But he is real. He has to be. Now could we forget all that and get on with our job?"

Thorold aimed the device at the door, pressing the button. Then he moved it slowly, going up one side, across the top, down the other side and across the bottom. "Nothing. You sure the batteries are working?"

"You see it light up. If you're warm blooded it puts on a show of blinking and flashing lights. Point it at me and you'll see what I mean," instructed David.

"So maybe they're cold blooded," Thorold responded, slipping the device inside his shirt pocket where it really did fit, then checked his handgun. He replaced it in his holster, picked up the shotgun, and prepared to enter.

"Should we call for back-up?" David asked.

"I thought you said the place was empty. Your machine sure seems to think so."

"It's not my machine. It's a prototype the agency's resident genius put together. Besides, there isn't a machine going that can beat a cop's intuition," he said, drawing his weapon, then stepping aside as Thorold turned and used a Karate side kick to smash at the wooden door.

"One more and we're in, David," he said, striking it again. This time the wood splintered around the handle and they were able to push their way inside.

▲

The three men were deep inside the warehouse in a room that had been specially lined with materials that would reflect outside detection equipment. There was metal shelving covered with electronic equipment meant both for broadcasting and tracking. A large reel-to-reel tape recorder was attached to a scanner capable of intercepting cell phones, CB radios, and all other broadcast signals. There were several VCRs, some equipped to record television broadcasts, others connected to satellite dish receivers and high performance remote controlled video cameras. There was also a spotting scope observation window so tiny that it was invisible when a sliding panel covered it. When open, the men could see anything taking place in the schoolyard hundreds of yards distant. There was also a couch, some battered chairs, a table on which sat a radio control trigger, and other furnishings. A small refrigerator held soft drinks, sandwiches, and other snacks for periods of prolonged observation or monitoring.

The building entrance was far enough from where Thorold and David had broken through that the men were oblivious to the intrusion. It was only when their own door was suddenly opened, by the two agents moving inside, keeping their backs to the wall, and their weapons outstretched, that they realized they had been discovered.

"FREEZE!" shouted David Smith. "O.N.E. Put your hands up." He held his gun in one hand, his photo identification in the other.

Startled, the three men reacted in a way that made it obvious they were as well trained as David and Thorold. The first drew his weapon, firing a shot that just missed Smith. At the same moment, Thorold fired the shotgun, striking him in the chest and killing him instantly.

The other two men used the distraction to bring out their own weapons, firing rapidly as they sought cover. Thorold and David shifted their weapons, returning fire as they, too, tried to find protection.

The bullets went wild. One struck a computer monitor. The screen exploded with the impact. Others tore into the couch and chairs, the walls, and the light fixtures. The shotgun held only five rounds. Thorold had to abandon it for his handgun.

One of the men tried to escape by throwing himself to the floor, rolling towards an exit, then jumping to his feet as he shot wildly until the clip of his automatic was empty. As he rounded the corner, he dropped the clip on the floor and jammed another clip into the handle, ready to shoot anyone who followed.

Also using a flurry of bullets for cover, the other man raced up a back stairwell as David fired rapidly in his direction. With the movement and his adrenaline pumping, Smith's rounds struck the stairs ineffectually.

Thorold knew the procedure. They had shots fired, one man down, and two armed men moving in two different directions. They were to stay where they were, radio for back up, and not pursue until the building was surrounded, all avenues for escape sealed off.

The trouble was that the men and women who established these procedures were not street agents who had just experienced a shoot-out. Their adrenaline was not pumping when they made up these rules. They were not experiencing the fear that if the bad guys reached the street while the officers waited for a back up, innocent civilians could be hurt. They were not experiencing the sense of duty that told them to stop such violent individuals at any cost.

Nodding at one another, David headed for the stairwell and Thorold jnodulljmoved towards the opening through which the other man had disappeared.

David Smith moved cautiously, his back to the staircase wall, his right arm stretched out ahead of him, holding his weapon, ready to fire if necessary. He had heard the gunman running to the next level. He heard a door open and shut, but he had no idea what lay ahead. He should have stayed back. He should have called in for someone to check the layout of the building. He should have....

It was too late to worry about that now. David realized Thorold might have been right about the Haters. He had come to the warehouse expecting to be in a shoot-out. He was certain that people who bombed a school bus would be armed. People who denounced the Messiah, who had seen the way he had saved the world from self-destruction, had to be comfortable with violence. Yet when they arrested the Haters, they had found no weapons of any kind. That's what didn't make sense. Perhaps there was more to this than the obvious. Perhaps.

Smith reached the top of the staircase. A door opened outward onto the landing. There was no window, no way to see what was on the other side. Even worse, the door opened towards him, creating an awkward situation.

Positioning himself so the opening door would offer some cover, Smith reached across his body with his left hand, then pulled the handle as swiftly as he could while standing on the other side. He could see nothing but a seemingly empty room from his limited angle. He listened, but all he heard was silence.

Steadying himself, slowing his breathing, Smith waited. Then, keeping his back against the open door, his gun forward, he moved around the side.

It was only training that kept David Smith from pulling the trigger, only training that taught him to look first, to register the target as neutral or an enemy. Without these special courses, David Smith might have shot his superior officer, Len Parker, the head of the One Nation Earth security force, the man often considered second in power only to the Messiah himself.

"Overlord Parker. Sir, are you all right? There was a man who came up these steps just moments ago. He tried to shoot Agent Stone and myself."

Even as he spoke, David realized something was wrong, very wrong. The building was supposed to be the center for Haters. At least that is what they thought when they made their arrests. But seeing Overlord Parker there; knowing that the man he had just been chasing had to have passed Parker, seemed suspicious. The man had to come this way, and he should have been arrested if....

"I think you understand my precarious position, Agent Smith. You did some excellent detective work to find this place. I know the DNA meter would not have registered through these treated walls. I must congratulate you. Perhaps you will even be buried with a medal."

David was shocked as Parker raised his gun. "Mr. Parker. No! You don't understand. I...."

Len Parker fired the first round into David's chest. He fell back against the wall, his mouth agape, his eyes staring. David's weapon slipped from his hand as it became lifeless. Parker shot a second round through David's skull. "I'm afraid you're the one who doesn't understand."

▲

CHAPTER 5

▲

The Hunter Becomes The Hunted

▲

▲

▲

▲

For a moment Thorold thought of going back. Some thing was wrong with what was happening, terribly wrong. His place was with his partner. Together they could handle one man, and worry about the other later. Together they would be safer, each covering the other's back. He had made the killing shot that saved his partner's life. The next time it might be David who saved him. They should not have split up like that, not with no other back-up available.

Thorold held his gun with his finger along the

trigger guard the way he had been taught in the academy. Holding the trigger before he had to could lead him to fire accidentally. And in a situation like he was in, every bullet mattered.

"Fire fights aren't like on television," he remembered his instructor telling his academy class. "You're both scared. Your hearts are pumping blood like crazy. You think you're aiming carefully and you're really pulling your shots all over the place.

"Police departments around the country have found that most shootouts take place at nine feet or closer. And most times both parties miss. That's how worked up you'll be. Everything you can do to get control of a situation first, and that means not accidentally firing your weapon before you're ready, may give you that slight edge that makes the difference between living and dying."

Thorold waited, trying to slow his breathing, faintly hearing the other man doing the same. Then, when he knew he had to make a move, Thorold lowered his weapon, put his finger on the trigger, and fired two wild rounds into the room. Moving in, he fired again as he spotted his assailant doing the same.

The man Thorold was after no longer had a handgun. He was now holding an automatic rifle, and though the clip was short, the weapon was far deadlier than Thorold's.

Just as Thorold had done, the man let loose with a burst of bullets in Thorold's direction. The bullets struck the wall. The sound echoing about the room seemed to grow louder with each reverberation, a cacophony of death. Thorold fired again and retreated back around the corner. He prayed he was by a firewall, or a support wall; any wall thick enough and strong enough to provide real cover.

Thorold counted to himself. One, two, three, four, five...Then he looked around the corner, fired, then retreated as another burst of bullets came in his direction. Again he went out, but when he started to shoot, he found his weapon was empty. Smiling, his attacker aimed more carefully, pulling the trigger as Thorold scrambled back to the room where he had first confronted the gunmen. He remembered a stack of crates against a far wall and thought he could use them for cover.

Thorold kept moving, expecting at any minute to feel the burning sensation and searing pain of a bullet entering his body. As he reached the stack of crates, he heard the same clicking sound his own weapon had made. The attacker was out of bullets.

Suddenly Thorold's eyes spotted a gun on the floor that had been dropped by the first man killed. Before he could run for it, the gun shook slightly, then flew across the room, into the hand of his attacker. For a moment he was mesmerized by what had just occurred. Then he realized the attacker was aiming the weapon, and he moved behind the stack of crates on palettes just as the other man opened fire.

Momentarily hidden from view, Thorold climbed the crates. He didn't know what was inside, but whatever it was, he was thankful it was heavy enough to hold his weight without swaying or creaking. He had never been very athletic, posting the lowest passing scores for strength and agility in the academy. Now he found himself moving swiftly and quietly. "Trying not to die makes Olympians of the worst of us," he thought as he moved.

The man with the gun moved boldly, making no attempt to seek cover. He knew Thorold was out of ammunition. He knew there were only two ways out of the room and from his position, he could easily cover both of them.

Part way up the stack, perhaps ten feet off the ground, Thorold paused, reached into his shirt pocket and took out the DNA detector. He hurled it across the room, hoping to momentarily distract the gunman.

The ruse failed, though the gunman glanced away anyway, amused by the desperate attempt to gain a few more seconds of life. He had the upper hand. He knew he would shortly spot Thorold and kill him.

Then he heard the sound before he could react. Thorold had managed to dislodge one of the crates, shoving it down towards the gunman. He moved to the side, leaping as the crate fell. He scrambled towards the gunman whose shoulder had been struck, and knocked him to the ground.

Thorold knocked the gun from his hand, then twisted the man's arm up behind his back while pushing his head against the floor, knocking him unconscious. He jerked his cuffs from the case at the back of his belt, then locked the man's wrists together behind him. Thorold was taking no further chances.

Breathing heavily, Thorold pulled the man from under the crate, then began going through his pockets. In the gunman's jacket he found what he suspected he would find, a small electronic box with a collapsible antenna and a detonate button.

"A detonator," said Thorold, breathing hard. "So you did set up those Haters. They didn't blow up any bus. That was you. But who are you?" He continued searching the pockets of the unconscious man, seeking some form of identification. What he found was not what he expected.

Thorold pulled out of the man's pocket a standard issue leather folding case containing a badge on one side and a photo identification card, complete with fingerprints and description on the other. It was a holder he knew well because it was identical to the one he carried. "You're working for the O.N.E.?" he gasped, staring at the man.

Frightened for the first time, Thorold dragged his assailant to a wall where a pipe ran up one side. He freed one of the still unconscious man's hands, then cuffed him to the pipe. He took the dead man's spare ammunition, reloaded his handgun, then found the DNA detector he had used for a distraction. He turned it on, watching the lights work. It was far sturdier than he realized. He moved it around the room and saw that it registered where it should. Thorold placed the device back inside his breast pocket. There was no way of knowing when he might need it. Then he started back towards the stairs where his partner had gone.

▲

Thorold Stone moved automatically as he reached the top of the stairs, opened the door, and saw the sprawled, bloody body of his partner and friend. He had known from the moment he found the O.N.E. identification holder in the pocket of the assailant he subdued that this would be the outcome. He did not know why, nor did he dwell on what it meant. There would be time for grieving later. There would be a place for righteous anger. At the moment all that was certain was that he was alive in a game of cat and mouse in which the cats had the upper hand.

Thorold moved with the same choreographed precision that preceded his partner's death. This time there was no surprise when he saw Overlord Parker. This time the gun was aimed at his superior. Thorold was ready to fire if Parker raised his hand. "Overlord Parker, sir. I'm going to have to ask you to drop that weapon."

Parker continued to hold his weapon loosely at his side. There was a smile on his face, a look of unconcern Thorold suspected was meant to psychologically disarm him.

"What tipped you off, Agent Stone? What led you here?" Parker asked.

"Drop it, Mr. Parker," said Thorold, ignoring the question. "Drop it right now!"

"You're in way over your head, my friend," said Parker, speaking quietly.

"Why are you doing this?" asked Thorold. "Why are you setting up the Haters? Why is the O.N.E. lying to the world?"

Parker was silent for a moment, then slowly raised his gun in Thorold's direction. But before he could sight, Thorold fired.

Nothing happened. He heard the explosion of the bullet being struck by the firing pin, felt the kick of the weapon, saw the smoke come from the muzzle. But that was all. He might have been firing blanks, except even blanks shoot something from the muzzle.

Thorold, shaken, steadied himself and fired again and again. Round after round went through his gun the same way. It was as though each bullet vanished upon leaving the muzzle of his weapon.

With the clip empty, Thorold lowered his weapon in shock. He was certain he was about to die; equally certain there was nothing he could do about it. "Who are you?" he asked quietly. <u>What</u> are you?"

Parker spoke quietly, his voice now strangely different. Deeper, more resonant, it seemed to rise from the depths of Hell, filling the room with its power. "I am a servant of the Messiah. I'm here to help him rid the world of anyone and everyone who stands in his way. And now, Agent Stone, that includes you."

Parker raised his gun and fired. Thorold was thrown back by the impact, dropping to the floor. He lay unmoving, mouth agape, eyes wide, while Parker turned and walked purposely towards the brick wall, passing through it as though it was a projected image, not bricks and mortar.

For a moment Thorold was still. His chest felt as though someone had thrown a brick at him. Gradually he gained the energy to roll on his side and feel for blood. When there was none, he touched his pocket and realized the bullet had struck the DNA detector. It was shattered, but it had deflected the bullet. His chest was bruised from the force, but the skin had not been punctured.

Thorold removed the now worthless electronic device, then carefully stood up, staring at the place where Parker had passed through the wall. Certain it was an illusion, he walked over to the brick. Either it was a projected image, like a hologram, or there was a trap door.

Moving his hands against the brick, Thorold realized the wall was real, not an image. He found the deep indentations where the bullets he had fired from his gun had struck. He had thought they had disappeared, but they passed through his target. They passed through harmlessly, yet with enough force to shatter some of the brick.

He carefully rubbed, poked, and probed, trying to find a hidden switch, a loose brick or some evidence that the wall was hinged. He desperately wanted something that would show him Len Parker had passed through a secret door, not through the wall itself. There was nothing. Thorold had seen what he thought he had seen. Len Parker had passed through solid brick.

In shock, Thorold started to walk over to the body of David Smith, then found himself so light headed, he dropped to his knee, lowering his head. His face was covered with sweat. He hadn't been shot, but the impact of the bullet striking the DNA detector in his pocket had been stronger than he realized. He was in pain, his body felt as it had during his early martial arts training when he had failed to block another agent's kick, the man's foot striking and breaking one of his ribs.

Forcing himself to breathe slowly, not to let himself hyperventilate, he looked over at his partner's corpse and said, "You were right, buddy. Macalusso's not the only one doing miracles." He paused, feeling the bruise on his chest, wincing from the pain of his own touch. Then he said, "I won't let them get away with this, David. First my family and now my best friend. I won't let them get away with this."

Thorold wanted to be still. Each movement he made was as painful as when he had first been struck. There was no time for such self-indulgence, though. He had a prisoner downstairs. There was a dead man to be reported. There was work to be done.

Thorold stood, steadying himself, then moved to the stairs, walking as swiftly as he could. When he reached the bottom, he headed for the pipe where he had left his prisoner, then stopped, amazed. The man was gone, though the cuffs remained. Both were still locked, one around the pipe, the other sitting empty where the missing man's wrist had been.

The building was an architect's wonder. The twenty-seven stories of steel and glass looked so futuristic, it seemed as though it could be launched into space and used as an orbital home for workers in the 22nd Century. It had been built as the corporate headquarters for a multi-national media conglomerate acquired by Franco Macalusso's business interests just before he bought WNN and performed the first of his miracles.

The sign at the top included what had become the most familiar logo in the world – the pyramid and eye symbol with the banner for "One Nation Earth" below. The windows enabled passers-by to watch the happy employees doing their jobs. It was a place that seemed to radiate joy, inclusivity, and a new beginning for all. There were people of all races, all ages, and all walks of life, each thankful for the opportunity to serve the Messiah, and serve the new world he was creating. What could not be seen was the conversion that had been done in a massive lower level which formerly had been an underground parking garage.

The conversion had been made because the construction of the garage allowed for it. There were no windows, and access to the lower floors was already limited to a single elevator and a single stair well. Building high security holding cells, sound proof interrogation rooms, guard areas, and other necessities for dealing with the Haters had been a relatively simple matter. The entrance ramp had been converted so that a massive steel door prevented any but authorized vehicles from coming into the area. It was through this entrance that the Haters arrested by Thorold Stone, David Smith, and the others were brought for processing.

The eighteen members of the Davis congregation were quiet as they walked past a row of holding cells accompanied by a single guard. They were no longer handcuffed, but it was obvious from the design of the holding area that resistance was futile.

The guard ordered the Haters to stop at a processing window. A bulletproof glass enclosed structure served as the monitoring headquarters and processing point. A bank of television sets revealed all parts of the holding area and interrogation rooms, hidden cameras and banks of special video recorders kept track of everyone's actions, including those of the guards and O.N.E. Special Agents doing business there.

"Another eighteen Haters," said the guard, handing the man at the desk the papers. "They've all been processed."

"Don't sound so annoyed, Bill. Eighteen more Haters locked away means we're eighteen steps closer to world peace."

The men and women were silent. This was not the time to take a stand. This was not a time to publicly praise the Lord. They would do that quietly in their cells, regretting only that they had seen the light too late to avoid this time of trial.

As the Haters were taken to their cells, an angry man approached. He was holding a frightened teenaged boy by the arm, and escorted by an armed guard.

"He insisted on bringing the boy down here," said the embarrassed guard. "And I agreed to bring him here to you, even though I know it's improper. It's just that, well, he's a good man from my neighborhood. We often are at each other's house to celebrate the arrival of the Messiah."

"It's the boy…" the man said.

"Dad, please. Please don't do this. You don't und…"

"Tough love. That's what he needs," said the man. "Drugs. Alcohol. Christianity. It's all the same. When a boy goes astray, the punishment has to be swift and sure. It's the only way he'll learn."

"Are you saying your son is one of the Haters?" asked the man at the booking station.

"Claims to be. Has their literature. Sings their songs. His mother and I raised him better than to be a no good punk hanging out with a bad lot."

"If you don't mind my saying so, Bill," the guard said to his friend. "I think you may be over reacting. I've known Joey since he was born. He's basically a good kid. A little rebellious like so many of them. Too young to really grasp what's happening."

"He had a Bible in his room. A Bible. He knows our family's values. We don't allow such obscenity in our home."

"Sir," said the booking agent. "I admire your love and respect for our Lord and Savior, Franco Macalusso, praise his blessed name, but from the looks of him, he's awfully young. How old is your son? Fourteen? Fifteen?"

"Fifteen, but what does that matter? First the Bible, and tonight, when he thought I was downstairs, I caught him kneeling by the bed, head bowed, hands clasped together. He said he was thinking about a test coming up at school, but we all know better. We know what he was really doing. That's when I cuffed him good and hauled his butt down here. He wants to be one of the Haters, let him take the consequences while he's still got time to learn."

"But Dad, I was praying for you."

The guard looked sadly at the boy. He had been to his home many times. He had taught him how to play basketball. He had taken him to baseball games. He guessed you just couldn't tell about kids. Some make a father proud, and others turn out to be…"I think your

Dad's right, Joey. This is an awful place. A terrible place. It's no place for children, but it is where Haters have to come. Maybe if you're here a few days, maybe when some of the people here talk with you…."

"Dad…."

For a moment the older man had second thoughts. He looked around the holding area, and sensed for the first time how bleak and foreboding it was. He'd be terrified to be taken here. To do it to his son, even if the boy was with the Haters…"This is the right thing, isn't it, Kent?" he asked, looking at the guard.

"You're not the first father to turn in a son. Probably half the Haters in captivity were turned in by family members. It's what we have to do in these times when we're so close to world peace."

The father looked at his son, then hugged him, holding the youth against his chest, burying his face in the boy's hair. "I love you, son. I know it may not seem like it right now. I know that saying I'm doing this for your own good sounds hollow. But if I didn't love you, I wouldn't care about your immortal soul. I wouldn't care that you were reading the book, praying…I…."

The boy pulled back, tears in his eyes. "I know how you feel, Dad, and I respect that. I'll be okay. Jesus will protect me and I'll pray for Him to look after you, too."

The father stared for a moment. His son, his beloved son had become almost a stranger. The Haters were dangerous. Of that he was certain. He just hoped the shock of being in jail would return the Joey he wanted his son to be. Then he hugged the boy once more and left the holding area.

When the father was out of sight, the guard looked at him with great anger. "What's the matter with you, Joey? Can't you see what's going on in this world? Why would you want to be part of such a hideous cult as this? Look at these idiots. We just booked eighteen Haters who blew up a school bus full of kids just like you. It's hard to imagine anyone being so full of hatred when someone so good has come among us. You keep your nose clean around here. You watch and listen. You think about what's really going on. I think you're going to be glad your dad brought you here."

The guard put his arm around the boy's shoulder and took him to a holding cell. As they walked down the hall, two of the women who had been arrested earlier were being taken to a shower room with several other prisoners. Quietly, hoping no one else would hear them, they began singing "Jesus loves me, this I know, because the Bible tells me so...."

Startled, the guard walking with Joey turned and drew an electric stun gun from a small holster on his belt. The weapon was meant to achieve swift control over violent prisoners without killing them. When he pulled the trigger, two darts connected to the weapon by a long, thin wire, imbedded themselves in the arm of one of the women. Then a high voltage, low amperage current jolted her body, causing her to scream in agony and lose all muscle control. Then he detached the wires, readied the weapon for another use, and replaced it in his holster.

"Yes, Joey, I think this is going to be just what you need."

▲

CHAPTER 6

▲

On the Run

▲

▲

▲

▲

Len Parker paused at the newsstand just outside of the O.N.E. building and stared at the display racks. Stretched across the top were copies of *Time* magazine, each bearing his photograph on the cover. "Len Parker: One Nation Earth Top Cop" read the caption.

He was startled. He had known when his picture was being taken that there was talk of a story in the works. He had known that people were being interviewed. He had just assumed that the interviews were a normal part of the Macalusso publicity machine.

There were always stories being written for placement in some newspaper somewhere around the world. But this was different. *Time* magazine had acted independently. There was certainly some cooperation by the Messiah's staff, though they did not initiate the cover decision. This was about Len Parker and only Len Parker, thanks be to the Messiah.

Ever since he was a kid living in some of the poorest, toughest sections of Chicago he had wanted to be a police officer. His father was a laborer who took the most dangerous jobs he could get because they paid a few cents more an hour than safer work. He went on assembly lines where the safety shut-offs were disabled on stamping and cutting machines which periodically cost one or another co-worker a finger, a hand, or worse. He cleared asbestos from buildings for a company that underbid everyone by going in without special protective equipment for the workers, paying a bribe to any inspector who came by. He worked construction where the materials and equipment were often substandard. And always he called himself lucky because he had never had anything more serious than a dislocated shoulder, a broken leg, and a few cuts and bruises; at least on the outside. What he did not realize until his collapse at the age of forty was how badly he had hurt his lungs and other organs from the waste he inhaled. He was a bedridden old man within three years and dead before his forty-fifth birthday.

Parker's mother cared for the family as best she could with jobs cleaning homes, offices, and apartments. There were six kids in the family, Len being the youngest, and too often there was a choice between eating and rent. His mother always chose food for her children, so they lived in a succession of cramped apartments, sometimes leaving in the middle of the night, sometimes watching the Sheriff's department move their few belongings onto the front lawn in response to an eviction proceeding.

Father Mike at Our Lady of Perpetual Devotion, to which his mother dragged the family every week, thought Len's interest in law enforcement was the result of a higher calling. Father Mike had a grandfather and several cousins in law enforcement. He talked about the motto a number of departments had adopted—"To Protect And To Serve"—and praised Len for wanting to be a part of that tradition. Len, by contrast, thought Father Mike was full of it.

Len's role models were the swaggering street cops of his neighborhood, the ones who took whatever fruit they wanted from the stands they passed or had the butcher give them five pounds of prime rib and charge them for five pounds of chicken. They got envelopes filled with cash from bars that had illegal back room after hours joints and meted out justice to errant teens by taking them into an alley and beating them with a rubber hose.

"Won't leave marks, punk," said Officer O'Malley the day Len got caught shoplifting in Woolworth's. Len had returned the toy, said he was sorry, and thought that would be the end of it. When O'Malley was done with him, he could barely walk and it hurt when he tried to pee. The punishment hadn't fit the crime. It was a sadistic beating the cop got away with because of his uniform. And Len wanted that same power.

There was a police cadet program when Len went to high school. Do-gooder cops, men that Father Mike thought should serve as role models. They worked with kids, taking them on ride alongs, giving them tours of the station, teaching them athletics, and helping them with their homework. They were trying to give the best and brightest of the ghetto poor a leg up in life, and Len Parker embraced them for all they were worth; not that he wanted to be like them. He just knew that these were the men who held the key to his future success. He watched, listened, and learned, working his way through college in civilian jobs within the department, then going to the academy when he turned twenty-one.

Len knew the system by then, knew how to work his arrests so he could move up quickly. He'd play the bars, the after-hours joints, the brothels, and the drug houses one against the other. Whoever paid him the most stayed open without a bust. The only exception were the ones utilized by local power figures—city council members, county commissioners, the heads of corporations, and the like. Those went untouched, though he made certain both the owners and the "guests" knew what he was doing. He knew no one would turn him in. He also knew that many, especially the high stakes gamblers and the men who brought a different "wife" with them on every visit, would feel beholden to him.

Len also made certain he never collected from the power players. He only went to see them when he needed something special, such as a good word as he moved up the ranks into administration. Usually he waited, knowing that the ambitious councilman with the conservative constituency and a secret lust for living beyond his income was moving into state politics. Some of the people who owed him became Congressional Representatives, Federal judges, high state officials, and inside money sources for both major political parties. By the time he was ready to move from city officer to Federal cop, he had supporters in place who would do anything for him just so he wouldn't reveal what he knew.

The trick was one J. Edgar Hoover had used to protect his power base. Hoover had been the master in a day when the media could be controlled. Parker had to tread more treacherous waters, knowing that there was always some hot shot reporter who wanted to "earn his chops" by exposing corruption he couldn't enjoy first hand himself. It was a fact that had come to the attention of Franco Macalusso when he was still with the United Nations. It was the reason Macalusso elevated Parker to the top position after revealing himself as the Messiah of One Nation Earth.

Now, with his picture on the cover of *Time*, with his ability to take a life at will and have no one question his actions, with his ability–praise to the Messiah–to walk through walls, he felt like one of those ancient gods. He felt he had been elevated to Mt. Olympus, a deity in human form greater than anyone other than the Messiah himself.

Smiling, Len Parker walked into the O.N.E. building. In the lobby a television monitor was programmed to play the Macalusso-owned WNN, now the voice of One Nation Earth. WNN was now broadcast in more than 1,000 languages and dialects throughout the world. "Coming up on WNN–Macalusso mania is sweeping the globe. Around the world, celebrations continue every minute of every day as citizens of One Nation Earth revel in the wake of the Messiah's latest series of miracles…."

Parker entered the elevator, removed a key from his pocket, put it into a slot marked to the twenty-seventh floor, then pushed the button. Even here at headquarters, the limited access floor, the luxury private office, the equipment to instantly access anywhere in the world, all set him apart. A god…Len Parker was like a god. He was….

"Overlord Parker, sir, we have a problem," said Agent Warren Spencer, Parker's chief of internal security. He and his partner, Agent Wayne Dempsey, were waiting just outside Parker's office door. Their comments interrupted his moment of reverie. He did not appreciate that fact.

"What sort of problem is so important that it requires you to delay me on my way to my office?" he asked, annoyed.

"The second agent, Thorold Stone…."

"Yes, I'm familiar with Agent Stone. We had the misfortune of meeting him when we were setting up the Haters, but I made certain he will cause us no further trouble."

"That's why we're here. I sent a clean-up crew to the scene and they…. They suggest that things didn't work out the way you might think."

"You mean there were witnesses? There were others with them?" asked Parker, angrily.

"There were only two. Agent Smith is dead, but, sir…."

"Will you get to the point?"

"Agent Stone is not dead, sir. He's gone."

"What do you mean?"

"Gone. His body wasn't there. His blood wasn't there. It's as though…."

"I shot him myself. He wasn't wearing a flak jacket. That bullet had to have hit him in the chest." He stared at the two men, clearly stunned. A man with his power should be fully in control of every situation. He took a deep breath, exhaled slowly, then turned to Dempsey and said, "Kill him. Find Agent Stone and kill him. I want him dead. No arrest. No warning. He's as well trained as you are so you'll have to use caution, but make certain he doesn't escape us again. The man knows too much for his own good."

"Yes, sir," said Dempsey, hurrying out.

"There's something more, sir," said Spencer. "There's something else, too."

Parker glared at his chief of internal security. For a moment he thought about taking out his gun and shooting the man. No one would question the death. No one would dare. Yet he also knew that the problem was not the fault of Spencer. He was the one who had shot Agent Stone, then left without checking to be certain he had left a corpse. The missing man was his responsibility. It was wrong to kill the messenger even if there would be no one bold enough to question such an action. He had to stay calm, to listen, to figure out how to rectify whatever had happened.

"What is 'something more?'"

"The CD, sir. We strip-searched all eighteen of the Haters. We checked every inch of the warehouse where they were hiding. We sent crews to search each of their homes, their offices, their cars....anywhere they might have hidden it. The CD is nowhere to be found. The only thing we can imagine is that our intelligence information was wrong. The woman didn't have it when we thought she did."

"Oh, she had it, all right. She worked for me, the lying Hater. She worked for me, knew about it, and pretended to love the Messiah as much as we do. Then she stole it from me. She stole it and it has to be somewhere those Haters go."

"We'll recheck our steps and widen the search, sir."

"You'll do that. You'll do that and you'll find it or I swear I'll charge you with being an accessory to its disappearance.

"The Day of Wonders is less than seventy-two hours away. If that CD makes its way into the underground, and if those Haters manage to find out what's on it, they'll do everything they can to expose the Messiah's plan."

"I understand, Sir," said Spencer, wondering how the Messiah's Day of Wonders could be so dependent upon such a human object as a computer disk. This was the great one who had raised his arms and stopped missiles in their flight, destroyed weapons in the arms of soldiers, and saved billions from horrible deaths. Why was the Messiah so concerned with a computer disk? Why would it matter?

Spencer started to ask, then thought better of it. Len Parker was barely in control. He could see that. The man was too dangerous to rile any more than he already was. "I understand," he repeated.

"No, I don't think you do," said Parker, angrily. "If you did, you'd be here telling me you found the disk."

Had Thorold Stone been thinking more clearly, he would have left his car and stolen someone else's to make the trip home. Going home was more of a risk than he should be taking, that he had known since he made the decision to go back. What he had not thought about was the homing device on every O.N.E. agent's car. It was meant to assure help could reach them quickly if they had an emergency. The control center would be instantly notified if they crashed, and satellite sensors could pinpoint their location within ten feet. There was also a remote panic button they carried with their keys, which would enable them to alert the monitoring center if they were in trouble. What he had failed to consider was that the system could work in reverse. Punch in the vehicle's code number and it would be found in a matter of seconds. He was home, and Agent Dempsey was not far behind.

The television was on when Thorold entered what had been the family room, which he partially converted to an office when his family...disappeared.

He always left the television on when he left, a carry over from his training. The sound meant that someone was home. Anyone seeking to break in would have second thoughts if they heard the television. A ringing telephone might be ignored. An unanswered doorbell might mean that the person had fallen asleep in front of the set. It was a device that would cause second thoughts, though this time Thorold was sorry it was playing. The stories were all about Macalusso, someone Thorold was increasingly convinced was either evil or a complete fool. Since he did not like to think that a Messiah, a real Messiah, could be naïve about the actions of his underlings, Franco Macalusso had to be a false…False what?

"A look at the new Europe," said the newscaster on the television. Thorold glanced at the set for a moment while he said, "Not since the days of the Holy Roman Empire has the continent found such peace and unity. Now, without a single shot being fired, Europe, under the leadership of the Messiah, Franco Macalusso, once again rules the world."

The camera switched to the pyramid and eye logo of One Nation Earth, then dissolved into a seemingly endless row of flagpoles, each with the flag of a different nation mounted on top, as a voice over intoned, "One World. One Network. This is WNN." Then the newscast continued.

"Coming up this hour, we will be looking at the following stories: The incredible transformation of the Middle East in the wake of the seven-year peace treaty between Israel and her neighbors.

"Construction continues on the Temple of Mankind in Jerusalem as One Nation Earth officials struggle to ensure that the expected crowds can be managed.

"But first, our lead story: Another Hater strike has shocked the world. More than seven-hundred elderly patients at a veterans hospital near Rome are now confirmed dead in this latest attack by Christian extremists."

"Yeah, right," muttered Stone. "And Santa Claus steals toys from orphanages."

Thorold stared at the organized chaos that passed for a work area, trying to decide what he had to take with him. The desk, actually a solid wood door laid over several fire resistant file cabinets, was covered with papers, books, video and audiotapes. A top of the line personal computer rested next to a sophisticated laptop. There were three VCRs in a rack arrangement, the wires passing through filtration devices to boost the picture quality for copying. There was a television monitor, a duplicating audiocassette deck, and speakers mounted on the wall.

The rest of the wall space was partially covered with newspaper clippings related to the coming of Franco Macalusso. The headlines read, "Messiah's Miracle Saves World." " Messiah Arrives; Nukes Vanish In Flight." "A New Beginning: 187 Million Enemies Of Peace Vaporized." "A Last Message Of Hate." "Haters Block Spiritual Breakthrough." " Messiah Heals 7,000 In Athens." "If Not God, Who?"

There were also family pictures of him in his

rookie uniform surrounded by his academy graduating class, of the appointment ceremonies when he joined O.N.E.'s enforcement division, and Wendy when they were on their honeymoon.

Thorold stopped to pick up a photograph of the four of them together, smiling happily. "I'll never stop looking for you," he whispered, lingering to look at the picture longer than he should. "I'll never stop loving you."

Placing the photograph on top of the notebook computer, he pulled it from its docking bay, quickly removing the wires from the back so he could take it with him. He set it by the door, then hurried to his gun closet. Unlocking it, he removed a small revolver and ankle holster that would keep the weapon under his pants leg and out of view. Then he added an automatic and several clips of ammunition for the police issue weapon he had been carrying when he got into the shoot-out at the warehouse.

Finally he went to the bookshelf, searching for the volume he wanted to take with him. It was a book he had purchased out of curiosity, a supposedly scientific study he thought might be fun to read some day. Now its title—*Aliens Among Us?*—seemed to relate to what he had seen Len Parker do following the shooting. He would read it when he got somewhere safe.

As Thorold prepared to leave again, he heard a sound in what should have been an empty house. Grabbing the television remote, he pressed the "mute" button to silence the set. Listening closely, he realized it was the sound of creaking floorboards. Someone else was in the house, trying to move silently towards where he was working. Still holding the remote and staring at the entranceway for a moment, he started to move swiftly to where he had left his weapons. Before he could do it, Agent Dempsey walked into the room.

"Freeze, Stone," said Dempsey. He was wearing a bullet resistant vest and a flak jacket. He had a radio in a holster in his belt, the microphone/speaker clipped to his lapel. If he had trouble, he would be able to press a button on the radio and be in instant two-way communication with the tactical commander. "Get your hands up where I can see them."

"Those Haters didn't blow up that bus," said Thorold. He recognized Agent Dempsey, knew he worked for Len Parker, and knew he might die. But if he could distract the man from whatever his mission might be, if he could get him talking...

"That doesn't matter. They're still Haters. If they didn't do that crime, they did another. They're all alike."

"No, it's not like that. They were set up. Probably the same is true for others. It's happening with Parker's knowledge. But why? And why are you helping him?"

"Let's just say that keeping attention focused on the Haters helps keep the world motivated. Now get your hands up above your head."

For a moment Thorold just kept talking, hoping to distract Dempsey from seeing the remote he still had in his hand. "Keeps the world motivated?" he asked, slipping his finger on the volume setting. Out of the corner of his eye, Thorold could see the television set that was almost directly behind Dempsey. The word

"Volume" appeared at the bottom of the screen, along with an ever-growing scale to show that the sound was being increased. "Motivated to do what? To hate them?"

"Get your hands up now, Stone."

Thorold shrugged his shoulders, then slowly started moving his hands. Dempsey, nervous, realized he had better kill Stone while he still had some semblance of control. He moved the weapon from a one handed to a two-handed grip, preparing to fire, when Thorold released the mute on the remote. The sudden explosion of sound from the television set startled Dempsey who jerked around, accidentally firing a round into the wall as he moved.

Thorold leaped at Dempsey, grabbing the wrist holding the gun with both his hands, twisting his body into the Agent, then raising his knee and bringing the man's arm down sharply against it. The movement broke the arm. Dempsey dropped the gun and screamed in pain. Thorold let go of the arm, then delivered a blow with his elbow into Dempsey's stomach. Turning back so he faced the agent, Thorold punched him twice more in the gut, then grabbed him by the hair and collar, smashing him into the wall. Dempsey fell to the ground, unconscious, landing at an angle that triggered the broadcast/receive button on his radio.

The brutality of his action surprised him. Thorold was well trained, one of a limited number of men who was allowed to help the Secret Service when the President had come to the city prior to the day when Franco Macalusso changed all the governments of the world. Still, he thought of himself as a peaceful man, a gentle man, the only type of man he could imagine Wendy loving. What he had done to Agent Dempsey was vicious, and as he looked at the unconscious figure on the ground, he realized he didn't care what happened to the man. Perhaps the stress of the loss, of the confusion over the Haters, and of the violence that had come from the man he thought was on the same side of the law had all become too much for him.

Had he become one of the predators, a man as evil as Len Parker? Had he....

"Agent Dempsey... Agent Dempsey, do you copy?" came a voice from the unconscious man's lapel. Thorold realized immediately what had happened. He didn't know if he should shut off the radio or leave it alone.

"Agent Dempsey, report, please. Agent Dempsey...."

It was not the time to think. He had to move, had to act.

Thorold picked up Dempsey's gun, aimed it at the computer monitor on the desk, and fired a round, exploding the glass and electronics. Then he stuffed the weapon in his belt, stepped over the unconscious agent, grabbed his laptop and the photo of his family, and left.

"All tactical units in the vicinity of 357 Park,. Cross street Lawn, Park and Lawn, we have a possible 721. Suspect is armed and dangerous."

Thorold could hear the sirens as he raced to his car. The way the city had been divided into grids for the tactical response units, he knew he had no more than a minute before at least one unit would arrive. He opened the car door, tossed in the computer, and started the engine. Hoping no one was on the street, he shot backwards out of his drive, then drove in the opposite direction of the louder of the two sirens he was hearing in the distance.

He turned right at the corner, left at the next, then pulled into the drive of a house with a "For Sale" sign on it. The place was empty, the owner having moved to Florida a month or two before the Messiah had appeared. With the garage in the back, it was the perfect place to hide until the responding agents were at his house.

Breathing hard, Stone sat in the car, engine running, gun on the seat next to him, and the windows open so he could listen to the sounds of the street. That was when he remembered the homing device. Once his house was searched, once Dempsey was found, they would call in his car.

Frightened now, Thorold got out of the car, taking the computer and the photo of his family. He crossed the lawn and looked around at the houses. The neighborhood was popular with families, and many of them had three or four cars. The husband would drive one, his wife another, and it had become a status symbol among teens to buy a car as soon as they had both a license and their first job. Frequently one or two would be left in the drives while the families were away.

Thorold spotted several by houses that looked empty. Hoping he was right, or that the person inside was absorbed with some activity more interesting than watching the street, he moved rapidly to each house.

He did not run and he tried to look as though he belonged there, but once he reached the first car, all pretense was lost. After trying the door handle and looking at the ignition to see if a key had been left behind, he ran his hand around the inside of the bumpers as well as under the car at the driver and passenger sides. He knew that a number of his neighbors had purchased Key Safes over the years. They were small metal slipcases just large enough to hold a spare car or house key. A powerful magnet enabled them to be attached to the underside of the car so they would be available in an emergency.

There was no key in the first three cars he checked. A house key was hidden under the forth. It was on his sixth try that he found what he was after. Being careful to keep the magnetic holder away from both the computer and the CD he still carried in his jacket pocket, Thorold removed the key, quietly opened the door, and then started the engine. He slowly drove down the driveway and onto the street. He continued for another two blocks before he fully reached the speed limit.

▲

CHAPTER 7

▲

The Search For Answers

▲

▲

▲

▲

What Thorold Stone needed, he thought, was a fifteen-year-old kid. He had been using computers for years. He had been given additional training when he was asked to join the elite One Nation Earth agents because their work involved too many citizens to keep track of any other way. Yet as simple a task as getting a CD to play on his laptop's drive was beyond him. Or perhaps it was beyond the software inside his machine. He didn't know which, didn't know how to determine where the problem might be, and didn't know as much as some teenaged hacker.

At one point Thorold thought about going to a shopping mall, walking inside, and setting up his machine on one of the benches. He'd pretend to be working as the kids milled around, talking with friends, going in and out of stores, and buying soft drinks, burgers, and fries. Eventually some kid would come by and make a remark like, "Get a life, Pops. That machine is ancient history. It hasn't been on dealers' shelves for at least three weeks." That would be the kid who could help him. That would be the kid who could play the CD or show him which among the latest units he needed.

Had Stone not been a marked man, he might have gone to the mall and hung out in plain sight, stayed as late as he could, then slept in the car.

The trouble was that he was condemned. Before Macalusso, before there was One Nation Earth and its force of special agents, the law would not have tolerated what was taking place. The police would issue an all points bulletin for a wanted man, alerting all appropriate departments by fax and by telephone. A bad guy such as a rapist or robber known to be working in a particular area would have his description and photo circulated to every cop in the region. Sometimes this meant a certain section of town. Sometimes this meant a multi-county region. And sometimes, if the man had relatives or friends known to have given him shelter in some other state in the past, the bulletin would include law enforcement agencies in various parts of the country. Stone believed he would be handled differently, though. He was certain that the alert would go only to the elite units already looking for him.

Len Parker dared not admit that someone who worked as a special agent for the Messiah's own law enforcement agency had doubts about who Franco Macalusso really was. The Haters were an easy target. Their minds had been deluded from reading the Bible and other forbidden religious books. They had watched forbidden videos, and been corrupted by the Christians who no longer walked the Earth. They were few in number and so intractable that most people found them boring, even obnoxious at times. They didn't participate in celebrations for Macalusso. They didn't praise his holy name. They could only discuss the forbidden Jesus, a man most people saw as impotent and dated.

To have a cold, hard, elite member of the Messiah's own security forces say that Macalusso was a fraud, that something was wrong with the story of the glorious times they were experiencing, could create problems. Alive, Thorold Stone, speaking of his doubts, could do more damage to the Messiah's work than could vocal Haters. They were seen as the voice of fanaticism. Stone's was the voice of reason. That was why his defection could only be whispered to an elite few.

Thorold knew that he did not have to fear the regular law enforcement officers. Men and women driving the city in their patrol cars would not know who he was. He was only in danger in crowded areas where special agents were dispatched in plain clothes in order to blend in.

That was why Thorold had to avoid the shopping mall. He was too likely to run into a fellow officer who knew he was wanted, and who knew his career would be enhanced by making the arrest. The Special Agent spotting him might even share some of the same doubts and concerns as Thorold, but he would not let that hinder his actions. All of them knew that their income, and their chance to rise in power and favor with the Messiah, depended upon their giving the impression of total loyalty, and total dedication. It was the way he had been, the way David had been. And now David was dead and Thorold was on the run.

Abandoning the mall idea, Thorold drove to a well-stocked electronics store in a small strip shopping area in a part of the city he had never frequented before. He parked in the midst of a cluster of cars where he did not think there was a chance of the plate being read by anyone searching for the missing vehicle. Later he would have to get a different car or steal different plates. For now, he had to act as though it was his own, especially since he did not know if the theft had been reported. There was just no sense in being too casual, and he knew from his days as a street cop no one ever looked for a stolen car in the middle of others. For some reason most thieves parked the car away from anything else, not thinking that the very isolation aroused suspicion.

A bell sounded as Thorold entered the store, but the sound was all but drowned out by the sound of Franco Macalusso's voice being repeated over and over on two dozen television sets positioned along one wall. "But remember this. I have come to save you. Not just your earthly bodies, as I did when I removed your terrible weapons of mass destruction, but your heavenly bodies as well." The televisions ranged in size from a two-inch pocket portable to a five-inch black–and–white AC/DC desk model to a 31-inch color giant that showed the Messiah's head larger than life.

The effect was frightening. For a moment Macalusso seemed to be an all-seeing, all pervasive presence. He had to remind himself that having all the television sets turned on to the same channel was normal in retail stores. There had been times when he and Wendy brought the kids into such a place and then couldn't drag them away from the endless images of Barney, the purple dinosaur. Today the sets were turned to a speech by the Messiah. It was a chance decision, not some special threat.

Thorold tried to ignore the televised speech. He walked to the computer section and looked at the different machines. The store was crowded, and he was aware of people looking at him as he moved. He wondered what they saw; if they knew something was wrong. He felt like he was back in high school again, the self-conscious adolescent who is certain he is the center of everyone's attention and that each passer-by somehow finds him wanting. He had to remind himself that people are curious. They just look at one another. They didn't know him, and didn't care about him. If he did nothing out of the ordinary in the store, no one would remember what he looked like.

"And in order to save your souls," the television Macalusso intoned, "I have had to remove those who stood in the way. Now it is time to step forward, a step that will lead you into a world of wonders."

Thorold found a demonstration model computer and checked the specifications on the advertising sign posted just below it. He didn't know if it was state of the art, but it was obviously more sophisticated than his laptop, sophisticated enough for that kid he fantasized about to not consider it an antique. He quietly found the CD-ROM drive and inserted the CD. The machine made a whirring noise as it worked to reveal whatever was hidden on the CD.

"The world of wonders is a world unlike anything you have ever imagined," said the two dozen Franco Macalussos. "Finally those things that until now have been hidden will be revealed. Those things of darkness will find the light."

"Yeah," mumbled Thorold. It was a speech he had heard before. The Day of Wonders was to be the biggest event the world had ever seen, whatever that meant. But if creatures of darkness fear the light, he wondered how Len Parker would handle the spotlight such an event might put on him given his position with the Messiah.

"Can I help you, sir?" asked a sales clerk, startling him. She had approached Thorold while he was deep in thought. He did not realize she was there until she spoke.

Relax, he told himself. Relax. Most people don't know who you are, and even if they did, probably most would not care. Relax. "I didn't notice you," he said, forcing him to smile. I…"

"I'm sorry," said the clerk. "I didn't mean to startle you. You looked so preoccupied with our Millennium 2120 I thought you might need some help."

"No. That's okay. I don't really…." Take a deep breath. Exhale. She's trying to earn her pay, get a commission. She's not the enemy, Thorold told himself. "I'm sorry. I've been looking at this model for some time," he lied. "I'm just getting the cash together to buy it only a problem came up before I could do it."

"We handle our own financing if that will help," she said. "Ninety days same as cash with approved credit. Or we can give you a lease arrangement letting you turn it in on the latest model available after 24 monthly payments. The ninety days same as cash is the best way to go if you're planning to pay it off quickly. The interest rate kicks in after that and it's retroactive. We're not supposed to say this, but if you can't pay it off that quickly, you're better off using your Visa or MasterCard."

"No. I'm sorry. The cost isn't the problem. I'll be paying cash. It's just that I have this problem about a week before I can make the purchase. I was given a CD-ROM that I thought I could run on my dinosaur of a laptop and I find that it won't read it. I figured since I'm buying this and it's the latest model, I'd pop it in the drive and see what came up on the screen. But as you can see, it gives me a message stating 'Error reading from specified device.' It's the same message I get on my laptop."

The sales clerk looked at the screen then leaned down and took the CD from the drive. She studied it for a moment, then said, "This isn't your normal CD. It fits the player which is where you probably became confused. But when you've worked with these things as long as I have, you notice subtle differences. I'm certain this was designed for another driver. Maybe for the Macintosh."

"You don't know?"

"I'm supposed to. They hired me to be their computer guru, but the truth is all my training's been on IBM clones and mainframes at college. Give me a PC and I'll make it dance a jig. Give me a Macintosh and I know which buttons to push to impress the customers. That's not the same as really knowing it. Still, if this is for the Mac I should be able to get it up and running."

The young woman took the CD to a different section of the computer department, selected the most sophisticated Macintosh they sold, and inserted the CD. The same error message appeared.

"I guess I'm better than I thought."

"What do you mean," asked Thorold. "That's what we were getting on the Millennium 2120."

"Exactly. I did as well on the Macintosh as I did on the PC."

Thorold stared at the woman, not comprehending.

"It's a joke," she said. "A computer joke. I couldn't get either of them to work right. That means I'm equally skilled."

"Yes," said Thorold, forcing a smile. She was trying to make a sale. How could he tell her that he was trying to save the world? "About the CD..."

"Look, the CD you have is one of two types. It could have been written on a special CD-ROM machine, maybe an experimental model. That would be why it doesn't work on these.

"That's unlikely, though. Nobody can beat the

system. All the PC makers are using the same drives. The rise of the generics is what let the independent companies destroy the monopoly market Apple and Macintosh once held. To bring in something that's not compatible with anything the public is used to buying is to risk losing the farm in Silicon Valley."

"So what's the other possibility?"

"That it's a proprietary CD."

"What does that mean?"

"It's a special security encoding unique to one computer. You have to have the computer that wrote it in order to read it. Do you know where it came from?"

"I...I got it from...a friend of mine. I can't imagine she'd give me a...Proprietary CD? Is that what you called it?"

"Yes."

"I can't imagine that this CD would be like that. Is there someone else on the staff who might be able to..."

But the sales clerk was no longer listening to Thorold. Instead she was staring at the bank of television monitors. Her face was ashen, her mouth slightly agape. Curious, Thorold turned and saw his face on monitor after monitor. Underneath, in large letters, were the words WANTED FOR MURDER. A toll free number was listed for anyone who might spot him.

Thorold cursed. They had thought of the one way to get him he had not anticipated. Instead of bringing attention to the fact that he was one of the top security people connected with Macalusso's law enforcement arm, they focused on the simple crime of murder. Anyone could murder another person. The heat of passion could lead to violence unrelated to politics, religion, or anything else. They weren't going to cover-up his defection from the Messiah. They weren't going to quietly take care of one of their own as he anticipated. They were just announcing that he had killed another human being and the public was being asked to turn him in.

"O.N.E. officials are looking for Thorold Stone, a Hater responsible for blowing up a school bus earlier today."

It was worse than he thought. He figured they would charge him with the O.N.E. agent he had killed when the man was trying to shoot David. Now they were making him take the blame for the school bus incident. They were declaring him to be one of the Haters. That meant they were hoping for vigilante justice. They were depending on some radical Macalusso follower who would think he or she was earning extra points from the Messiah for serving as executioner.

"Thorold Henry Stone reportedly left a note in his office confessing not only to this blatant act of terrorism but also to killing his partner and long time friend, David Smith. Citizens are warned...."

Thorold turned back to the girl who was carefully studying his features. Normally people would assume that someone who looks like a wanted poster or a celebrity photograph couldn't possibly be that individual. They miss the opportunity to get an autograph from the celebrity, or they miss the chance to gain a reward from turning in a bad guy. The sales clerk was not like that. She knew he was the same man whose face was being shown on television.

"It's him!" the clerk screamed. "The one they're showing on television. Call the police! Call the police!"

Thorold turned and fled through the aisles. Terrified, he ran blindly, bumping into people, careening off displays, focused solely on escape. A young store employee stepped in front of the door to block him, but the teenager had more courage than skill. Thorold stepped around him, then pushed him off balance, opened the door and ran to the car. He would have to assume the license had been spotted. He would have to leave it somewhere, and steal another one. He would have to continue running without knowing what was on the CD, or what it might mean.

▲

Thorold had found a Volkswagen station wagon left running while the owner ran inside the Post Office. He felt badly about taking the car, knowing how hard it might be for the person who owned it. That was the trouble with being honest. You had compassion for the people who were victimized. The compassion was one of the reasons he had gone into law enforcement. To be acting as a thief, even for a good cause, was distasteful to him. He only hoped he could somehow make up for the unpleasantness he had caused the people from whom he had stolen the cars. If he could find a way to read the CD: if he could stay alive....

Thorold had left the city and driven into a rural

area where he and Wendy once enjoyed taking the children. At one time the area had nothing but large family farms, everyone knowing everyone else so that a stranger was instantly spotted. Many of the farms still existed, along with the general stores and local craft shops. But there were also new housing developments. City people were seeking a rural experience by stripping the land of trees, filling in the natural ponds, then constructing a home and garden magazine's idea of "real" country living. So many new people were coming into the area, where once strangers were noticed, now they were accepted or ignored.

Exhausted, Thorold had parked the car behind a roadside billboard featuring Franco Macalusso's face and the words, "The Day of Wonders is for all of us. Do your part. Report Haters." It seemed adequate cover for the world's newest "Hater."

Desperate to take a nap yet determined to solve the mystery of the CD, Thorold worked with his laptop one more time. He inserted the CD and tried every different way he knew to access the drive. Always the screen announced that the machine was "unable to read file." Finally he removed the CD, closed the drive, and shut down the computer. He set it on the seat next to him, removed the photo of his family, and risked turning on the interior light long enough to take another look at Wendy and the children. Then he turned off the light, slumped back against the seat, and gave in to the overwhelming tiredness.

Sleep came rapidly but fitfully, Thorold moved in and out of dreams. He found himself back in the warehouse, talking with Mrs. Davis. The others were there, her husband, the rest of the congregation, David, the SWAT team, yet all were in shadows. It was as though they were all on stage, only Mrs. Davis and Thorold were in spotlights.

"It's perfectly clear to anyone who's not too afraid to open up a Bible," said Mrs. Davis. Her words were like loving rebukes, a parent arguing with a petulant child.

"I heard enough of this Bible prophecy nonsense from my wife," Thorold said in his dream. "And look where it got her."

Mrs. Davis gradually faded from view, replaced by Wendy. "It got us to Heaven, Thorold."

Thorold reached out to embrace Wendy, but instead he found himself holding his handgun, firing a round at Len Parker in the upper room of the warehouse. He watched the bullet leave the barrel as though in slow motion. He watched it move flawlessly towards Parker's chest. It was a round that would reach a kill zone, exactly as he had been taught and practiced on the range. But the bullet never reaches Parker. It just seems to fade from existence.

Angry that Parker has taken Wendy from him, he fires again and again, not stopping until the weapon is empty. Parker just stands there, smiling, completely unharmed.

Enraged, Thorold heaves his gun and starts to charge, only to find himself cradling the body of David Smith who is dying even as he speaks. "The answer's on that disk, Thorold. It's all up to you."

David's body seems to vanish, leaving Thorold on his knees staring at a gun on the floor of the warehouse. As he watches, he sees the gun shake slightly. Then it starts to move across the floor, going faster, as though in an invisible game of shuffleboard. It rises from the ground, and as he follows its movement, it lands in the hand of the terrorist. Grinning, the man takes careful aim, and as he starts to pull the trigger, Thorold throws his body forward, hoping to miss being struck by the bullet while knocking the terrorist over.

Thorold connects and....

HOOOONNNNKKKK! The sound of a blaring car horn jolted Thorold awake. He had thrown himself onto the steering wheel, the weight of his body sounded the horn, awakening him. He pushed back and sat up, with his back aching, and his neck stiff.

For a few seconds Thorold looked around, forcing himself to remember where he was and why he was there. He was still in that twilight area between sleep and wakefulness when all is confusion.

Thorold looked down at the seat, glanced at the photo of his family, then picked up the CD. He stared at it for a few moments, as though he might be able to will it to work for him.

"I almost died over you," Thorold said to the CD, as though it had a life that could understand his words. "If it hadn't been for that DNA detector...."

And then Thorold remembered his partner's words. "The guy in the wheelchair. He's the one who makes these things. That guy can do things with a computer that would blow your mind."

Willy....Thorold remembered. Willy Holmes. That was his name.

He stepped from the car, and stretched his body. He worked his head, his neck, and his body. He moved his arms and twisted at the waist. There was no time to stop at some fast food place for coffee or food. That would have to wait. What he needed was a restroom and a telephone. The first was a personal necessity. The latter would enable him to get Willy Holmes' address.

▲

The house was on a non-descript street that had been developed right after World War II. All the homes were small, containing two or three bedrooms and one bath. The idea was to fill them with GIs, newly married, attending school on the GI Bill, and taking advantage of veterans' benefits. The houses had seemed like a dream come true at the time, even if the price did strap them to the limits of their finances.

Over the years the neighborhood had become a cohesive community, with kids racing across the yards, going in and out of each other's homes, as all the mothers watched out for them and as the fathers went to work in the city. Homes were expanded as people could afford. A bedroom was added here, a second full bathroom there. What originally seemed like a starter home became a place that was used for retirement, for family gatherings. Only when the original owners died, moved to warmer climates, or were forced into nursing homes did the houses come up for sale.

The neighborhood had become a mix of young families, couples without children who wanted more space than an apartment, and the remaining elderly. Among these, in a house distinguished only by the wheelchair ramps both at the front and rear doors, was 668 Waverly, the home of Willy Holmes.

As Thorold approached the drive, he saw a van with a handicapped plate and wheelchair lift. There was a bumper sticker that read, "Protected by Siamese fighting fish."

A sign on the front door declared, BEWARE OF THE DOG. Beneath that, in smaller letters, were the words "he's small but he knows Kung Fu." Smiling despite his emotional state, Thorold opened the screen and raised a heavy knocker. Before he could use it, he heard a series of gunshots inside the house.

Somebody got here first, thought Thorold, instinctively moving to the side and drawing his gun. He touched the door handle, found it unlocked, and quietly pushed open the door. Forcing himself to control his breathing, he moved swiftly but quietly inside, listening, looking, and staying silent while he tried to orient himself to what was happening.

More shots were fired. They seemed to be coming from the back of the house, but he had no idea of the source, or how many people were in the house.

Moving to his right, Thorold entered the sparsely furnished living room. Everything had been arranged for maximum mobility. Here and there handgrips had been added to areas where Willy obviously liked to leave his chair. He seemed a man who valued independence.

Nothing in the room indicated that a helper of some sort was in his employ.

There was a door to one side, and as Thorold approached it, he flattened his back against the wall to avoid being shot when he opened it. Again he felt for the handle. Again it was not locked.

"Well, I'll tell you, Pilgrim. We don't have room for guys like you around these parts."

Thorold recognized the words and the accent, a very bad imitation of the late actor John Wayne. As he stood, confused, there was one final shot.

Not certain what he was facing, Thorold held his gun so the barrel was pointed in the air, his finger off the trigger. What he was hearing still troubled him, but it sounded less and less like an attack on Willy or anyone else.

Thorold pushed open the door, stepped inside, and found himself staring at the back of Willy Holmes. The electronics expert was dressed like a kid going to a Halloween party. He was wearing a white cowboy suit with a ten-gallon hat, fringed shirt, gun belt, and surprisingly small cowboy boots on his shriveled legs. A small dog was running around the chair, tail wagging, jumping up against the chair as though trying to play whatever game was taking place.

What made the scene even odder was the large pair of electronic goggles that Willy was wearing, along with the silver .45 caliber revolver in his hand. There was a small receiver pack and antenna attached to the side of the goggles. The revolver had a thin wire running down from the grip across the floor to an elaborate, hand made electronics device of some sort.

As Thorold took in the room, he realized it was some sort of workshop. There were highly sophisticated computers, electronic testing devices, a variety of miniature tools, micro chips, circuit boards, wires of various types and sizes, soldering equipment, and devices Thorold had never seen before. The room looked like a sophisticated laboratory, where everything was arranged for the ease of a man trapped in a wheelchair.

Suddenly, Willy turned the chair with his left hand while aiming his revolver in the direction of the doorway where Thorold was standing. At the same instance, the dog stopped, for the first time realizing he was not alone with his master. It was obvious the animal was a companion, not one kept for security. Any self-respecting watchdog would have been fired for acting as he did.

"Whoa there, Pal, I come in peace!" shouted Thorold, not even certain if Willy could see him through the goggles he was wearing.

Startled, Willy screamed, throwing off his goggles so he could see the man who had entered his home. "Who are you?" he asked.

"Thorold Stone," he said. "Is that gun real?"

"Only with the goggles on. And yours?"

"I'm sorry," said Stone, putting it back in his shoulder holster. "I heard the gun shots and thought someone was..."

"The gun shots were real. They were created by a digital recording I made at the range. I have to pause and reload every six rounds. It's just that the only thing this fires is an electronic signal," said Willy. Then, pausing for a moment, he said, "You're the one who killed David Smith, aren't you?" There was no fear in his voice. It was just a question from someone who had long ago come to believe that there was little more life could do to him than had already happened. It made him fearless and direct.

"David was my friend!" Thorold said, angrily. "I could no more have killed him than you…you…you could get out of your chair and run a marathon."

"Then you've seen my trophies?" said Willy.

"What…?"

"Just kidding." Willy's face was somber as he studied the agent in front of him. "If he was your friend, why is he dead?"

"We were in this warehouse, trying to find who else was in there after the Haters were arrested, and we ran into what we thought were terrorists. I killed one, but the leader killed David."

"The leader killed your partner? Then why are they saying that you're wanted for the murder?"

"They have to say that. The leader was still there when I found David's body. I recognized him when he tried to kill me, too," said Thorold. "He's being protected."

"And who is this leader who apparently is setting you up?" asked Willy, cautious.

"Len Parker," said Thorold, watching Willy's face for a reaction. It was impassive. The only change in attitude came when he slapped his lap, signaling the dog to jump on him. The animal snuggled down while

Willy petted him, watching Thorold, thinking.

"You're saying that the Messiah would authorize a lie?"

"I'm saying Len Parker lied. I don't know beyond that.

"I can tell you that's not the only lie you've probably heard today. If you'll just give me a few minutes of your time, I'll prove it to you."

"Why should I listen to you?"

"Because I need your help."

"Are you a Hater?"

"I'm a man in a crisis that's not of my own doing. I need your help because there seems to be no other place to turn."

"And if I choose to say no?"

"My gun is real."

"Yes, but somehow I think you won't use it."

"I don't think it's a good idea for either of us to see how serious I am."

The system was brutal but effective. Keep the Haters together in small clusters. Let them have their foolish prayers and their songs to the false one who came before the Messiah. Then find a way to separate them, psychologically if possible, or with violence if necessary. Get them alone, helpless and in terror. The truly faithful should die anyway. The weak ones could be used to subvert the others.

Not that Len Parker had any use for either type. Anyone who could be a Hater after witnessing what Franco Macalusso did that day in Megiddo was a damned fool in the fullest sense of both words. Why should anyone care what Macalusso really was or what he meant to the world? Raw power of the magnitude he had shown was to be respected even if you did not have the sense to call him the Messiah. They were fools for clinging to their Bibles and their stories of one who was so weak that he could be hung on the cross until dead that he deserved to die. They had nothing to offer One Nation Earth.

As for those so weak that torture would convince them to declare their allegiance to Franco Macalusso… These were not people you could trust. They spoke the name of Jesus one-day, the name of the Messiah the next. They would worship at a statue of a howling dog if they became frightened enough of what was happening to them.

Let them serve their purpose by undermining the will of their fellow Haters. Let them parade around as examples of the Messiah's love, then quietly kill them in the night. They were a blight on society, not people you could trust in a crisis.

This time he had to deal with the Davis family. This time there would be no mercy no matter what happened. The man was a leader, a serious convert after the day of the Disappeared. He was one who would die praising his false god, joyously sharing the pain of the one he called his savior. Such people were like cancerous growths on the face of society. They had to be crushed before they infected others.

The wife was something else. She had worked for One Nation Earth. She had been a part of the office staff during the high level planning for the Day of Wonders. She did not have access to the details, but she did have access to the materials being prepared.

Not that the woman had the knowledge and equipment to learn anything. She was not at that level. She was not that well trained. It was even possible that she or someone connected with her had stolen the CD just to win favor from her husband. The person might have no idea of the importance of the disk he or she had in hand.

What mattered was that Anna Davis had worked for the Messiah. She had been a part of the One Nation Earth headquarters where she was now in a holding cell with her husband and daughter. To do what she had done proved her to be weak at best, a common criminal at worst. She was also the one among this group of Haters he felt would respond most favorably to the application of pain, the one who could reveal the network they had developed in the underground. All he needed was the right balance of terror, isolation, and pain.

Parker walked down the corridor of holding cells with two uniformed guards. As they passed various Haters, some looked from behind the bars with pity, their lips silently moving in prayer for the eternal souls of their captors. Others were angry, their faces filled with disdain, as though they had just stepped on something soft and foul smelling while jogging through the park. And a few, those who had experienced his methods, scooted to the farthest corner of their small cells, huddling in a near fetal position, staring wide eyed, in terror, relief flickering in their eyes only after the three men had passed.

The Davis family showed none of the reactions of the others. They were too new to know what could happen, too filled with trust to believe their lives could be any worse. The so-called "Elder" Davis had even given his name as "Paul" when being booked, saying he would share the prison experience of one of the earliest leaders in the young Jesus movement.

The procedure was routine. One guard opened the cell, the other stepped inside and grabbed the prisoner who was to be taken.

"Mrs. Davis!" said the guard, firmly gripping her arm. The woman did not resist. She looked at the man, then stepped forward.

"No! She has done nothing. I am the one you want," said her husband. He had been ready to pick up the cross and follow in the footsteps of Jesus, knowing the outcome of his decision just as Jesus had known His. What he had not anticipated was to be left behind in the cell while his wife was taken for…for…

He could not let himself think. He could only act. He stepped in front of his wife and grabbed the wrist of the guard, unaware that Len Parker had drawn a small handgun from his pocket.

"No, Daddy! No!" shouted the Davises' daughter, but it was too late. Len Parker placed the weapon against the man's chest and fired a single round.

Elder Davis stepped back, his mouth moving, no sound coming out. He stared at his wife, his daughter, then sank to his knees, clutching the wound. Slowly, painfully, he found the words he sought. "I love you," he said, blood coming from his mouth as he fell forward, trying to hold himself upright for just a few more seconds. "I'll be waiting."

Mrs. Davis shook off the surprised guard, took her dying husband in her arms, cradled his head, and kissed him. But there was nothing she could do, nothing anyone could do. Tears came to her eyes, yet when she looked at Len Parker, she seemed to have more pity than hate, a look that surprised him.

"Murderers!" screamed the daughter. "You filthy, stinking slime! You killed my daddy. You..."

"Leave him!" said Len Parker, nodding to the guard who had been holding the door. "Take the daughter out of here. We don't need some hysterical teenager."

The guard reached for the girl who raked his face with her fingernails. The guard gripped her wrist, then twisted it around, pressing his other hand against the back of her shoulder. He pulled the arm behind her and forced her to her knees as she began screaming.

Still holding her despite her efforts to free herself, the guard brought his knee sharply against her throat. She dropped, frantically gulping for air, all the fight knocked out of her.

The guard kneeled down, lifted her onto his shoulder, and carried her from the cell. As he moved down the corridor, Parker looked at Mrs. Davis and said, "Good afternoon, Mrs. Davis. It's been a while since you left One Nation Earth and I've been most interested in talking with you. I have a few hours free on my schedule today so I thought I would drop by to see you. I hope we haven't caught you at a bad time."

To Parker's surprise, Anna Davis did not yell or scream or beg for her life. Her face was filled with anguish and pain, but her voice was soft and controlled. "Leave my daughter out of this. She hasn't done anything to you. My husband and I have always been the ones you wanted. Now he's dead and you have got me. Just leave her be. She's only a child."

Parker looked at the woman silently, as though he was considering what she had requested. Then he smiled and said, "She won't be a child for long."

Only then did the woman before him begin to scream.

▲

That they had been talking for more than an hour did not surprise Thorold. No matter what Willy may have thought of him, wanted for murder according to the media reports, Willy was an intensely lonely man. Physically deformed yet brilliant of mind, his opportunities in life had been drastically limited. Even when he had achieved his dream of working in law enforcement, he was used for his genius, spending many hours a day thinking, tinkering and developing the electronics meant to help the men and women in the field do their jobs better. He had never married and apparently had never developed any truly close friends. Even now, when he was respected by all who knew of his work, his idea of recreation was a virtual reality game shared only with his dog. The close attention of another human being was a rare treat. The fact that his visitor might be a dangerous killer did not matter.

Thorold and Willy sat at a table, drinking coffee and talking while Willy smoked a cigarette. "Nasty habit," Willy told him when he lit the first of several he had consumed in the last hour. "Doctor says they'll stunt my growth. I'd apologize for the second hand smoke, but you're the one who came to see me, and in my home, non-smokers have to go outside if they want a breath of air."

"Fair enough," said Thorold. "I'll remember that any time I think I need a breathing break." He had become more relaxed as they talked. Willy not only listened closely to what Thorold had to say, but he also asked questions that required Thorold to explain how he had proof of what was taking place.

"So the Haters weren't responsible for any of these things—the school buses, the orphanages, the old age homes..."

"None of it."

"And the last one, the children, you're saying you personally saw Len Parker in the warehouse where it was triggered?"

"Yes. He killed my partner and best friend. He would have killed me if that gizmo you made to detect DNA hadn't taken the bullet for me."

"Truly a noble piece of electronics. It's a good thing you were carrying the prototype. If we go into production, I'm going to encase it in lightweight plastic. It's supposed to find humans, not save them from bullets."

"I just wish David had been wearing... something."

"When Len Parker shot him?"

"Yes," said Thorold.

Willy stared at the agent, thinking, saying nothing. Then, softly, he asked, "Why?"

"What do you mean?" asked Thorold, taken aback.

"Why Len Parker? Why One Nation Earth? Why anything connected with Franco Macalusso? You saw the same news coverage I did. We all see clips of that day in Megiddo two or three times a week. How could such a man...? How could he go to such...unimaginable lengths to...."

"Make us hate the Haters?"

"Yes."

"I don't know. The easy answer is to say it's happened before. We've had Hitler and the Jews. We've had Stalin. We've had Idi Amin. We've had...."

"Those were mortals. Hitler and the rest could never stop missiles in mid-flight. He was a hate filled man who united a people ready to be led into conspiring with the Devil himself. But he was still a man. He could not do..."

"I don't know. Okay? I can't explain Franco Macalusso any more than I can say why I'm so certain he's all wrong. All I know is that we've all been lied to about the Haters. And if the O.N.E. is lying to us about this, then who knows what else they might be lying about. For that matter, what might Macalusso himself be lying about? Think about it. If he's deceiving us, he can't be who he says he is. You can't be god and a liar."

"Wait a minute! You can say what you want about Len Parker and anyone else at the top of O.N.E. Then you're talking about humans, and humans have always managed to corrupt themselves in the name of power and money. But the Messiah? What makes you think he knows anything about this?"

"Look at this logically. We had the miracles. Everyone's witnessed them and we're all overwhelmed by what we experienced. The man saved the planet from a hell that would have assured that anyone surviving the initial battles would later die from a lingering, agonizing death. We were ready to destroy every living creature in the name of…who knows what.

"Now the way I see it, Willy, is that anyone who can do what he did has nothing to fear from anyone. If he's the Messiah, why does he need the big police agency, the interrogation rooms, the SWAT Teams? Why can't he just vaporize his enemies? Or stop them from their violence. Or… I don't know. I don't believe that a god would need someone like Len Parker. I don't think a god would be fomenting hate. I don't think…"

"So what do you think, Thorold Stone? You're the great investigator. Who do you think this guy is?'

"Someone from another planet. Macalusso, Parker, all of them at the top."

"Okay, the Messiah's a space alien and I'm a long distance runner. Both make sense to me."

"All right, make fun of what I'm saying. But what's a better explanation, that he's Satan? The reincarnation of Harry Houdini?

"Look, I saw bullets strike Len Parker with no effect whatever. I saw Len Parker walk through a wall. I have seen things with my own eyes…"

"And so have I. You walked in when I was having

a shoot-out at the OK Corral. I saw everyone, smelled everyone. When I shot them, they went down and 'took their deads' as we used to say as kids. It was just like when I was a kid playing cowboys with my sister. Only now I can walk across the prairie, ride a horse, kick the gun out of a bad guy's hand. You saw me, didn't you?"

"I saw you wearing goggles and some sort of electronic gadget on your head. I saw you holding the revolver. I saw...."

"The wheelchair, my rolling prison, was your reality. The goggles brought me an illusion as lifelike, for those moments I was wearing the equipment, as what you saw was real to you. What we think we see is not necessarily what we see in reality.

"Franco Macalusso saved the world. We all know that. I think he's the Messiah. You think he's a little green man from Mars. And as for Len Parker...."

"If you saw what I saw with my own eyes, not some virtual reality contraption, you'd wipe that smirk off your face in a hurry."

Willy looked sadly at the agent. "You've been through hell, I'll grant you that. You either killed your partner or you didn't, but either way you're in trouble, so I can understand your emotional state. What I want to know is why it's easier for you to think Franco Macalusso is an alien than to believe he's God."

"Because I don't know if there's life on other planets, but I do know there's no God.

"Look, I didn't come here for a philosophical discussion. I know I'm right and I know the answer is somehow on this disk. I got this CD from one of the

Haters who worked for O.N.E. She claimed that the O.N.E. was trying to kill her over it." Thorold removed the CD from his pocket and handed it to Willy.

"It's an O.N.E. disk all right," said Willy. "It will fit on a standard CD-ROM player, but it will never show anything."

"I learned that the hard way. I almost got myself arrested trying it on the newest machines I could find."

"You need a special drive and code access." Willy wheeled himself over to one of the many computers in the room. He selected a separate drive mechanism, inserted the disk, and then began working the keyboard.

Thorold watched the monitor Willy was using, expecting to see the same error message that had been frustrating him. Instead it said, "O.N.E. internal control. Enter your password."

Willy pressed several buttons. His fingers seemed to fly on the equipment. Thorold could understand why the man was so highly regarded.

"Casement code," read the screen, and a picture of the disk inside what looked like a block of see-through concrete appeared. This was followed by the image of a man with a hardhat holding a jackhammer against the side. After positioning the tool, the cartoon figure looked up as though staring at the computer user. Then a tiny voice said, "You have one minute. Then I pack up and go home."

"You sure you can do this?"

"I designed the security graphics myself. A man's got to have a little fun when he's slaving over a hot keyboard all day," said Willy. He pressed several keys

169

and the workman image on the screen went to work. The jackhammer began pounding against the block, suddenly freeing the diskette.

The computer beeped, and the pyramid and eye symbol appeared on the screen. Then a rainbow appeared and the words "Welcome to the Day of Wonders Project. Press any key to continue."

"This isn't just the security system I helped design. This is the project I've been working on. You say the Haters had a copy of this?"

"Yes. What is it?"

"It's what the Day of Wonders is all about. Look."

The screen requested a password to continue. Willy typed in his authorization and waited.

"Please type your password," read the screen.

"So maybe I went too fast," said Willy, shrugging his shoulders and typing in his access code. Once again it failed to work.

"What do you mean, no? I helped make you. I'm like your parent. I hold all the keys. You've got to let me in." His fingers seemed to fly on the keyboard. He tried his own code. He tried something he called a master key. He shut down the system and rebooted, always getting as far as the Day of Wonders symbol on the screen before his security code would not work.

"What's wrong?" asked Thorold. "Why can't you get in?"

"Do you realize what this is?"

"I was lost when the salesclerk was telling me the problem in the computer store. You're way beyond that. What is it?"

"It's a new program for the Day of Wonders Virtual World System."

"You said you worked on it. Why can't you get access to it?"

"My password doesn't work. No password works. They've changed the Interlink system."

"Could you start over using English?" asked Thorold.

"You know about the Day of Wonders."

"I know it's being advertised on half the billboards in the city, on the radio and television stations, in the newspapers...."

"Then you know about it."

"It's like some preview of coming attractions where they tell you how much you're going to love a new movie without telling you anything about it. It's supposed to be the best day of our lives, the start of something even greater than when the bombs were stopped and the world was saved.

"You know about as much as everyone else including myself and I worked on the project."

"If you worked on it, why don't you know more?"

"Because of Interlink. There were a couple of dozen of us working around the world. All of us had been in law enforcement. All of us had been hired by One Nation Earth the same way you went from street cop to Agent for O.N.E. And all of us were given a small piece of coding to develop. We all had special access codes I developed, and I did what I usually do as well. I created a secret passage, a master code so that if there was a problem with someone forgetting how to get access, I could open the trapdoor. I shared it only with Overlord Parker because I knew the Messiah might want it.

"Interlink is the key to the way we worked. Each day, when we felt we had finished our task for the moment, we would type a special code that would send our work to Interlink. There it would be stored like a giant jigsaw puzzle. Interlink assembled the pieces to create a more and more complete program. A week ago it was done and we all had access to everything so we could troubleshoot."

"Then this equipment should let you play the CD?"

"Not exactly. Even assembled, none of us are able to play the entire system. That is being saved for the Day of Wonders. What we can do is reach any single part, just as though it had not been assembled, so we could fix any overlooked glitch."

"Couldn't you download each piece with that ability, storing it and reassembling it to see what is on the full CD?"

"No. Interlink is coded in a way that allows it to tell which special player/recorder is being used when we make access with the full disk. It sends a signal to Overlord Parker's system when we try to work on two different parts, and it shuts down when we reach three separate parts. Permission to continue would have to come directly from the Messiah's top people. He wants this to be as much a surprise for those of us who worked on it as it will be for you and the other citizens of One Nation Earth."

"So what happened? Why can't you get into even one of the parts?"

"This is a new program. Someone's made extensive modifications to the interior system."

"This Interlink you talked about?"

"This is something else. Something different. The player still works, and some of the access codes. But it's like they kept the casing to a music CD and changed all the music."

"Would Len Parker know?"

"Of course. He would have the key. He answers directly to Bishop Bancroft who's in charge of the whole Day of Wonders project. And Bishop Bancroft reports directly to the Messiah. Why do you ask?"

"I told you. He was there."

"Your story's true, isn't it? Your partner wasn't a rogue or a Hater? You guys aren't connected to that bus bombing in some way?"

"I'd feel better if I was guilty of something other than having apparently been at the wrong place at the wrong time. Whatever's going on, something tells me that the Day of Wonders is not going to be the joyous time we keep hearing about. Something tells me...."

▲

CHAPTER 8

▲

For The Love Of Jesus

▲

▲

▲

▲

Only those who had been through interrogation understood the ominous nature of the special room in that Len Parker had placed Anna Davis in for questioning. The floor was smooth concrete, sloping gently towards a large drain in the center. On one wall hung what looked like a garden hose with an adjustable nozzle to assure a hard stream of water could be aimed at any point in the room in order to wash away blood and gore. A small wall cabinet held containers of disinfectants and specialized cleaning compounds. The walls themselves were covered with seamless material similar to the type used in hospital operating rooms to allow for complete cleaning. It was all rather sterile, all rather odd to the person being questioned. Until the person became stubborn that is; until something harsher than words had to be used; until the blood began to flow....

Anna Davis was sitting on a metal chair, her wrists tied behind her to the back of the chair. Len Parker sat on a chair opposite her, his legs straddling the seat, his arms folded across the back, his chin on his arms. His posture was relaxed and casual, like he was sharing a conversation with a friend.

"It would seem we've chosen different sides, haven't we, Anna?" His voice was quiet, gentle, no different than when he used to see her working at her desk in O.N.E. They might have been sitting in a coffee shop together, meeting for lunch or after work, discussing shared experiences from the past.

"It's like we're both soldiers hoping to win a war that only one side can win...."

Anna Davis stared at Parker, her face registering no emotions. Her face was bruised and slightly swollen. There was dried blood on her lip. She had been slapped and punched just enough to cause pain, to let her know that there could be an escalation of the discomfort she had been enduring. This was the man who had murdered her husband. This was the man who had taken her daughter to God knows where. This was an evil unlike any she had ever encountered, an evil so monstrous....

She dared not think. She could only endure.

God had brought her to this point. She would have to trust in the Lord that whatever happened, He would be with her. He would be with them all.

Parker rose from his chair and walked slowly around the small cell. When he was behind her, he touched her shoulder, leaned forward, and spoke so softly it was almost a whisper as he said, "I thought about joining your side once. I was raised in a church, you know. I used to memorize Bible verses every week. I even won prizes for my memory when we kids had contests at the annual church picnic.

"Yes, I came very close. But do you know why I did not join you?"

Parker kept walking, pausing for effect before looking at Mrs. Davis. "You're living a lie! God claimed to be the only God. I know what the Bible says. I know about Genesis where it says that God made us in his image. Then he backtracks and we have Adam and Eve being chastised for seeking the fruit of the tree of the knowledge of good and evil. There is so little difference between God and man: just one piece of fruit. He is so insecure, he has to use intimidation to prevent us from seeing our rightful inheritance, our ability to be just like him.

"Don't look so surprised, Anna. I told you I was raised in the church. I know the Bible. I was almost deceived by its lies. Can you imagine? I could have been a Hater like one of you, though thank our Messiah, that did not happen.

"The Messiah opened my eyes and let me see the truth. We can all achieve godhood. Every single one of us. Look at what I've become through believing in the teachings Franco Macalusso has brought to enrich us.

"That's what God's afraid of. That's why we had all those stories which were meant to keep us fearful, humble, and thankful for the crumbs when we could really have the whole loaf.

"The Messiah has shown us that God is afraid that we will realize that he's not so special, that the power lies within all of us."

"Is it this god within you that gives you the power to cold bloodedly murder a gentle, unarmed man whose only crime was to love his wife?" asked Anna Davis, quietly. Her mouth ached and it was difficult to speak. She realized that she was hurt worse than she had thought. She also understood that this was only the start of what would happen to her that day. "Is it this god within you that gives you the power to take a helpless teenaged girl? Is it this god within you that gives you the power to tie me to a chair, or to use a gun and batter helpless people? Is that what you have sold your soul for? Cain had such power. So did Pharaoh. So did the father of Salome, who gave his daughter the head of a jailed, gentle and helpless man. Bullies and tyrants, petty little men in positions they could use to hurt others have always had such power. You are not special."

"You have not seen the powers with which I have been gifted. You have no idea what awaits you unless you denounce the false one and join with us," threatened Parker. "Your co-workers, your neighbors, many of your friends have all done this. How could so many citizens of the world be wrong? You must see that."

"I see that God loves the outcast, the person who has the courage to stand alone for His sake. The prophets were all unlikely vessels of His holy Word. They were shunned, scorned, or so lowly they lived in terror of speaking out against the establishment. Yet God was with them, and because He stood by their side, their words impacted on the world. The way of the cross was a gift of strength, not a sign of weakness. Jesus was murdered. Paul was murdered. Their lives touched mere handfuls of people compared to how many were alive throughout the globe. Yet the word that was left, and the churches of five and six members Paul gathered, have spread in ways that prove God's hand is in all the world. Your false Messiah can only triumph by killing those who would speak against him. <u>Speak</u> against him, Len. Not take up arms. Not foment revolution. They just walk humbly, speak truthfully, and love the Lord our..."

Len Parker rose from his chair, stepped over to Anna Davis, and slapped her hard across the face. Then, with a calm voice, he said, "So let's try this one more time. Did Thorold Stone join your deluded cause? And what is he planning to do with that CD?"

Mrs. Davis sat quietly. Her arms were beginning to become uncomfortable from their tethered position. She wanted to shift in her seat. Yet she knew that any indication of discomfort would be a victory for the forces of the false one.

"Come on. Stop playing games with me. I know you gave him that disk. Your daughter told us all about it."

This time Anna Davis reacted as Parker had

hoped. This time he had touched on emotions that were overwhelming. Her daughter was not a strong child, but like many teenagers she was belligerent, especially in the face of someone she disliked. If her daughter had told about the CD, that meant they had hurt her in ways no one has a right to hurt so innocent a child.

"What have you done with her?"

Len Parker ignored the question. "We confirmed the information with statements by a clerk in an electronics store who waited on Stone until she saw his face on a television broadcast. She recognized the CD because he tried to read it on one of their computers.

"Now I want to know what he is planning to do with it? I want to know his role with you Haters."

"I want to know what you have done with my daughter. I will tell you nothing until you answer me," said Mrs. Davis.

"Stop worrying about your daughter. I checked on her before coming to see you and I can tell you that she is in absolutely no pain whatever…." He paused, looking deeply into the eyes of the woman he considered a traitor to the O.N.E. where she once worked. He could see her nervousness, the sweat forming on her forehead. She was breathing faster, her heart racing, frightened now for the first time. Then, softly, slowly, he added, "She is in no pain…now."

The sound was like a high pitched keening. It was soft at first, and then it rose to a wail that seemed to penetrate the walls of the interrogation cell. She began rocking her body, as though the movement might provide comfort when none was possible.

"Noooooooooo…."

Parker's face held a look of disgust. "Don't sound so upset, Anna," he said. "It's not like any of you Haters have rich full lives ahead of you. None of you will live long enough to see what The Day of Wonders is really all about. A pity, too. Had you been loyal, you would have been among the first.

"Your Mr. Stone has no idea what he's up against. He thinks this is all about technology, about who has the most sophisticated computer equipment.

"But we know it's much more than that, don't we, Anna? We know why I will do anything to get the answers I need from you.

"Now let's talk about Thorold Stone some more. Did he make a decision to join the Haters?"

▲

Thorold could sense a change in Willy's reaction to his presence. The man was more relaxed, animated. They were talking more like two long time colleagues. He did not know if he had convinced Willy of the danger from Len Parker or if Willy was alone so often that he felt grateful for any company, even from someone he believed to be a criminal.

"So what is this Day of Wonders Project? What does it do?"

"Nobody knows exactly."

"I know you said that each of you worked on different parts of it, never seeing the whole. But someone with your genius, someone who designed the security system, must have an idea," noted Thorold.

"All right, I know more than a couple of pieces, but I don't know anything about the final program," Willy responded.

"Would you stop talking double talk and explain what you mean."

"There have been test versions," said Willy. "We've checked for sound, for graphics, for neural awakening."

"What do you mean?"

"Test versions. We have made CDs that simulate some of the things that might be on The Day of Wonders disk, but that's different from the content." Willy saw that Thorold still was puzzled, so he said, "We tested concepts like the Virtual Reality equipment you found me wearing when you came here. I said that it was just a computer game, but it's really quite a bit more. It's a technology that is advanced light-years from what we thought was possible before the day the Messiah revealed himself.

"Our test versions of The Day of Wonders programming have involved the technology. It's like working in the field of rocket propulsion, shooting off rockets with new types of propellants to see which one goes fastest, farthest, highest. And then there's someone else making bombs. They make big bombs, little bombs, chemical bombs, atomic bombs... Then, for a test, you explode a bomb one day and a rocket the next. But when they're brought together to make a missile, you don't know the target, the damage it will do, and the problems that might occur in the aftermath of the blast. The tests of the separate parts don't prepare you for any of that. "

"So what is this about? Virtual reality? Bombs? I just don't see...."

"Come with me," said Willy. He took Thorold over to the Virtual Reality platform on which Thorold had found him earlier. Willy rolled his chair over to a console of elaborate dials and switches, turned on the power, made adjustments, and then moved to a computer keyboard and tapped rapidly on the keys. "Pick up the goggles on the left. I'll use the others," instructed Willy.

"I remember something like this from when Wendy and I went to an amusement park a few years ago. It was a virtual reality auto race. It cost us a fortune to play, but it really felt like you were in the midst of a racetrack. The floor we stood on moved with the cars so that it added to the illusion."

"Select Desired Virtual World," prompted the on-screen menu. Underneath were the choices "O.K. Corral, Aspen Ski Challenge, Climbing Everest, Olympic Games, Walk On The Beach." Willy selected "Walk On The Beach" as he said, "You don't realize how far Macalusso's taken us. What you saw was like watching one of Thomas Alva Edison's first motion pictures back at the end of the nineteenth century compared to a modern motion picture. What you're going to experience... Put on your goggles. I really can't explain otherwise."

Thorold Stone put on his goggles and stared straight ahead. This was not the virtual reality machine he and Wendy had tried. This was....

Thorold took a deep breath. His lungs filled

with the moist, warm air from the breeze coming across the beach from the ocean. He was barefoot, in swim trunks, and he could feel the sand between his toes. The sun was shining brightly, and in front of him was Willy Holmes, also in swim trunks. Willy was no longer in his chair, no longer had withered legs. He was a man without a disability, his body powerful from regular exercise.

Thorold reached up and lifted the goggles, suddenly certain he had been transported somehow to a real beach with an able bodied companion. Willy was sitting in his wheelchair, still in his cowboy suit, his withered legs still useless. The only difference was that Willy was wearing an identical pair of goggles and they were both plugged into the same machine. Startled, Thorold lowered the goggles over his eyes.

He was at the beach again. The sun was more intense and Willy was taking precautions, spreading sun block lotion on his face, arms, and legs. "Lotion?" Willy asked casually, holding the tube up to Thorold.

"Do I need it?" Thorold asked. Wherever he was, whatever was happening, this was a world where he believed anything was possible.

"No more than I needed the cowboy suit to play at the O.K. Corral. I'm just a big fan of ambiance. Good thing you didn't come on nudist beach day," Willy teased.

"This is…This is real. I mean, I can feel the water, smell it…It's like…If I had one of these, I'd never leave the house," Thorold said.

Willy looked at him intensely, then quietly said, "If I didn't have one of these, I'd never leave my chair."

Thorold did not reply. Willy's pain and the meaning of the system to him were not in his thoughts. He was too in awe of the technology, too amazed by what he was experiencing.

Willy began moving down the beach, signaling to Thorold to join him. As they moved through the waves, Thorold realized that their goggles were wired directly to the machine. He figured that any moment they would both be jolted back to whatever reality might be as they reached the end of the cord. Instead, their walk took them at least a half-mile through the surf before a stunned Thorold asked, "How can we do this? The cord to the goggles is what? Six feet? Seven feet?"

"It's ten feet, actually," said Willy. "And yes, we've gone a lot farther than that."

"So how…."

"Your legs aren't moving. I told you this technology makes everything that came before it look like something our great-grandparents might have used. Sports medicine doctors have long known you can strengthen muscles by direct stimulation with a small electrical current. It's how they keep athletes in shape while an injury is healing and preventing them from working out with that part of their body. This does something to the brain that changes what we think, how we feel. You can run ten miles along this beach and you're going to feel every step of the way. Your breathing will change. Your heart will pump more rapidly. Your leg muscles will 'burn' with the exertion. And I wouldn't be surprised if you produce the biochemistry of running. You probably make the beta-endorphins that diminish the pain of long distance running. Yet if you take off your goggles, you'll find you haven't moved a foot."

"But how can we…I mean, how…What makes any of this possible? Where did the technology come from? How have we come so far so fast? Is this from some secret project the government's been working on for years?"

"It's not what or how this came about. It's who gave it to us," responded Willy.

"Macalusso? Are you saying this technology came from Macalusso?" Thorold asked.

"Incredible, isn't it? He's so far beyond where we were with our electronics, it's like we've just come out of a time machine set on fast forward. It's like we can climb into a television set and interact with the actors we normally watch from a distance. Your brain can't tell the difference between this and the real world. You know you have on the goggles, but after a while it's no different than if you were wearing eyeglasses or a hat. It's just there.

"I've been around computers all my life, but this stuff is beyond my wildest dreams…"

Both men ducked as some birds swooped low, to catch fish swimming just below the surface.

"Actually, it is my wildest dream. The beach, my legs, the birds…. Everything is exactly how I imagined a perfect world to be," said Willy.

"How far can you go with this?"

"You mean, can you go into a restaurant and pick up women? Have a harem? That sort of thing?"

"Well, yes…I mean, I can see some teenager

using this and thinking he had gone to heaven before he has the nerve to ask a real girl for his first date."

"I've never tried anything like that. You saw the list of programs. But my guess is you can do anything you can imagine. I can even see prisons using this for uncontrollable, unrepentant criminals. Let them commit all the crimes they want if they're behaving well when the goggles are off. Let them commit mayhem. Whatever you want to do is possible, I'm sure. It's like living your dreams."

"I don't want to be living the dreams I've been having lately," said Thorold, suddenly jolting back to thoughts of the world outside of the virtual beach he was experiencing.

"Lost loved ones?" asked Willy. "Some of the disappeared?"

"Yes," said Thorold sadly. He noticed a stone lying on the sand, picked it up, and chucked it towards the water. "But I know that everyone lost someone. There doesn't seem to be any lives that weren't touched by that day." Then, smiling, he added, "Of course, not everyone is mourning. I have friends who are so delighted that they lost certain co-workers or family members that they regularly go to bars to celebrate their good fortune at being left behind.

"I can understand it, I guess. It's just that with Wendy…well…Wendy was different. Sure, she was a believer. She would be classed as one of the Haters if she were still…here. It's just that she was….

"I loved her. I still love her. As for the kids, well, I still don't understand about a couple of innocent children. I know I should get beyond it, especially with the tragedies I've seen others have to overcome. I just can't seem to do it, though.

"What about you, Willy? Who did you lose?" Thorold asked.

"My grandmother and my sister."

"Were you close?"

"I was close to my sister. She practically raised me, even when she started on her career as a newscaster and television anchor. She used to call me all the time when she had to travel on a story. We had a lot in common."

"And your grandmother?"

"A nut," said Willy, derisively. "One of those Holy Joes, always looking for the good side in things. Called my legs a blessing. She said that they were God's way of guiding me to where my true genius was. She said that one day I would understand, and in the meantime I should praise the Lord for His blessings.

"Like I said, a nut!"

"Still, you lost two and your sister's loss must hurt. We both have reason to look into this stuff.

"When I found out Parker was setting up the Haters, it was the first glimmer of hope I've had since the vanishings. Suddenly, for the first time, I had something to hold on to. Maybe my wife wasn't some evil person whose heart I had never really known. Maybe she was just…different, better, more insightful. I don't know. Good people are a threat sometimes just by their refusal to go along with those they think are doing wrong.

"For a long while I knew I was not going to see

her again. Like your grandmother and sister, I figured my wife and kids were dead. Of that I was certain.

"Now I'm not so certain. If I can prove Macalusso knew about all this, that he's been lying about it, then that opens up a whole new can of worms. Suddenly everything he's saying would be called into question, including what happened to our families and what we can do about getting them back."

The two men continued walking on the beach, Willy deep in thought, Thorold distracted by what he was seeing. In the distance were sail boats moving lazily on the water: birds were flying overhead, and a few white clouds were drifting through the blue sky. He looked further up the beach and saw small children laughing, running, and building sand castles with their plastic buckets and shovels. A large dog ran along the beach, barked at birds, and raced into and out of the water, pausing only long enough to shake himself off.

It was the kind of day when there should be no cares, with no one missing, dead or dying. In here there were no police, no weapons, no chance for violence or pain to mar the passing hours. It was a place of rest, of solace, and for Willy, a place to exercise legs he had never used in the other "real life."

"I just can't believe this," said Thorold. Despite all the emotions of the day, putting on the goggles was like being given a new life, a new chance for happiness, for...he didn't know what. "Five minutes ago I would have sworn this was absolutely impossible. Everything looks so real. It's as though if I take off the goggles and see your house, that will be the illusion and only this the reality. So much for the idea that seeing is believing."

"That's the whole point of this equipment. You can't trust your senses when you're in here. Any world that can be programmed becomes life itself. Sometimes I wonder if I left the goggles on all the time, would I survive by eating in this world, sleeping in this world, or would I slowly starve to death and never know it. Can death even take us if we are wearing the goggles."

"Probably," said Thorold. "At some point the electric company's going to get mad about you not paying your bill. When they cut off the power, there goes your virtual world and there goes you."

"That's why I like it in here. It's a world without responsibilities, a world without consequences. You can do anything...anything at all and there's no price to be paid."

"What do you mean? Have an affair? Kill someone?" asked Thorold.

"More than that. Look at this." Willy walked over to where he had spotted a broken seashell in the sand. The break made one ragged edge sharp and pointed, almost like a knife.

"Give me your arm," said Willy.

Thorold held out his hand, exposing his arm. Willy grasped Thorold's wrist, then used the shell to cut the flesh. A thin red line formed in the wake of the shell, and blood slowly oozed from the split flesh.

Thorold stared at the wound for a moment. "It...It's bleeding," he said. "You cut me."

"That's right," said Willy, laughing. "But you didn't feel a thing, did you?"

"No. There's no pain. But the blood. It's real, isn't it? I really do have to put a bandage on, don't I?"

"Take off your goggles," Willy suggested.

Thorold removed the goggles, forcing himself to reorient for a moment. His eyes had become accustomed to the bright sunlight at the beach. He had to close them, then open them, letting himself acclimate to the darker room.

Everything was as he remembered it, from Willy in his wheelchair to the elaborate computer equipment along the walls.

Willy removed his own glasses, then said, "How's your arm?"

Thorold looked at his shirt and realized the sleeve was long and buttoned. He loosened it, rolled it up, and stared at the undamaged skin. There was no hint of any sort of injury. "This is incredible," he whispered.

It was the sound of the doorbell that startled both Willy and Thorold back to their full reality. Thorold Stone was a fugitive from justice, a man wanted for murder. Willy Holmes was a sworn law enforcement officer, even if his job involved sitting all day and working on electronics. He had been through the academy, trained on weapons, learned modified self-defense techniques, and carried a badge. If he were found to be harboring a man wanted for murder, he would be lucky to get out alive.

A pounding at the door followed the bell. Thorold, suddenly frightened, looked about the room for a way to hide. If Parker's men had somehow followed him there, tracked him, they would attempt to kill him in the house. There would be no witnesses except a man who also worked for the O.N.E. forces. The public would never know about what Parker was calling a rogue agent.

Thorold thought he had covered his trip well enough to avoid detection. He was certain Willy had no secret alarm to alert headquarters to an intruder. However, for all he knew, when Willy tried to gain access to The Day of Wonders disk, some homing signal was sent out.

Willy, seeing Thorold's panic and recognizing his own vulnerability, wheeled over to a small black-and-white monitor. The exterior of the house was rigged with surveillance cameras, something Thorold had not noticed when he approached the house. As he looked over Willy's shoulder, he saw a deliveryman standing, waiting for someone to answer. His uniform read "World Post."

Willy quickly changed the channels, checking every other camera to see if the deliveryman was legitimate or a cover for the police. There was no one else in sight anywhere around the house.

"Relax. The cavalry hasn't arrived," said Willy, wheeling out of the room and to the door.

"Mr. William W. Holmes?" asked the deliveryman when Willy answered the door.

"That's me," said Willy.

"Are you still the only occupant of this building?"

"Just me and my dog. I keep waiting for some gorgeous woman to come here, declare undying devotion, and move in so she can cook my meals, soothe my fevered brow, and look adoringly into my eyes. I know she's out there. She's just too shy to knock. But until then…"

The deliveryman laughed and said, "I need you to sign for your Day of Wonders package. Can I see your Global ID card, please?"

"No problem," said Willy, wheeling back inside to take it from his desk. When he returned, the World Post man took the card and swiped it along the edge of a small box he carried. The information matched what had been programmed in for that day's delivery route.

"It's you, all right."

"I could have told you that. I check each morning in the mirror. So long as it's me, I know I'm going to have a good day."

The delivery man laughed, then handed Willy some papers to sign. "If you'll just fill in the spaces marked and sign I'll be on my way."

"I used to worry about just being a number," said Willy as he began filling in the blanks. "With the new system, I'm now three numbers, a dash, five more numbers, another dash, and seven more numbers. If my mother was alive, she'd be so proud to see how far I've come."

"At least kids being born today are sure of learning their math," said the delivery man, taking the papers and checking to be certain they were fully filled out.

"I guess this stuff is keeping you guys pretty

busy. A lot of overtime money to spend on The Day of Wonders?"

"Who knows what money will be worth then. But it's not so bad. We have a little overtime, though not so much as we used to have during the old holiday seasons. They hired thousands of part-timers around the country to help with the delivery. There are 300 in this area alone. It's really a no brainer. They don't handle the office accounts that we do. They just take around the boxes, check I.D., get the papers signed, and get their pay. It's like delivering phone books. By tomorrow everyone will have a set of these glasses. I just can't wait to see what it's all about."

"You and me both, pal," Willy said, watching as the driver returned to his truck, then shut the door and wheeled himself back to where Thorold was waiting. He was surprised to see him sitting by the computer he had used to try and gain access to the CD.

"Getting anywhere, Agent Stone?" he asked.

"Nope. Same thing every time. 'Password required' I figured that maybe if I used the right CD player and other equipment, dumb luck would take me where skill and brilliance failed."

"Like that old idea that if you gave a hundred typewriters to a hundred monkeys, eventually they would write all the works of Shakespeare?"

"Something like that."

"Maybe you're not dumb enough to do it," said Willy, tearing the wrapping off the package, then opening the box. Inside was a streamlined version of the high tech glasses he had been wearing when playing with his home Virtual Reality equipment. But instead of the larger size and attached wires, the glasses were small, lightweight, and ultra-sophisticated. A tiny radio transceiver was built into one earpiece, an antenna integrated into the frame of the lenses. There were what looked like contact points at the bridge of the nose and where the goggles would touch the forehead. Willy recognized them as skin sensors that conceivably could interact with the human brain.

Willy put on his pair, hoping to see something. The fit was snug but comfortable. They were much better designed than the prototype with which he had been working. The material was so highly malleable it seemed to shape itself to his forehead. The goggles were truly one size fits all, something not achieved with previous materials.

"See anything?" Thorold asked.

"Nothing. These are the real ones, though. They'll be activated when the O.N.E. computer transmits the signal at noon on The Day of Wonders. That's when the whole world will see whatever's on that CD of yours."

Willy set down the goggles, took a cigarette, lit it, and began smoking. He was nervous and needed to relax. Everything about what was happening required time to think; time to analyze. He was used to an unpressured existence. The stress of having to deal with a fugitive, a new disk design, the arrival of the goggles, the news about the Messiah….It was all more than he wished to handle, yet there was no choice. He had to think. He had to do something.

"Do you understand why I'm so concerned about knowing what's on that CD before The Day of Wonders?" asked Thorold. "This is a CD that came from Len Parker's office. We know he's a liar. We know he's a murderer. He killed little kids. He killed Smitty. He'll stop at nothing."

"Or so you keep telling me. So far it's your word against O.N.E. I've seen their report on you and I've heard you out. The rest...I don't know."

"You don't care about Len Parker any more than I do. What you're worried about is Macalusso. If I'm telling the truth about what happened, you want to know if the Messiah knows the Overlord is overstepping his authority, if he's the rogue in all this.

"I'll tell you this, no matter how high this goes, what's on this disk, or what's in store for the world... It's not going to be a walk on the beach," worried Thorold.

Willy stared at him, unsure of what to say or do.

▲

Anna Davis lay on her side on the floor, her wrists still bound behind her back and to the frame of the chair. She had been knocked off balance, landing painfully on her shoulder, the side of her head striking the concrete. Her throat was parched, there was a ringing in her ears, and one eye was swollen shut. She could no longer speak, though it did not matter. Len Parker knew there was nothing more she was going to say.

Perhaps he suspected that there was nothing

more she could say.

Anna had slipped Agent Stone the CD because she did not know what else to do. He was a man she sensed she could trust, and apparently she had been right. But there was a difference between trusting Agent Stone and having him be one of them.

Had Thorold Stone joined the Christians? Was he a man who had come to love the Lord his wife and children had known with such joy? Somehow she doubted it, though she fervently prayed he would find his way. He was still hurting, too angry, too confused to do more than act in a moral and righteous manner, standing alone against unjust orders.

That was why she had trusted him. She felt he would want to know what was on the CD, to evaluate it for himself, before giving it to his superior officer. And if he was able to play it, if he was able to learn the secret, she hoped he would go against his training and loyalty oath to deliver it to the others. They would know what to do and how to use it.

But all this was speculation, the hope of a desperate woman. She knew he had not given the CD to Overlord Parker. She knew that Parker had not yet found him. Beyond that she was as lost as her former boss. All she was certain of was the fact that Stone was still missing.

"Overlord Parker. Please meet Agent Dempsey at your office!" came an announcement over the loudspeaker.

Parker looked down at the semi-conscious woman on the floor. He had treated her gently, with the utmost control. What he wanted to do was break every bone in her body, then to fling her from the top of the O.N.E. building. How dare she challenge the Messiah? How dare she challenge him? Did she not know the power he held within, the godlike abilities he had revealed to Agents Smith and Stone before killing one and thinking he had killed the other? How dare she create a situation that might cause the Messiah to lose faith in his ability to help Bishop Bancroft achieve the objectives of The Day of Wonders? Parker straightened his necktie, rolled down and rebuttoned his shirt sleeves, and left the interrogation room. He'd send a guard to take her back to the cell when he was good and ready to do it. Until then, let her lay there on the floor.

"Overlord Parker," said Agent Dempsey, hurrying down the hall to meet him.

"What is it, Agent Dempsey?"

"Sir, the security system has been shut down on the Day of Wonders Project. Someone has hacked in."

"Shut down? What's the back trace? The only people who can hack in are from our design staff. They're the only ones with the equipment." He hoped this was not another traitor in their midst. Anna Davis was bad enough. This was worse.

"The trace leads us to the home of one of our computer engineers, sir. A William Holmes, the man who designed the security system and password encoding system for The Day of Wonders," said Dempsey.

"We've patched Holmes through to a secure cell phone, Overlord Parker," said Agent Spencer, hurrying down the hall. "He says it's urgent that he talk with you.

Parker grabbed the telephone, uncertain what was happening, though knowing the day was not progressing the way he desired. He was livid and nervous about how the Messiah would look upon his actions in all this.

"Parker here. What's going on, Holmes?"

"Some crazed lunatic named Stone busted in here about an hour ago. He knew I was one of the engineers, and he knew I was in a wheelchair so I couldn't fight him. He forced me to hack into The Day of Wonders database. But don't worry, I got far enough so he thought I was helping him, then deliberately gave the wrong password to prevent full entry."

"Your break-in was registered here, Holmes," said Parker.

"As I knew it would be. When you can't walk, you have to find ways to protect yourself."

"Is Stone still there."

"I wouldn't be calling if he was. He got frustrated when he didn't get in, and when I told him I was setting off an alarm, he fled. I did manage to plant a microchip on him before he took off. If you have someone in my area, tell him to set the scanner at 123.33 megahertz. The battery on the chip is good for at least 40 or 50 hours. He should have no trouble following the Hater wherever he goes."

"Nice work, Holmes. Stay right there. We'll send some men down to talk to you and make sure this doesn't happen again," he said, turning off the telephone and handing it to Agent Spencer.

"Spencer, do you know where Holmes lives?"

"Yes," said Spencer. "I'm aware of the area."

"Good. Then get over there and take a scanner. Holmes said that Stone is traveling with a transmitter set to 123.33 megahertz. Get to them both and kill them."

"<u>Them</u>, sir?"

"You heard me. Them. Stone and Holmes. They're both finished with O.N.E. and The Day of Wonders. We can't have loose ends like that for the Messiah's big day."

As Spencer turned to leave the building and go to his car, Agent Dempsey asked, "Do you want me to go with Spencer, Sir?"

"Don't you think you've done enough?" yelled Parker, angrily.

"Sir?"

"You had him in your hands and you let him go. Remember? Special Agent Thorold Stone was nothing but a lapdog, someone we could use to do whatever was ordered. Then he discovered you and that idiot partner of yours, and suddenly the man starts to think. Now he's a real threat to The Day of Wonders. I think your letting him go has been more than enough."

"But, sir, you were the one who had him last. You shot at him. You…"

Parker's voice became very soft, belying the intensity of his eyes. They seemed almost to glow like lasers. His body tensed, like a panther waiting to spring. "That kind of talk can get you killed, Agent Dempsey."

"But, sir, I…"

"I don't need you, Agent Dempsey. One Nation

Earth doesn't need you. The Messiah doesn't need you. Now what do you think that means?"

"That I'm fired?" he whispered, terrified.

"Too much paperwork," said Parker, taking out a gun and shooting Dempsey in the head.

▲

"That's all I can do," said Willy, "buy a little time."

"Do you think they believed you?"

"Who can say? We knew the risks when I decided to hack into the security system at the O.N.E. building, then jump to the password files. Once I had access to them, we were able to download that list I gave you. But though the files were vulnerable to hacking, they had an alarm system. It was like breaking into a house with a security system. You can get in, though once you're there, the alarm is ringing and the police are on the way. By calling I gave them an excuse for what happened and maybe bought us some time. They're sending someone over, but I think he has to come all the way from headquarters, so that will buy us some time. "

"What do you mean 'us?'"

"Look, Stone, whatever these guys are doing, they don't want anybody to know about it. Let's say I believe a lot more than I did, and if things are the way I think, killing your partner was a way to avoid loose ends. Who do you think is going to care if a guy in a wheelchair ups and disappears? Like it or not, you've got yourself a partner. It's the only way I can stay alive."

"Then let's roll, Willy," said Thorold.

Willy took the CD, the player, and some other equipment, placed it in a case, set it on his lap, and began moving towards the door. He paused at the entrance and whistled for the dog. "Let's go, Elvis. We're going to have an adventure that would make Lassie jealous."

▲

CHAPTER 9

▲

Into The Valley

▲

Of The Shadow of Death

▲

▲

▲

It was dark outside. Night had settled on the city. In the basement of the O.N.E. building, though, harsh lights burned 24 hours a day, disorienting prisoners and guards alike.

"How long has Overlord Parker had the Davis woman in the interrogation cell?" asked Ned Phillips, the third shift replacement. He had arrived early and was trying to determine what he faced that night.

"Since some time after dinner," said Austin Cardwell as he prepared to sign out and go home.

"She must be very important to him," said Phillips, amazed. "This is not the type of questioning he normally handles himself. I would have thought he would assign it to someone else."

"Something to do with a Day of Wonders CD. She used to work in the department that was involved with the planning. That's where he knew her before. I'm guessing they were friends. From what I've been hearing, he feels personally betrayed. I think she took a disk."

"I can understand that. She was probably trying to get a jump-start on Heaven or whatever else the Messiah has for us to enjoy. If I was in a position to get one early, I can't say I wouldn't take it myself. "

"I wouldn't say something like that too loudly. From the sound of her screams, I don't think Overlord Parker sees it as a minor offense. My guess is she gave something to the Haters. Her husband was one of the leaders, you know.

"Anyway, it's not my problem. My shift is over, and I've got a wife and a good dinner waiting for me at home. All I want to do is get out of here and relax. See you tomorrow night."

Austin Cardwell passed the interrogation room as he headed for the locker room to change out of his uniform. Anna Davis was leaning against the far wall, barely able to keep herself erect. Her wrists were tied behind her back; her head sagged forward, and both her eyes badly swollen. The chair had been moved to a far corner of the room.

Len Parker hovered over Anna, all pretense of

calm gone. His face was covered with a thin sheen of sweat. His shirt was disheveled, his necktie askew. He was tired, overwhelmingly tired, and unable to understand why the woman didn't just give up and die.

"What are you hanging on to, Christian?" said Parker, breathing hard. "Don't you see, you've lost? God has lost!

"It's so simple. We will defeat your God by destroying his people. After the Day of Wonders, you and every other Christian will be dead or converted. The battle will be over, the war lost. There will be no living Christian, no one to tell the story; no one to celebrate the foul name. It will be a new era, one in which we who have made our decision will rule with absolute authority.

"Why will your God have any reason to return if there are no people to welcome him? His prophecy will have failed. There will be no souls for him to claim and we will have won.

"That's why I can't understand your resistance. You can save your life, Christian. Renounce Jesus Christ and live, I tell you. Renounce Christ! There is no reason for you to have to endure any more pain." As if to emphasize his point, he slapped her hard across the face. She screamed as her head jerked to the side, striking the wall. She lost all control, slid to the floor, and whimpered as she collapsed in a heap. Her clothing was torn and filthy. Her body so battered that the few patches of flesh not bearing bruises actually looked out of place.

"You can't escape my fists. He could not bring his pathetic self down from the cross. There is no power in his name. You are dying because of a meaningless prophet. So what's your decision woman? I'm running out of patience and you're running out of time."

Anna Davis raised her head slowly, as though being called by a voice only she could hear. She painfully shifted her body, and rolled on to her back so she could look past Parker. She seemed to be staring at something on the ceiling.

"Renounce him!" Parker screamed.

Slowly the hint of a smile changed Anna Davis' swollen lips. "I can see Him," she said, her voice a hoarse whisper. "I can see Jesus standing at the Father's right hand."

"You're delusional!" Len Parker shouted as he looked at Anna Davis, then slowly raised his own eyes in the direction where she was looking. His mouth opened and he stared in horror, no longer mocking the woman he had battered so brutally. When he finally could speak again, his voice was deep, as though the sound came not from his vocal cords but from some entity resonating from the darkest depths of his soul. Barely conscious, Anna Davis realized she was hearing a voice similar to that of "Legion," the demonic presence Luke mentioned in the country of the Gerasenes. Just as they had been unable to avoid Jesus' ordering them into a swineherd, so she sensed the fear within the heart of the man who had so brutally hurt her. "What have we to do with thee, Jesus, thou Son of God? Art thou come hither to torment us before the time?"

Then, shaking himself as though trying to regain his earlier defiance, he raised his hand to strike the woman one more time.

"How long do you think they'll follow the false lead I gave them?" asked Willy. He was sitting in Thorold's car. His wheelchair was folded in the back next to the electronic items he knew he would need. Only his O.N.E. scanner was plugged into the lighter socket, allowing them to listen to all calls being dispatched on any of the tactical units. Willy felt as though he was having an adventure for the first time in years and he loved the excitement.

"Five minutes. Five hours. It really doesn't matter, Willy. We have to assume that they'll throw a net over this city so tight that no one will escape. Right now we're probably considered the two most wanted men in the world." He drove the car aimlessly, trying to stay in areas where they could blend with traffic. Thorold knew that the later the day became, the fewer the people on the road, and the harder it would be to hide. They needed shelter. They needed a place to plan what to do next.

"I've never been wanted before," said Willy. "It's a good thing I was still wearing my cowboy outfit. Now when we ride into town to meet the bad guys in the center of Main Street, no one will have to guess who's on the side of peace, justice, and the American way."

"I thought that was Superman," laughed Thorold.

"And who do you think inspired Superman?" asked Willy. "Wild Bill Hickock, Roy Rogers, Bat Masterson, Hopalong Cassidy, Wyatt Earp….Without we cowboys taming the west, there'd have been no

Metropolis."

"Okay, I'll concede the point. The question is what do we do now? We can't go back to my place or yours. We can't go where we're known. We can't go where we're obvious strangers. And with that chair of yours…"

"I know. Even if I disguise it as a Sport Utility Vehicle, they'll still figure it out.

"The fact is I've got to have a computer to do anything. I took the special peripherals, but I've got to get them onto something bigger and faster than your notebook. That means only one thing. We're going to have to join the Haters."

"What do you mean? Break into jail? The Haters are locked away in that Hellhole in the basement of the O.N.E. building. Assuming we could get in, we'd never get out alive.

"I'm the one who arrested them, remember? I'm the one who turned them over to Len Parker to do God knows what with them. If I thought we could get into the holding cell area and free them, I'd have headed for there instead of driving out here. I never wanted to be a party to such a terrifying miscarriage of justice."

"I'm not talking about those Haters. I'm talking about the ones that are still free," responded Willy.

"And just how are we supposed to find these Haters? I'm an Agent of the O.N.E. assigned to Hater round up and I don't know where to find them. What makes you think we're going to locate them, much less be welcomed by them.

"The Haters aren't angry with the world the way Parker wanted us to believe. They're peaceful people trying to love their God and stay alive. They've also been persecuted by me and tracked by the devices you've made for O.N.E. If we could find them, and that's stretching a point to think that we can, what makes you think they won't hate us? If I were them, I'd want nothing to do with you or me."

"Don't make so many assumptions. I think we'll find ourselves most welcome," said Willy.

"Why? Because you're wearing a white hat?"

"Just you wait. In the words of Quasimodo, it's just a hunch."

▲

Warren Spencer moved cautiously on the fringe of a wooded area a few blocks from the home of Willy Holmes. He was carrying a shotgun along with his sidearm, both ready in case he spotted either of his targets.

"They're tricky," said Agent Mel Walker who had accompanied Spencer. Thorold Stone had already escaped from what should have been certain death. And Willy Holmes, though an electronics expert, had received enough training to be deadly if armed. It was better for Walker and Spencer to work together.

"Is Stone still backtracking constantly?" asked Spencer, looking down at the tracking monitor Walker carried.

"It's like Stone's going from tree to tree, doubling back, then moving in a new direction." As he spoke, Walker watched a LCD screen with a grid of city streets. At the top of the screen were the words: "Transponder

Frequency 123.33." On the screen itself was a small blip moving in a seemingly random pattern. The satellite tracking monitor could be switched for increasingly narrow areas of coverage, or for a citywide pattern. The satellite tracker could take them to an area within fifty feet of the broadcast unit. It could also extrapolate the direction in which the person was moving and the possible destination by constantly extrapolating data from the recorded movements. All the back tracking and other efforts to mislead them would mean nothing so long as Thorold continued to move more in one direction than another.

Walker changed the control to give them a smaller and smaller area to study. They were closing in. The screen indicated they were within 100 yards of Stone and, presumably, Holmes.

The men moved forward, separating slightly as Walker drew his gun. They would position themselves to keep Stone and Holmes off guard. They wanted to be certain that no matter which way one of them shot, Walker or Spencer would be behind him. Procedures called for two more O.N.E. agents to be involved in the takedown. With four, there would be no risk of the arresting officers getting shot; no risk of Stone and Holmes fleeing. Parker refused, though. Parker could trust Walker and Spencer to handle the matter without ever revealing that an O.N.E. agent had lost his faith in the Messiah. Many other agents, like Thorold until a few days earlier, were seemingly loyal, yet remained unknowns. Parker felt the risk of failure was too slight to consider, especially if Willy Holmes had been telling the truth about being

Stone's prisoner. Willy would embrace Walker and Spencer as rescuers and delight in the shooting of Stone. By the time Willy realized he, too, was expendable, he would be dead.

Spencer pressed the broadcast control button on the tactical radio unit he had attached to his belt. The microphone/receiver was clipped to his lapel. The sensitivity level was turned up so he could whisper and still be heard in headquarters. "We've got him on the monitor, Mr. Parker. We're within a few yards of being able to kill him," Spencer whispered.

There was a pause while he listened to Parker, then said, "No, sir. We don't have them in line of sight just yet. This is a wooded area, but the tracking unit is giving us excellent directions.

"No, sir, we won't lose them. They're moving in an odd pattern. Walker thinks they're backtracking to keep us from following them. But from the grid map, I suspect they're setting up some kind of electronic relay that will work through the phone system. Stone keeps stopping at every telephone pole.

"Yes, sir. Spencer out."

With each new direction Willy gave Thorold, the car moved back into the city, back where the surveillance was likely to be most intense. "What do you think you're doing, Willy? You're taking us back towards WNN property. Is this some sort of set-up? Are you trying to get us killed?"

"Turn right at the stop sign," said Willy, but this time Thorold ignored him, going straight ahead for a block, then turning off the car lights and pulling to the curb.

"Like hell I will," said Thorold. "I want to know what is going on around here."

"We're going to visit some Haters."

"In the heart of where Macalusso has his media headquarters? This is a set-up, Willy, isn't it?"

"Will you get back on the road?" said Willy, nervously. "Whether you believe me or not, I happen to know some Haters. They're hiding out not far from here."

"Like the eighteen I arrested? Willy, we do a great job of running them down. I'm ashamed to say that now, but it is true."

"Not that good. I know for a fact that they've been using this one hideout for a few months. Parker's men don't know about it at all."

"Since you have been loyal to the Messiah, I don't want to know how you know about it."

"We all have our burdens and our secrets in these times," said Willy.

"Assuming you're right, what makes you think they'll let us in? From what we've been hearing on the radio tonight, if they're smart, they'll most likely shoot us both, then dump our bodies as far from their hideout as possible. We're too much trouble. Why should they risk their lives for us?"

Willy looked down, saying nothing. His sudden quiet was so unexpected, Thorold looked at him in surprise. "One of them is my sister," Willy whispered.

"Would you say that again?"

"My sister. One of them is my sister," said Willy,

both embarrassed to have to admit it and a little proud that she was doing something so against the rest of the world. "I told you I lost her. I never said she was one of the disappeared. Why do you think I even listened to you when you told me the Haters were being set up? Because you're such a smooth talking salesman?

"When you're as isolated as I am, having a sister go underground is almost as big a loss as having her die. You have no idea how lonely my world can be without her."

"But you know where she is?"

"I visit her whenever I think it's safe. Right up there. Pull over in front of that green house."

"This is the place where they're hiding?"

Willy ignored Thorold. As the car stopped, he opened the door and whistled.

"What are you doing?"

Willy said nothing and whistled again, only this time louder. He stared into the darkness, growing nervous when there was no response. Then, just as he was about to whistle one last time, Willy's dog, Elvis, came bounding to the door.

"Up!" said Willy, and the dog jumped onto his lap.

"What the..."

"I have a friend who lives there. Elvis and me, we go visiting here all the time. I told him the name when we let him out in the woods. It was so close, I knew he'd go there to wait for me."

Willy took the collar in his hand and carefully examined it. There was nothing there. "It looks like someone found the tracking chip."

As he petted Elvis, he heard an excited

dispatcher on the radio. He leaned over and turned up the volume.

"Attention all units, investigators have located Thorold Stone's microchip. They report that it was placed on another party as a diversion. The entire downtown core has been sealed. Orders remain unchanged for both Agent Stone and William Holmes who was falsely reported to be a hostage. Both men are to be considered armed and dangerous. Both men are to be shot on sight."

"That's kind of neat," said Willy as Thorold eased the car back in traffic. "Somebody thinks I'm dangerous. This is more exciting than a gunfight at the O.K. Corral."

▲

John Goss was sitting at a large table, with a blueprint unfolded in front of him, pondering the enormity of the organization for The Day of Wonders. It was when the goggles began to be delivered to the citizens of the world that the enormity of The Day of Wonders finally became clear to him. Every man, woman, and child in the world was being equipped with the viewing device. Broadcast units and transponders had been established on tall buildings and in desert regions, in the rain forest and in the frozen north. Wherever there were people, there were goggles being delivered and a method for broadcasting the activator signals.

Just the manufacture of the goggles was impressive. Regional factories had been established worldwide, each producing a different part for the special viewing goggles. Prisms might be manufactured in Brazil,

South Africa, Australia, China, and Germany. The radio receivers might be made in Paraguay, Spain, Egypt, France, Japan, and Canada. There were more than sixty separate parts in all, and more than six hundred regional factories turning them out over the course of three shifts working seven days a week.

The assembly plants were equally scattered. Care had been taken to assure that no one who worked in a parts manufacturing plant would be related to anyone in an assembly plant. In that way, no one could recreate the details of the electronics. No one had more than one-sixtieth of the knowledge he or she would need to learn the secret of the goggles.

Then had come the packaging, the shipping, and the identifying of every human on earth. The identity cards helped, of course. It was doubtful that more than a handful of people in any given region lacked the proper identification. And if someone had been missed in the effort, no one really cared. They were likely marginal individuals at best, who slept over steam grates to keep warm in winter. They were likely alcoholics living on cheap wine and too little food, or drug addicts who preferred their pharmaceutical fog to dealing with real life. None of them were Haters. None of them were connected with the Messiah's enemies. Besides, given enough time, it was probable that they would all be dead.

The Day of Wonders was an undertaking like no other in the history of the world. Goss had read once about an effort to bring mass communication to Third World countries. Simple radios were designed to be given out to remote villagers. They cost only a few cents each to manufacture and distribute. The sets were little more than the crystal sets kids once played with before the invention of the transistor. Even though it was a crude and inexpensive undertaking, the cost and the logistics were overwhelmingly difficult to handle. The project never got very far. That one person, even one with the powers of Macalusso, could plan, mount, and arrange for the execution of the invention, manufacture, and distribution of the goggles was beyond his comprehension.

It was only the fact that he and the others remained in hiding that gave Goss hope. Anyone who could mount so elaborate an event as The Day of Wonders but could not ferret out Christians in hiding was vulnerable to being stopped.

Not that there was consensus on his beliefs. John Goss looked upon Franco Macalusso as his mortal enemy. He didn't know what kind of man he was, where he was from, or how he had gained his powers. But he was a man, of that John was certain. He was a Hitler, a Stalin, and an Idi Amin. He was the embodiment of all that was evil in the world, and if he couldn't find the hideout in which Goss, Helen Hannah, and the others were working, Macalusso could be stopped — some how, some way.

John Goss frustrated Helen with his reasoning. "You've got to read the book," she kept telling him in frustration. "Franco Macalusso is the Anti-Christ. He is the fulfillment of prophecy. You call him your 'mortal enemy,' but he's anything but that.

"John, the Bible says the Anti-Christ is going to

win. Many Christians will die by his hand, just as they are doing now. He is going to succeed in getting many people to take on the mark of the Beast. We're going to see people who once were our friends and neighbors, co-workers we thought we knew, all worshipping the image of the Beast. And those of us who refuse will be killed.

"The time of the Anti-Christ has come and must unfold. It has been foretold, and none of us can do anything about it," Helen had continued vehemently.

"And where does The Day of Wonders fit in?" John had asked.

"I don't know," said Helen. "That's what concerns me. If it's part of the prophecy, there's nothing we can do about it. I just haven't found anything in my studies that seems to make it part of prophecy.

"Besides, look at us. We haven't been found by Macalusso's men. That must mean The Day of Wonders is either something else or God wants us to learn the truth and expose it, stop the event...I don't know. Whatever can be done.

"Look, John, we've been safe here so far only because of the Lord's presence in our lives. There must be rightness to our cause, to the need to tell His story. Certainly we must preserve the knowledge of Jesus Christ, the true savior. We can not let that die, and I'm convinced that so long as we walk the path with Jesus, we have nothing to fear."

"And I think we've avoided capture because we picked a good place and we've been very lucky. I've been reading Revelation like you asked me to, Helen. I've been reading in other parts of the New Testament, too. I want to believe. I want to have your faith. Right now I just...I guess that if I think of all this as inevitable. I mean, what's the use? This Macalusso is an evil man, the most evil the world has ever seen. Maybe we can't stop him. Maybe he is the Anti-Christ. But if we can frustrate his plans, stopping things like this Day of Wonders, maybe others will see him as a fraud. Maybe others will..."

The argument always ended the same way, with Helen sighing in exasperation, giving him a hug, then handing him more reading, more tapes, whatever she thought would knock some sense in his head. And John would return to his plotting to defeat the plans for The Day of Wonders, thinking of himself as a guerrilla warrior, never allowing himself to truly consider the issue of the Anti-Christ.

Now, with all the time that had passed, with the closeness of The Day of Wonders, John Goss felt discouraged as Helen Hannah walked over to him to check on how he was doing. "Any word from Ronny?" John asked.

"Not yet," said Helen. "We know he's cleared every hurdle in the background check. No one has connected him with us, praise the Lord. He's now officially a part of Len Parker's security staff, which will give him the greatest direct access possible to finding out what was on that CD. The question is whether or not there will be anything to find in the areas to which he is assigned.

"How about you? Anything yet?" Helen asked.

"I'm still trying to figure out this goggle stuff.

Part of me wants it to be something silly, like giving every person in the world a new computer game to play so they will become obsessed with the electronics and forget about what has happened to the world. It would sure work with kids who play their Game Boys and Play Stations and other toys in all the stores that sell them. They're absorbed for hours. Maybe that's what he's doing."

"Right, John. And the Bible never warned us of the Anti-Christ."

"Okay. Okay. I said that's what I want it to be. I know it's far more, far worse. I just keep wondering what a pair of fancy glasses could possibly have to do with the Day of Wonders. The only way we're going to find any answers is if we can break into the O.N.E. computer system, and there seems to be no way we can get in there."

As the two talked, they were unaware that Willy had just rolled into the room. "I can get into the computer," said Willy, quietly.

"Willy! Oh, thank God, Willy. You're alive. You're safe. You're…" said Helen, rushing over to the chair and hugging her brother.

"Handsome. Debonair. Hell on wheels, if you'll forgive the expression," said Willy.

"We heard that you were missing, kidnapped, believed murdered by a renegade O.N.E. Agent named…"

Helen stared at the man who entered moments after Willy. Startled, John drew a .25-caliber automatic from his pocket. It was a poor choice for a revolution but deadly in close quarters.

"Hey, John, put that gun away," said Willy. "Thorold's okay. He doesn't need to get killed by an amateur when there are professionals trying to do it. Give him a break."

"He's a cop, Willy," said John, still holding the gun. "An O.N.E. Special Agent. I heard on the news..."

"That he's the one who kidnapped and probably murdered me," interrupted Willy. "Unless you think resurrection strikes twice on the same planet, Thorold Stone isn't the man they claim. He apparently knows too much and now he's an embarrassment to the O.N.E. Special Agents."

"But he's a cop. What if he's undercover. What if...."

"John, put that thing away. I'm not Jesus. You're not Peter. And this man isn't a Roman soldier come to arrest me in the garden. Even there Jesus made his friend put away his sword," said Helen.

"I'd really appreciate that," said Thorold.

"Come on, John. This guy may dress funny compared to the sartorial splendor with which I left my house, but he's one of the good guys now," said Willy. "I'd take him to the O.K. Corral with me any time, and my compliments don't get much better than that."

"John, you know Willy. Put the gun away," said Helen, walking over to Goss, holding out her hand, and taking the weapon from him. She clicked the safety catch back on, then tucked the small weapon in his shirt pocket.

"Thank you," said Thorold. "I never thought

I'd be beholden to Helen Hannah, the world's most wanted woman." Then, turning to Willy, he added, "You really should have told me, Willy. When you said your sister had been in television news, I pictured some small town Barbie Doll whose one skill was reading a monitor without giggling each time she mispronounced some name. I never thought you meant one of the most respected people in the business."

"That sure is sexist," said Helen. "Maybe John was right. Maybe we should have shot you when you came in."

"Would you have told me if the situation was reversed," asked Willy, seriously. "Helen and I have had very different religious beliefs since our grandmother disappeared. You know how I feel about the Messiah, no matter what Len Parker has been doing, and Helen is as devout a Christian in her own way as our grandmother was in hers. But Helen is my sister. More than that, she's my friend, something a chance of nature does not create. The money being offered just to learn where she's hiding would make anyone rich beyond his or her wildest dreams. Until I thought I could trust you, there was no way I would tell you everything."

"At least introduce us," said Helen. "All I know is that your name and face are all over the news. Apparently people in high places don't like you very much. And these days I have to say that I admire that quality in a man."

"Helen, this is Thorold Stone, the crazed lunatic who killed me and cut me into little pieces which he mailed to a little old lady in Pasadena who mistook the package for stew meat that she prepared for her cats."

"How do you do?" said Thorold, shaking her hand.

John stared at the three of them, then said, "If being a Christian means risking my life for nuts like you…"

"We all have our cross to bear," laughed Helen. Then, looking at Willy, she asked, "But where's Elvis. You didn't have to leave him behind, did you?"

"He was out exploring the front of the building," said Willy. "He should be along any time…."

His words were cut off by a curse escaping John's lips. Then, embarrassed, he said, "Sorry. Old habits die-hard. I'm trying to learn, but Willy, this dog of yours…" John was staring down at his shoe as Elvis, standing nearby, happily wagged his tail. "You were right, Thorold," said Willy. "We should have let him relieve himself at the fire hydrant before we came inside."

At least the computer equipment was state of the art. That was the one advantage to his sister and some of her friends having worked for the world's largest television broadcast system. Still, it had taken Willy almost three hours to rewire some of the computers and install the special hardware he had brought with him.

The work was especially tedious because he had to find ways to keep from being traced when he hacked into the O.N.E. system. There already were voltage boosters in place to help with wired telephone lines, but some of the work had to be dispersed in a manner that could not be discovered. He wired in a cellular phone unit, then altered a wired line so he could use the computer to move the feed around the country. It wouldn't prevent a trace, but it would confuse the normal computer system, taking extra time to locate the route of the hacking.

Willy dared not think about the passage of time. Willy dared not think about the people looking for him. Willy dared not think about anything, which was why he was startled when he heard the voice of Cindy Bolton say, "If you guys are hungry, there's some leftover salad in the fridge."

Willy turned and saw the blind woman Helen had mentioned. What she had not said was how beautiful she was. Of medium height and build, she moved with the grace of a dancer despite her inability to see. Her voice had a lilting quality to it that was a delight to the ear. And her face was that of a movie star. Her beauty came through despite the dark glasses she wore. "Salad? That's it? I've worked all these hours for a chance to eat green stuff?" mocked Willy.

"It's what I made to share with everyone," said Cindy. "I don't eat meat."

"I don't think you're being rational. Hasn't anyone ever told you that if God didn't want us to eat animals, they wouldn't have been made of meat?"

"I'm not a vegetarian because I love animals," Willy. "I'm a vegetarian because I hate plants. When I walk into a supermarket, the entire produce section cringes as I approach. I can't tell you the power I feel knowing I will soon be taking a knife to some romaine lettuce here, some broccoli there...."

"So share your hatred with your therapist. I've worked hard to get to the top of the food chain and I didn't do it to be a vegetarian."

"Well that explains a lot. Vegetables are brain food," teased Cindy.

"Helen," called Willy to his sister who was sitting on the far side of the room, talking with Thorold. "Where did you find this woman? She's rude. She's sarcastic. She's downright obnoxious. And best of all, she can't see my shortcomings."

Helen laughed, smiling as she watched Willy take a break from his work to wheel over to where Cindy was standing. He looked into her eyes and asked, "Where have you been all my life?"

Helen and John had relaxed a bit with Willy present, recognizing that the passage of time no longer mattered. Nothing was going to change in their favor until Willy finished assembling the hardware and could go to work on the computer. He was almost done, working intensely with Cindy sitting on a chair by his side. They talked as he worked, Cindy occasionally reaching over to touch his shoulder.

John Goss continued working on schematics and charts, searching for alternative means of attacking the system if Willy failed. He knew in his heart that Willy's skills were the keys to their future success, if they succeeded. But it was comforting to him to feel as though he was contributing something with his efforts.

Helen was sitting with Thorold, the two of them drinking coffee, wrapped up in a deep discussion. "Thorold Stone, I'm surprised at you," said Helen. "You actually think that Franco Macalusso's some kind of space alien? This is real life, not some science fiction fantasy. The Bible has been warning us about this for centuries but those of us who have been left behind were too foolish to heed the word in time."

"I went to church a few times with Wendy and the kids," said Thorold. "I never heard about anything like this."

"You have to read the book, Thorold. I've had more time to read about what's happening than I ever wanted to experience," said Helen, picking up the book and thumbing through it. "This is history. This is prophecy. This is God speaking to us through the ages.

"You know all the things we've seen, the so-called miracles. Here in the 24th chapter of Matthew it says, 'For there shall arise false Christs, and false prophets, and shall show great signs and wonders; insomuch that, if it were possible, they shall deceive the very elect.'

"And in the second chapter of Second Thessalonians, it refers to the Antichrist. 'Even him, whose coming is after the working of Satan with all power and signs and lying wonders, and with all deceivableness.' Does that sound familiar?

"God doesn't use aliens to fulfill Bible prophecy. We're seeing what the writer of Revelation showed us in chapter 13 where he wrote, 'And I beheld another beast coming up out of the earth; and he had two horns like a lamb, and he spoke as a dragon. And he exerciseth all of the power of the first beast before him, and causeth the earth and them which dwell therein to worship the first beast, whose deadly wound was healed. And he doeth great wonders, so that he maketh fire come down from heaven on the earth in the sight of men, and deceiveth them that dwell on the earth by the means of those miracles which he had power to do in the sight of the beast.'

"Thorold, the first beast is Macalusso, the Anti-Christ. The other beast is the false prophet."

"Len Parker?" asked Thorold. He had been listening intensely, uncertain of what he believed yet realizing he had to seriously consider what Helen was saying.

"I don't know. Maybe, Thorold. What matters is that we are living in the days that were foretold for those of us who failed to be raptured like Wendy and your daughters."

"I understand what you're telling me, but I'm trained to deal in facts."

"These are facts. Why do you think it's illegal to have a Bible? Why do you think that people who dare to proclaim the word of God are 're-educated,' tortured, or killed? Why do you think he has targeted only those who have come to know the word of Christ? Black is white and white is black. Those of us who love the Lord are now known as Haters."

"Helen, I saw Len Parker walk through a wall. He shot me, then turned and walked out of the room and the only thing there was a brick wall. That's not a power any earthly man has.

"Why couldn't they have read the Bible and planned everything to fit?"

"You experienced the parlor tricks of the Beast.

There is only one truth and that's God's truth. These people aren't aliens who have come from some other planet, then seduced us by reading the Bible in order to recreate prophecy. God's hand is in this. People like Len Parker have made choices, horrible choices. They may have dramatic powers, but they were gained at the cost of their immortal souls.

"Stop trying to analyze everything based on your old beliefs. Think about what you've seen in light of what I've just read to you. You've been willing to accept some television show plot about space aliens as truth. Why not recognize that all you've seen, all we're experiencing, has been foretold? Why not recognize that God has been working in your life, too?"

"God? My life? What do you mean, Helen? Wendy? The kids?"

"I'm not talking about the rapture. That was something they earned, a reward for recognizing what the rest of us were too dense to understand until we had to experience these troubled times. No, Thorold, I'm talking about what brought you to our door. You don't think it was chance that brought you to our door. I truly believe that you're here because God has a plan for you."

"God? Not me," said Thorold, genuinely surprised by the idea. "No, not me. I didn't buy the idea when my wife was selling it, and I'm sure not going to buy it from you."

"That's a pretty closed mind you've got there, especially with all you've experienced in the last few days and the Bible passages I read you which show this time so clearly," said Helen.

Thorold was becoming annoyed, though whether it was with Helen or with himself he did not know. It made him uneasy to think he might be an important player in all this. It was one thing to have the CD. It was quite another to be somebody who mattered. He could not deal with that idea right then. "Helen, my mom believed in God with all her heart when I was a little kid. Then Mom got cancer. I didn't know what that meant other than that she began to spend more time in bed. She'd pray to God for peace, but all I could see on her face was pain and anguish. She got weaker and weaker. When she got too weak to pray, I prayed for her. I made all sorts of deals with Him. I promised to clean my room. I promised to be a good boy. I promised...

"I had always been taught by my mother that children were important to Jesus. I had been taught that if we asked without being selfish, God would grant us what we asked.

"And then Mom died. One night I kissed her and she weakly tousled my hair. The next morning my father came into the bedroom, crying. She had died during the night, he said. I ran to their room, but they had taken away the body.

"At first I refused to believe what was happening. I wanted to see her, to prove to myself that she was dead. I screamed at my father, calling him a liar. I told him I had made a deal with God. I told him that God wouldn't let her die. I told him....

"And then we went to the funeral home. Mom was lying there in the casket, all made up like a department store mannequin. When no one was looking, I touched her, trying to get her to wake up. I poked her, trying to move her.

"That's when I realized she wasn't my mother any more. Her body was cold, wax like I guess. It wasn't her, that was for sure.

"That night I went into my room and told God I didn't believe in Him any more. I told Him I hated Him. I told Him if he was real, He should strike me dead for yelling at Him. I told Him a God wouldn't take a good woman like my mother."

There were tears in Thorold's eyes, though he seemed unaware of them. His voice was soft, intense. He was looking past Helen, past Willy and Cindy, past the physical barriers of the room's walls. He was seeing the past, remembering his mother, the feelings he had.

Helen reached over and touched his hand. He gripped it unconsciously, still staring at the memories of pain long past. "I just couldn't understand how God could take my mother away from me like that. I couldn't understand why.

"I tried for a long time to answer that question, but I couldn't. Not anymore than I can understand about Wendy and the kids. That's why I think the answer is simpler than you want to hear."

"Go ahead and tell me, Thorold," said Helen, softly. "I lost both of my parents when I was young. My grandmother raised Willy and me. I understand more than you think."

"You and Willy," said Hannah, "refuse to see the hand of God in the way you've been brought here.

You refuse to see that there are situations that won't have the outcome we desire. Yet in God's way, they work out for the best. That's why I know you're making a big mistake, you <u>and</u> my brother."

Willy looked up from the computer, turned towards his sister, and said, "Let me ask you something, Helen. If a man speaks in the forest and there's no woman there to hear him, is he still wrong?"

Thorold laughed at the joke, Helen smiled and shook her head. "All right, you guys. So we all know where we disagree. Now get back to work, Willy. You can't make nasty remarks and save the world at the same time." Then, turning to Thorold, she said, "Let's keep looking at this situation we're in and see where we do agree."

"Okay," said Thorold. For some reason he felt peace with Helen Hannah. In his mind it was pure luck that they were still alive. If Helen had other thoughts on what was taking place, he would at least listen to her.

"Thorold, I've been in broadcasting more years than I want to admit. I've covered stories all over the world. I've met world leaders and people who no one ever heard of. I'm as cynical as you are, maybe more. And I lost the most important person in my life during what I now know was the rapture. With all that, I have to say that there is no question in my mind that Bible prophecy is being fulfilled exactly as it was written.

"You still want to believe that aliens from another planet are following Bible prophecy like a script, trying to throw us off track."

"Yes, a little, even with what you've shown me,"

he said, feeling a little foolish about what he was thinking. He did not feel comfortable with any other explanation, yet there was a certain silliness to his grasping at some Star Wars type story.

"Now no matter which one of us is right, we both agree that the Bible is the best place for us to try to figure out what's going to happen next."

"If they're following Bible prophecy," said Thorold.

"And they are. Either way, they are. So why don't we sit down and keep going over the research we've put together from the Bible?" said Helen.

"Just remember that the book was written long before anyone heard of Franco Macalusso, Bishop Bancroft, or the Church of One Nation Earth. This is the story of our past and the foretelling of our present and future. It certainly is the best place to start."

"I'm in your hands, Helen. I never considered dealing with any of this until I discovered what Len Parker was all about."

"The New World Order has had as one of its primary goals the creation of a one-world church. There would be no chance for dissent. There would be no way for scholars to disagree. The Word of God could easily be subverted in the name of unity.

"People have been trying to achieve this one-world church for over 150 years," said Helen. "Now it's becoming institutionalized as the United Religious Organization, or the URO. To show you the details…"

"Helen, Thorold, John, we're ready!" shouted Willy, excitedly interrupting his sister's conversation.

They hurried over to the computer.

"There's still one line encrypted, but it won't stop me from running the program. I'll keep trying to crack it, but at least now I can take this baby for a test drive," Willy told them.

Willy clicked the mouse, causing the block and jackhammer images to appear on the screen. This time the block was shattered, the diskette was freed, and there was no error message. Willy moved to a second computer inter-linked with the first. On the screen is written "Select Desired Virtual World". It was the same message that was on the screen in Willy's home when he showed Thorold what it was like to walk on the beach. However, there was only one option on the screen–"Day Of Wonders."

"This is it, isn't, Willy?" asked Helen. "You're into the Day of Wonders disk?"

Willy said nothing. Instead, he pushed the button to activate the program, sat back in his chair, and put on the goggles. From the computer came a voice saying, "Welcome to the Day of Wonders."

It was white. That was the first thing he noticed. The virtual world was overwhelmingly, blindingly white. There was no sense of up or down, no horizon or sun by which to guide him.

Willy squinted and shielded his eyes, trying to adjust to the intensity of the brightness. For several moments he stood where he was.

Then, as he could on the beach, Willy was able to walk. He began strolling in what he hoped was a straight line, looking about, trying to see…anything.

He tried to understand what was happening. Willy jumped up and down, walked this way and that, and always kept looking all around himself. Other than the white mist, there was nothing, no borders, no walls, no ceiling, just…nothing.

Willy called out, trying to hear if anyone else was in his virtual world. There was no movement, no sound, and no echo. "This is the Day of Wonders?" Willy said, as much to himself as to the others. "I wonder who's going to lose his job over this program?"

Willy removed his goggles, suddenly exhausted. He had worked too hard to experience nothing. Something was not quite right, but what he did not know.

"So what was it?" asked Thorold.

"Nothing," said Willy, dejectedly.

"What do you mean, 'nothing?'" asked Thorold. "Could you walk? Talk? Was it like when we went on the beach?"

"It was nothing, white nothing. There was white mist and white…nothing. Like one of those fashion magazine advertisements where the model is posed on white seamless paper that is airbrushed before publishing. She is in perfect color and all around her is white. That's what it was like."

"I don't understand."

"Picture the opposite of everything—no trees, no beach, no women. Nothing. Zero. Zilch. Other than the fact that I could stand and walk, there was nothing to this program at all."

"You're wrong, Willy," said Thorold. "There's something more to that disk all right. As good as you are, you missed the most important part of it."

"What do you mean? I told you what happened when I put on the glasses."

"And I believe you. But you're forgetting one thing. I may be new to this Christian thinking, but I'm a trained investigator. I know how to look at seemingly unrelated facts and interpret them. I know how to find patterns. Len Parker, Bishop Bancroft, and who knows who else are trying to kill us because we have this CD. You've gotten into it, but you haven't found whatever it is that's worth any number of lives to them."

Willy, frustrated, stared at the screen. "Can I help you, Willy?" asked Helen.

"I appreciate the offer, Sis, but I think you'd better leave this work to the professionals."

"I've heard that one before, Willy. Professionals built the Titanic. Amateurs built the Ark!"

Willy smiled, pulled the goggles back down over his eyes, tapped on the keyboard, then began moving his upper body first one way and then another. He was obviously exploring the nothing that had so frustrated him.

Helen took Thorold's hand and led him back to the table where they had been talking. She was determined to bring him to the understanding she had worked so hard to gain for herself. That he had been raised in church, that he had lost a parent when he was young as she had, made it easier to relate to him. She understood the pain he had carried since childhood. She understood the anger. She had been fortunate in having the grandmother the good Lord had put into her life, a woman who could find joy in any burden if it enriched someone else's life, especially the lives of her grandchildren. Helen may have strayed from Jesus in her anger, but she had a living witness to bring her back. Her only sadness came from the knowledge that her understanding, and her deep abiding faith, were too recent to be part of the rapture. At least wherever her grandmother happened to be, and Thorold's family, for that matter, she knew it was a place of joyful praise, without pain or animosity. Loved ones were to be missed, of course. They had touched too many lives to not be. But the sadness was for the inability to be with them at this time of trial when their faith would be so enriching. She only hoped that she was gaining what her grandmother and so many others had found prior to the rapture. Live or die, the Lord was blessing them all with one more chance to know His son, His love, and His way.

"We're going to finish our discussion while Willy works, Thorold."

"Okay," he said, enjoying Helen's company even if her ideas were painfully close to those of Wendy. "Let me make sure I've got this straight. Macalusso, the guy Willy insists is the Messiah and I think is an alien, the guy who seems to have done nothing short of saving the world from utter destruction, is actually Satan? Of course, instead of dressing in red he wears designer suits he picks up in Italy, London, and Hong Kong. And instead of brimstone, he smells of expensive cologne. But he's Satan, and if I got a search warrant for his home I'd probably find a pitchfork hidden in a closet?"

Helen smiled at Thorold. "You really are bull-headed, aren't you, Thorold Stone? I said he was Satan. I never said anything about the red suit, horns, or a pitchfork. That's a modern concept, like the drawings of Santa Claus. Why shouldn't he wear an Armani suit or some other designer's label? He blends in with the rich and powerful just as Jesus' appearance made him a comfortable presence for laborers in the Roman occupied cities He visited."

"And Wendy and the girls, in fact all of the Christians who knew God before the disappear... I mean the rapture...are now in Heaven?"

Thorold stood up and began pacing, trying to think, and trying to respond to Helen. "This all sounds great, Helen, like one of those old movies that ended with the music coming up and everything happy in ways that would never occur in real life. But you're forgetting one thing, Helen. I don't believe in God."

"God believes in you, Thorold. He's still God, He's still with us, whether you believe in Him or not."

"Well, if He's for real, why doesn't He just show himself. We've got Satan or the Anti-Christ or some little green man from the planet Zenon disguised as Franco Macalusso. Why doesn't He just show himself, blast Macalusso with a lightning bolt, and let us get on with our lives?"

"I hear that question a lot from unbelievers, Thorold. In fact, I used to ask it myself."

"Do you still ask it or have you found your answer

in this little bunker where we're hiding to keep from being killed?"

"Don't be a smart mouth, Thorold. It's one thing for Willy who uses it as a defense mechanism. It's not becoming on a man like you."

"Helen, your parents were killed. Your grandmother was taken from you. You've lost your job. You're a fugitive with a price on your head. If someone finds you, they can probably kidnap you, rape you, torture you, and kill you, and so long as the person brings a recognizable face to the O.N.E. headquarters, Len Parker will declare the person a patriotic hero. Where is God in the midst of this Hell?"

"He's all around us."

"I know that one. It's the one they used to throw at us in Sunday school. They'd talk about how He's present in the birds that fly, the grass that grows, the flowers that bloom, in the sunrise and sunset, in a soon-to-be mother's womb. We even had some songs about all that, though I don't remember any of them any more.

"Years ago, when Mount St. Helen's erupted, a friend of mine, a police detective, was flying his family up to Vancouver to see his wife's relatives. He saw the smoke and lava and horrible devastation that the eruption had caused. It was like some fire breathing dragon had belched intense heat and smoke over everything, he told me.

"Not long after that, my friend flew over the volcano again. Everything seemed as desolate as the moon, he told me. Then he said that he saw God on the side of the mountain."

"What do you mean, Thorold?"

"That's what I asked him. I figured there was some brooding, bearded figure looking down at his handiwork and wondering how he had gotten the recipe wrong. I mean, what's a volcano to God but something like a gigantic cook stove He could use to prepare His meals when He's visiting His creation."

"Thorold, is this getting to some point? I know you don't believe, but I'm getting offended by your attitude."

"Hear me out, Helen. This guy tells me that when he looked down this time, in the midst of ash and the rubble, a flower was blooming. It had burst through all that muck and mess to show that new life was possible, even there."

"Praise the Lord, Thorold. I didn't think you could be so understanding," said Helen.

"I thought he was being a jerk myself. So he saw a flower. Everyone knows that given half a chance and some time away from our screwing up around here, the planet tends to restore itself. And God has nothing to do with it."

"That's where you're wrong, Thorold. Dead wrong."

"All right. If there's a God, I should be able to put Him to the test. I mean, I'm sitting with some of the last believers still alive on the Earth. God wouldn't want to lose face with you, would He?"

Helen looked at him, noncommittal, uncertain where he was going with all this.

"And he needs to keep your faith strong, right?"

"We need to keep our faith strong, Thorold.

God's always with us. We just don't always reach out to Him."

"Fine. Whatever. The main thing is He needs you, and right now it seems He needs some converts." Thorold took a waterglass and moved it to the center of the table. "Now if God wants to show me His presence, have Him knock over that waterglass."

"If He did that, you wouldn't need much in the way of faith, would you?" asked Helen.

"But if it's all faith, where's the proof?"

"Oh, it's not all faith, Thorold. Far from it. God says all you need is faith the size of a grain of mustard seed and he'll do the rest."

"I've heard that one, too. But where's the solid proof?"

"No proof is enough if the heart's not ready. "

"What's that supposed to mean?" asked Thorold.

"It just means that whatever God may do, you won't believe it was Him anyway. You'll always manage to find another explanation."

"I don't have to find another explanation. I already have an explanation. There is no God!"

"Okay, Thorold. Let's get personal. I don't know what you've experienced in your life that would have shown you that God was present, if you had a willing heart. But I do know what's happened to us all.

"Remember the day when the Christians disappeared? We didn't call it the rapture then because we didn't know about the rapture, and maybe you're still uncomfortable with that term. But you know your wife and children. They were good people, believers, a woman and children with faith at least the size of that mustard seed."

"I'd rather not talk about that so much, Helen. It still hurts."

"Like my loss, and Willy's, and John's, and Cindy's, and all of us. There were Christians in all our lives. They were people we knew and loved. What we didn't do was accept the message that they had come to so intimately understand.

"They were good people, loving people. They had morals and ethics, hopes and dreams that were not limited to selfish greed. And they knew God in their hearts in ways the rest of us had to be hit over the head to discover. Isn't that right?"

"Helen, my wife was a wonderful woman, a loving woman. She believed in God. She talked of Jesus as a personal friend. She read the Bible and tried to talk to me about it all the time. I'll grant you all that. But if you're going to rip open my scars from that day, I hope there's a point to all this."

"There is. God took the Christians as He promised, but His love remained. He stayed with us, trying to lead us to His story, and with time, He succeeded. We found Bibles when we were ready to finally listen. We found tapes and books left behind by the Christians who were raptured. We read the Word, we listened to Christian leaders whose words remained even after they were gone. And gradually, one by one, we opened our hearts to the Lord even in the face of men like yourself when you were still an agent of O.N.E."

"That's how you see it."

'That's how Franco Macalusso sees it. You're determined to wear blinders to keep yourself from admitting the truth.

"Who is the enemy in the eyes of Macalusso? Christians. Who is he seeking to kill? Christians.

"This so-called Messiah claims to have taken all the people who were somehow evil. Surely you've had the training concerning why he took those who are gone. Now, with the people he calls The Haters, it's as though he's engaged in some sort of mop-up operation. But if this man can stop missiles in their flight, disarm millions of soldiers, stop poison gas, and neutralize the largest bombs ever created, he's not going to leave a few thousand people who he sees as a threat. He's going to know what's in their hearts just as he claims to have known your wife, my grandmother, and all the others. He's going to make us disappear without spending billions of dollars on law enforcement officers like you to search every city of the world.

"If Franco Macalusso is an alien, and if he made everyone he considered an enemy disappear before he stopped the war, then why can't he do that again? A power like that doesn't need law enforcement officers.

"But if Macalusso is Satan, the Anti-Christ, then his powers, though impressive, are as nothing compared with those who speak the name of Jesus. The very fact that there are people he calls Haters, a growing number of new believer Haters I might add, means that God is with us. His love protects us and keeps us safe while we tell His story and keep His word alive. Now I could talk about all the ways I see God in my daily life, the way I see the loving embrace of Jesus, but that would mean nothing to your experience. All I'm asking you to do is think about the people called Haters, the new Christians willing to go to jail or die for their beliefs, and tell me how there can be any explanation other than God. And then I want you to think about Macalusso, the things he says, the deaths he orders, the way he fears anyone having the Word or even the books, tapes, and literature quoting the Word that were left behind after the rapture. I want you to tell me how you can see anything other than the adversary in his heart."

Thorold was obviously deeply moved by Helen's words. At the same time, he was not ready to believe. There had been too many years, too many hurts, too much to think about in the last 48 hours and too little sleep to enable him to truly think clearly. He sat there looking at the glass, at Helen, and then at the ceiling. "Come on, God," he shouted. "Knock it over right now and I'll believe in you. You couldn't save my mother when I was a little boy, but maybe you can at least take the time out of your busy schedule to knock over one little glass of water. I know I don't have an appointment with you. And you're probably very busy somewhere else. But I don't need a conversation or to hear the meaning of life. You can take care of this in passing. I have faith. Isn't that what Helen said. She said you can do anything and all I'm asking is for you to knock over the glass. I'll even clean up the mess."

Helen's eyes were sad, her heart heavy. "Forgive him, Lord, he knows not what he is doing," she whispered as she watched Thorold stare at the glass.

"Looks like God's not up to the challenge," Thorold said. His attitude was one of cynicism but there was a catch in his voice, as though he was trying to not feel the emotions which were beginning to overwhelm him. "I guess Macalusso's the only one doing miracles these days."

Thorold looked at the glass once more. He was not happy with himself and his attitude towards Helen. He felt like a bully, someone who had deliberately used words to hurt her, and he was not proud of himself. Finally, not knowing what to say or do, he said, "This is ludicrous. I need some fresh air."

Thorold stood abruptly, sending the glass of water flying. The water sprayed across the table, as the glass itself spun to a stop.

Thorold stared at the glass. His raw emotions were at their limits of handling anything. He left the building, saying nothing further.

Thorold walked into the empty field behind the building. It was a clear night, the stars so numerous they looked like a quilt that could cover the earth with its warmth. Tears streamed down his face as he stared at the vastness of it all. "I'm not looking for God!" he whispered, the words coming haltingly. "I'm not. I'm just trying to find my family…."

▲

Len Parker sat in his office, with his door locked, and his computer on a secure link to the personnel files. On the screen was everything known about Thorold Stone, his wife, and his children. There were photographs, DNA chartings, and copies of dental X-rays. If there was any sort of record of anything that happened to him, it was Parker's for the pressing of a few keys. What he did not have was Stone himself, and he felt almost impotent without the man under lock and key.

The powers that had come with the Messiah were like those of one of the ancient gods of Mt. Olympus. So why could he not find one Special Agent?

▲

CHAPTER 10

▲

A Time of Decision

▲

▲

▲

▲

Cindy Bolton was a romantic who delighted in stories about medieval damsels being forced into loveless marriages by cruel fathers determined to create political alliances to benefit their kingdoms. Such stories had knights who so adored the beautiful daughter locked in the tower until the betrothals could be arranged that they would risk life and limb to save her. In Cindy's mind, she was the maiden who wore gossamer garments that flowed with the wind when the knight rescued her from imprisonment and carried her off on the back of his magnificent steed.

Cindy listened to every talking book she could find that had such romantic themes. Not that all were about knights and castles. She also pictured herself trapped on an isolated ranch in nineteenth century Wyoming until a handsome passing stranger fell in love with her. She imagined herself an immigrant girl arriving at Ellis Island, going to work in a garment district sweat shop, and being discovered by the handsome son of the owner of the mill. In that fantasy, the most egalitarian of them all, her new husband turns the ownership of the mill over to the workers, then takes the newly well-off employees to his country club dances where they can meet the elite bachelors of the city.

Real romance had never been a part of Cindy's adult years. All her life she had tried to be like others, to fit in, to be a part of whatever was happening, even if she did not agree with what was taking place. She had dated because her friends had dated. She had encouraged boys she should have discouraged because she fantasized that they found her desirable, not just that blind girl with a good figure who might be so grateful for their attention that she would let them do things they had no business trying. She had even considered marriage once, until she overheard the man brag to his friends that they should get themselves a disabled girlfriend, too. "They may not be great to look at, but they're soooo happy to get a guy's attention, you can treat them like dirt and they'll still cling to you like you're a god," he had bragged. And Cindy, in her pain, had known he hadn't been that much off the mark.

That was when she retreated once more into the talking books that fueled her fantasies. In her imagination, the boy who had hurt her became the callous son of a rival king to whom she was betrothed against her will. His vile actions would one day be avenged by a wandering knight seeking his lady fair, a man with whom Cindy was fated to have a lifetime of happiness in a kingdom far from that of her cruel father.

What Cindy did not realize, nor could she see, was that she had the type of face and figure that caused men to turn and look at her when she walked down the street. She was also extremely intelligent, successfully competing with sighted kids throughout her school years. Her parents had refused to isolate her in a school for the blind. "You'll have to live in a sighted world. You might as well learn how to adjust while you're young," they told her, a decision for which she was grateful despite the pain of never being a full participant in her friends' activities.

Cindy understood the risks she was taking after the day of the disappeared when she had found the audio tapes of the Bible and of sermons by a number of ministers who had vanished with most of the members of their congregations. She had listened out of curiosity at first, then realized the speakers were making sense. She heard the Word read by professional actors, the Bible coming alive for her in a way she had never before thought possible. Having avoided church all her adult life, she suddenly found herself drawn to the man called Jesus, a man who loved the outcasts best of all. When she realized that Franco Macalusso was a false Messiah, she knew that becoming a Christian meant she would spend the rest of her life in greater isolation than she had known from her blindness.

Now, after weeks and weeks in self-imposed exile where her past romantic fantasies were but hurtful jokes, she was amazed to find her knight in shining armor was a computer genius who rode a gleaming wheelchair. And rather than carrying her off to his kingdom far, far away, he had come to share her tower imprisonment.

Cindy knew that Willy's legs did not function, but beyond that she knew little of how he looked. She also knew that it did not matter to her. She had been angry with God in the past, often questioning how much He truly loved His people. But if God had brought her Willy, then she would give thanks for whatever joy would be possible in their self-imposed prison.

Cindy walked over to where Willy was working, massaged his neck, then found the chair she knew was kept by the computers. After touching the back to be certain no one was sitting there, she asked Willy, "Is this seat saved?"

"No, but I'm sure somebody here is praying for it."

Willy took off his goggles, then held out his hand to Cindy to help her sit down. He stared into her glasses, as though he could see her eyes, as though she could see his smile. He knew she liked him, and he knew she did not care about his physical limitations. Talking with her was like talking with someone he had known all his life. She shared his sense of humor, and the laughter that comes when trying to cope with overwhelming pain. "Let me ask you something, Cindy," he said when she was sitting. "If blind people wear sunglasses, why don't deaf people wear earmuffs?"

Cindy laughed, then said, "Let me ask <u>you</u> something, then, Willy. Do men in wheelchairs complain if you leave the seat up?"

Willy laughed, then slipped his hand from hers, reached up and touched her face. He stroked her forehead, then ran his fingers down her jaw line. She tilted her head against his hand as he touched her cheek. "Do you ever take your glasses off, Cindy?' he asked quietly.

"Only when I'm driving."

"No, really. I've never seen you without them."

"Neither have I."

"I'm serious. If you're light sensitive, this place is dark enough that there shouldn't be a problem."

Willy reached up and carefully removed the glasses from her face. He then put his hand under her chin, tilting her head so her eyes would catch more of the light. To his surprise, there was nothing but white. It was as though she was a doll made in a factory that came up short on eyes that day.

"You're beautiful," he whispered.

"I thought I was the one with the vision problem."

"You're the most beautiful girl I've ever seen. You don't need to hide behind dark glasses."

Cindy took Willy's hand again, holding it tight against her face. "Do you know how long I've wanted to hear someone say that and mean it."

"So what made you decide to become a

Christian?" he asked, wanting to change the subject. He had been lonely and unhappy for too long to want to linger on such words. He wasn't ready to linger on words that so deeply touched his heart.

"Actually I wanted to be an atheist but there weren't enough holidays," she joked.

"No, I'm serious. I'd have thought being blind was enough of a bother for you. You had to add being denounced as a Hater."

"Yes, but now I can say that everywhere I go there are men anxious to take me away with them."

"I'm serious, Cindy. My sister I can understand. When we lost our mother, she had to cling to something, and that something was our crazy grandmother, the missionary wanna-be. I can see where some of that constant talk about God's love rubbed off on her.

"Not that I wasn't impressed, too. She was the most loving woman I ever met, but she drove me crazy with all her talk about praying to Jesus to be healed.

"I tried it once. I even went to Lourdes. Big pile of you-know-what if you ask me. Not only didn't I walk, my chair got a flat tire. That was when the old woman talked about healing being self-acceptance, that God had a reason, a plan for me. Crazy stuff.

"You've found something with all this, haven't you? This is a big thing, not like joining some bowling league. I mean, look at the way you guys are living here. In hiding. Spending every day in fear. You must really believe it. I mean, you have to be getting something out of it."

"I met you, Willy. I never would have done that

if I hadn't been here."

"That's another reason to go back to atheism even if you do have to work overtime to cover for all those people taking off for Easter or Christmas or whatever. So why do you believe?"

"I think you're assuming more about me than you should. To be honest, I'm not sure what I believe. My Mom and Dad really believed it. They made the church the focus of their life. I know now that's why they were raptured, but it was different for me.

"You know how some people think that the blind can't hear? They talk real loud when they're speaking to you and in a normal tone when they're standing next to you but don't want you to hear what they have to say?"

"Yes, I've seen that," said Willy. "It's like when I'm wheeling down the corridor at work and I say good morning to people. They've been so busy looking over me, they're shocked that I speak. Then they have to lower their eyes and admit I exist."

"Some of the church people used to talk about my blindness as punishment for past sins. They would say that I must have done something to displease God. Or my parents must have done something wrong before my mother got pregnant. Or even that my family was cursed since the sins of the father go on for five generations.

"Not that they thought I could hear them. They'd share this great 'wisdom,' then raise their voices to talk with me. There were days I wanted to scream at them, to tell them how wrong they were, yet in my heart I feared they were right. I felt like God was punishing me for a life I hadn't really lived.

"My parents weren't like that, though. Nor was the minister. But when they vanished along with all of their other church friends, I had nowhere else to turn, really. Then John invited me to come along with him and...Well, I did. I guess you could say I'm just sort of along for the ride."

"Wow, you sure had me fooled. I've watched you listening to the Bible. I watched you last night–singing and praying with them."

"The songs are joyous and who's to say what happens with the prayers. But that doesn't make me a full believer. Going to church doesn't make you a Christian any more than going to a pet store makes you a cat.

"So what about you, Willy? What's your story."

"I don't like to think about the end. I just want to die in my sleep like my grandfather, not screaming and yelling like the passengers in his car."

Cindy laughed, then said, "But seriously, what do you believe about all this?"

"When Thorold came to me and started carrying on about the Messiah being an alien or something, I just thought he was a nut. But when he showed me how the Christians were being set up...well, somehow I felt like I always knew it. I just knew Helen couldn't be caught up in any of that terrorism stuff.

"There's a difference between not believing in Franco Macalusso and being willing to kill for your beliefs. I've been called a lot of names growing up just because my body looks like my parents got me at one of those shops that sells slightly damaged goods at a big discount. I figured it was one thing to call people Haters, and quite another to be certain those people are violent."

"So what do you believe now?"

"The truth? Despite my sister's faith, I still believe Franco Macalusso is exactly who he says he is – The Messiah. I also believe that right now, the Day of Wonders program is in the hands of some of the most evil men I've ever seen. They're not doing the Messiah's work. I doubt that the Messiah has any idea what is taking place with them. That's why I'm convinced it's up to us to find out what they're up to."

"Superman without legs and Wonder Woman without eyes?"

"Sort of. But let's face it, Cindy. So far as we know there's only one copy of the program that's gotten out and this is it. When you've got the only game in town, it's easy to be a super hero."

"And in the land of the blind, the one-eyed man is king."

▲

There was a risk in going out. That he knew. There was a risk in walking the back roads behind the WNN building where the Haters were hiding. Yet it was because of the risk that Thorold felt safe.

Thorold was a police officer, trained to think like a police officer. This meant he looked at life logically. He knew that if a man was on the run, he would always be certain he could flee quickly. This meant he might go to an airport, train or bus station. This meant he would drive everywhere, making certain the gas tank was full, that there was air in the tires, and perhaps money in the glove compartment should he need to make an unexpected purchase. Every thought would be on avoiding detection, avoiding capture. He would go nowhere without constantly looking out for other cops.

To walk some back roads leading to a quiet park like setting with a pond was not something a fugitive would do. To walk lost in thought, looking neither right nor left, unconcerned if a car approached, again was not something a fugitive would do. That's what he would have told himself if he was in the patrol car looking for a wanted man like he had become. That's what Smitty would have told him.

It was like walking a dog. A dog might have to be walked at any hour of the day or night. Thieves who understood police mentality knew they would be eyed with suspicion if on the streets at 3 or 4 in the morning. They also knew that if they had a dog with them, they might as well be invisible.

It was the cop's mentality. It was the reason Thorold felt safe sitting on the rocks by the quiet stream, looking at the photo of Wendy and the kids in the moonlight.

The pastoral setting was the type of place he and Wendy had gone when dating. They could hold each other, kiss, and plan their future. There was peace to such an area, a sense of safety and serenity, as though all things evil were not allowed.

He needed to think, to try and put what was happening in some kind of perspective. He was also tired, physically and emotionally drained from the events of the last few days, and from the ideas Helen Hannah had been using to challenge everything he thought made sense before entering her hideout.

Thorold picked up a stone and tossed it into the water, watching the way the reflection of moonlight seemed to break up into a shimmering mass as the waves rippled out from where the stone landed. He threw another, then another.

Suddenly a stone began skipping across the surface of the stream. Startled, Thorold turned to see who had thrown it.

"You've got to use stones that are flat on the bottom if you want to skip them across the surface," said Helen Hannah, smiling at him. "And you've got to fling them with a side arm motion. Boys are so busy trying to see how far they throw them, they never learn to finesse the rock."

She threw a second one and Thorold watched it strike the water, bounce up, strike it again, and bounce once more before sinking below the surface. Then, gesturing towards the rocks on which he had been sitting, she asked, "Room for one more?"

Thorold smiled as Helen sat down next to him. He was surprised that he did not mind the intrusion. Perhaps he was beginning to heal a bit. Or perhaps the loneliness of the last few months was far greater than he had wanted to acknowledge. Whatever the case, having Helen Hannah sitting next to him seemed right somehow.

Thorold stared across the water, not looking at

Hannah though relaxed by her presence. "Isn't it crazy the way you sometimes have to lose something before you really appreciate just how much it meant? Right now, I'd give absolutely anything just to have my girls wake me up from a nap on the couch with their fighting over who gets to hold the TV clicker. Can you imagine? That used to be the biggest frustration in my life, not being able to complete a nap without the two of them arguing. They had learned that Daddy was tired from working overtime. They had learned that they could watch television if they kept the volume low. But they couldn't stop themselves from screaming at the top of their lungs if one grabbed the remote when the other thought she should have it.

"How I longed for the day when they would be in adolescent rebellion and want nothing to do with being in the same room, much less the same house as their parents. Now I just wish for a chance to see them once more, to hold them in my arms and never mind naps, or temper tantrums, or remote controls, or anything else."

Helen did not respond for a while. She just sat, watching the water, with her knees pulled up to her chest, and her arms around her knees. Finally she quietly said, "I never had a family of my own. I was always too busy, too caught up in my career. I convinced myself that I was a modern woman, someone who properly valued success and achievement and money. They were what were important in life. Can you believe that?"

Helen looked at Thorold and realized he did understand. The pain was obvious. She suspected that he had been as ambitious in his own way as she had been. He had married and had children, but that didn't mean he had been the father or husband he wanted to be. For herself, she had wanted to be the most famous newscaster in the country. She wondered if he had been determined to be Supercop, and if as much as he loved his wife and children, he had given them less time than he now realized he should have.

"Tell me, Thorold, if you could see your kids right now, for just a second, what would you tell them?"

"That I love them," he said, his voice choking with emotion. "That I've always loved them and I always will.

"I'm incomplete without them, and empty. A part of me was torn away forever. I'd have given my life for them if that would have helped, and I will gladly give my life now to bring them back. They're the two good things I've done in my life and I cherish the time we had together. I would sacrifice anything if it meant they would be well, safe, and at peace."

"Sounds to me like you've pretty well figured out what's going on in this world," said Helen. She was smiling, but her words did not make sense to him.

"What do you mean?"

"I'm talking about God," she said.

Thorold remained silent. With anyone else he would have assumed they were trying to get from point A to point B by twisting around point Z. Helen was something else. A woman who had once made her living with sound bites would not waste time trying to explain something so important as his relationship with his daughters.

"Think about it, Thorold," Helen continued. "Just like Molly and Maggie were your creation with Wendy, we are all a part of God's creation. In fact, some people think it goes even deeper. They feel that God is so much a part of our lives that when a child is born, that birth is the result of man, woman, and God working together. That is why God loves us not only as His creation, but also because God shares in the creations of our bodies. And you know the story. He died for His creation just like you said you would die for yours. It shows that you and He both seem to agree on what is most important in life."

Thorold was not certain he wanted to stay with the conversation the way Helen was taking it. "Look, Helen, I don't..."

"No, you look, Thorold," she said, sternly. "You say you like to deal in logic. Then do it! Do you really think you're being logical about all your arguments concerning what's happening in the world today? Do you think you're being logical now?"

"So what are you saying? What's your point?"

"Think about Franco Macalusso. Do you think he knows what's taking place in his name? Do you think he knows what Len Parker and the others are doing?"

"Yes," said Thorold. "He doesn't know everything. If he did, you Haters wouldn't have survived so long on the run."

"Thorold, will you please stop calling us 'Haters.' I know we Christians have historically been a contrary people. We wear the cross, a symbol of the most barbaric way of killing the Romans had devised for the people they felt were the lowest of the low, and we celebrate it as a symbol of new life. It's like someone starting a religion in which a miniature electric chair or gas chamber is worn around the neck. It makes no sense unless you understand the story.

"Christians have been taught to love the outcasts and the sinners. We have been taught to go among the lowest and help restore their dignity, and to bring our Father's love to them. We believe that those who are in a position to lord it over others on earth may have already received their rewards if they do not recognize their obligations and unburden them of the trappings of a materialistic society. We have been taught that the person who dies with the most 'things' is not the winner of the 'game' of life.

"But we don't hate. Jesus was very clear about that in the story of the adulterous woman in the pit to be stoned. Jesus knew she had sinned. She knew she had sinned. But He also knew what was in the hearts and lives of the men who gathered for the punishment expected under the law. That's why He made them examine themselves first. He told them that any one among them who could honestly say he was without sin should cast the first stone. None of them could, of course.

"Oh, maybe we can hate hypocrisy. Maybe we hate those who would hurt others in the name of a false god. But the way that awful term 'Haters' is used, it's as though a group of people are engaged in all out war against the majority of good, reasoned people. We may think that the followers of the so-called messiah are horribly and tragically wrong. We may want them to see the light. We may want them to hear the Word instead of tolerating its destruction wherever it can be found. But we don't hate them. We're not trying to hurt them or kill them."

"Okay. I'm sorry, Helen. And you're right. He's trying to do to Christians what Hitler did with the Jews – depersonalize them, lump them all together and declare them to be evil, unclean, lowlifes who take from society but never give, who will act as cancerous leaches who must be plucked from the world and destroyed. Hitler was the embodiment of evil and so is Franco Macalusso. I'm just sorry I fell into using the same language we non-believers have been encouraged to use without thinking what it really means."

"Apology accepted. Now, about Franco Macalusso, think about what he's saying. He claims to be our creator, but at the heart of it, his message isn't about love at all. It's about power. It's about selfishness. It's about each person getting whatever they want and the rest of the people be damned.

"The only way people can act in the manner Macalusso is encouraging is to be willing to destroy anyone whose personal desires interfere with their own. It's the survival of the greediest, the most self-centered, and the most vile.

"Franco Macalusso's message is about having whatever you want regardless of the consequences to anyone else. Can you imagine if your daughters were with you and you had to teach them about life? Can you imagine yourself sitting down and telling your children that in the name of success, they should kill anyone who stands in the way of their dreams?"

"That would be a terrible message to pass on to them."

"Of course, yet when you think about it, isn't that exactly what Macalusso is telling the world?"

Thorold stared at her. What she was saying made more sense than anything he had heard since the Messiah came.

"It's the exact same lie the serpent used on Eve in the Garden of Eden," Helen continued. "Come on, Eve, eat the fruit. It won't hurt you. Look how good it looks. You know you want to. God's just afraid that if you eat it, you'll be just like Him.'"

Thorold thought a moment, remembering the story, remembering what happened. "I know that story. I guess every kid learns it. But as an adult, I see something else. I see this God of yours just sitting there, powerless."

"Oh, He's not just sitting there, Thorold. Far from it. The problem many of us have is that His love is so great, He can be with us and still let us stumble. It's like when your own children were babies, you were there with them all the time. You guided them. You nurtured them. You made the way a little smoother than they realized. But you still let them find their own way. You still let them stumble and fall. You still let them make bad choices in order to understand good choices. Your love was so great that you gave them the opportunity to grow on their own, hoping your guidance and the knowledge they gained from their small mistakes would keep them from creating major problems for themselves.

"Franco Macalusso's a parlor magician on a grand scale. He did a wonderful thing when he stopped the wars that were about to engulf the Earth and he deserves our thanks for that. But that's the same as thanking Amos for his message to us, or Jeremiah for his words, or John the Baptist for his. They are all fulfilling God's plan. They may have acted in courageous ways or dramatic ways, yet they all acted through the grace and with the power of the Lord.

"God doesn't need thought police willing to kill anyone who disagrees with Him. God doesn't need to dominate the media to tell us how wonderful He is, what joys He has in store, and how we should be so grateful that we are willing to destroy anyone who thinks differently. God doesn't make us believe out of fear. God doesn't write us off until we die unrepentant, and even then I'm not so sure. After all, Jesus went to the dead after He died on the cross, bringing with Him all those souls that wanted to accompany Him. Certainly even the worst of us can repent as death approaches, and if we are sincere in our hearts, we can join our Father in Heaven. Try that kind of reasoning with Macalusso and his followers.

"God doesn't want to win you with cheap tricks and flattery. He won't bribe you. He wants you to get to the very bottom of your heart and make one decision – Do you believe Him? And do you believe in Him? Do you believe He loves you? Do you believe that He died for you and for your sins?"

Helen reached out and took Thorold's hand. He continued looking across the water for a moment, then turned to her, noticing how soft, gentle, and loving was her gaze. She reminded him both of Wendy and of Mrs. Davis when he arrested her. He had been one of her tormentors, one of her persecutors, and yet there was no hint of animosity. It was not a look of which Len Parker or any of the other close followers of the Messiah were capable.

"It's time for you to decide what you believe, Thorold Stone," she said. She released his hand, rose to her feet, and quietly walked back towards the building. He stayed seated, again looking out at the moonlit water.

Sleep came as it always did for John, Helen, and the other people known as the Haters. It came in fits and starts. All the time spent indoors affected their natural biorhythms. Some slept during the day, some during the night, and some in snatches.

Thorold's body was still on a normal time schedule. The lateness of the hour, his emotional conversation with Helen, and the pain of memories with which he was still dealing all contributed to his complete exhaustion. He lay on the couch in the room where Willy had been working, looking at the photo of his family as he fell asleep.

Willy should have been as tired as Thorold, but the chance to take a few minutes to talk with his sister kept him awake. He and Helen were sitting at a table, drinking coffee and arguing in a way they had done shortly after their grandmother disappeared and Helen had read the material she had left behind.

It was hard for Willy, Helen knew. It was hard

for anyone who was physically different from others to relate to the idea of a loving God, a caring God, a nurturing God. It was so easy to become self-pitying, and to resent having to lead a good life filled with physical and psychological barriers that seemed almost overwhelming, while people who chose to act improperly, or to do harm to others, were seemingly rewarded with good health.

Willy had become a pragmatist, separating Franco Macalusso from all those who were his closest associates. He was convinced that Len Parker and the leadership staff of O.N.E. had become corrupted, and evil; the exact opposite of the man he believed to be the Messiah. He could not see that someone who truly was God would discern their hearts and not tolerate what was taking place. Still, Helen tried to reason with him. Willy was becoming increasingly frustrated by her efforts.

"I don't want to hear about it!" Willy stressed. "I don't know how I can say it any clearer. I know who Macalusso is. I understand your problem with believing because of those around him. But I know who he is and…"

Willy looked up as the door opened and a man in full O.N.E. top security uniform stepped inside. Willy knew the uniform well. "Storm troopers," he jokingly called them when he was still working for the organization. "Jack booted storm troopers," he had laughed. He had heard the rumors of what the men did and how they acted towards the Haters. But like everyone else, he believed that the stories of tortures and summary executions in the basement holding areas were wildly exaggerated. He was convinced that the cells were a stopping point before the people were taken to some large re-education camp, a few of which did exist for those weak enough to declare their allegiance to anyone who asked with strong enough threats if they did not convert.

Now that he was underground with his sister and her friends, and now that he understood the full danger they were all in, he thought differently. He realized that he had become a target of the O.N.E. forces. This man who had entered was there to arrest him. He was going to be joining the Haters and other victims of Len Parker in the notorious interrogation center.

"Thorold!" Willy shouted, bringing Thorold instantly awake.

Thorold sat up and oriented himself. He saw Helen and a terrified Willy sitting at the table. By the door was an O.N.E. officer. Thorold dropped, rolled, brought out his gun and aimed it at the policeman. He would kill as many of them as he had to in order to protect the others.

Ron Wolfman, the man in uniform, was startled by the reaction in the room. Instinctively he drew his own weapon, aiming towards Thorold. At the same moment, Helen threw herself between the two men shouting, "Stop! Both of you, stop."

Startled by Helen's actions, Ron and Thorold eased their fingers from their triggers and raised their weapons. Both were uncertain what was happening, neither ready to relax from a position that would still allow one to kill the other.

"It's okay. We're all on the same side here."

Thorold, confused, watched as Helen went over to Ronny and gave him a hug. He nervously looked at Thorold who slowly brought his weapon down and holstered it. Only then did Ronny put away his own gun.

"Thorold Stone, I want you to meet Ronny Wolfman. As you can see, Thorold, he has infiltrated Macalusso's forces, another reason not to give too many 'brownie points' to the powers of the so-called Messiah."

Thorold nodded, still uncertain of what was happening.

"So how'd you do, Ronny?"

"A lot better than Anna Davis," he said rather sadly.

"What do you mean?"

"I have access to the monitoring equipment used in the interrogation area. I managed to make a copy of the tape used in the internal security camera. It's part of a....

"Helen, it's worse than you think. Overlord Parker calls this a 'conversation.' The other guards call it 'interrogation.' What it is is torture. I doubt that St. Paul ever endured what some of these people have been put through. I'm only glad I wasn't there when the original tape was made. I don't know if I could have stood by and...anyway, I have a player. You'll hear Mrs. Davis for yourself.

Ron set down the machine, adjusted the volume control and pushed "Play." In a moment everyone could hear the voice of Len Parker. "We will defeat your God by destroying His people," he said. "After the Day of Wonders, you and every other Christian will be dead or converted. The battle will be over, the war lost. There will be no living Christian, no one to tell the story; no one to celebrate the foul name. It will be a new era, one in which we who have made our decision will rule with absolute authority.

"Why will your God have any reason to return if there are no people to welcome Him? His prophecy will fail. There will be no souls for Him to claim and we will have won.

"That's why I can't understand your resistance. You can save your life, Christian. Renounce Jesus Christ and live, I tell you. Renounce Christ. There is no reason for you to have to endure any more pain."

There was the sound of a violent slap, of a head striking the wall, of a gasp, a scream, another moan. Everyone in the room cringed at the sounds. Ron's face paled and he felt nauseated as he reached over and turned off the machine. "I'm sorry," he whispered. "I wasn't there. I couldn't stop it. I didn't hear it until after it was done. I didn't…."

Helen touched Ron's shoulder. "It's not your fault, Ronny. No one blames you for this evil. It's happening and we have to know everything we can if we're going to stop it."

"You couldn't have stopped it if you had been there," said Thorold, quietly. "I shot him. I shot Len Parker. I emptied my gun into him and nothing happened. He wasn't wearing a protective vest. He just… Nothing. And then he walked through a solid wall. The man has been given powers that.... Trust me. You couldn't have stopped him."

"I would have liked to try," said Ron. "All I know is that Mrs. Davis is still alive. I just don't know if she considers that fact a blessing any more."

"At least we know more about the Day of Wonders," said Helen.

"That it's about death?" asked Thorold, trying to grapple with the question that seemed so overwhelming for them all. "The Day of Wonders is about killing people? But how? With some fancy computer game?"

Thorold began pacing nervously. There was something more to all this, something they were missing. Even he had to admit that whatever these people were, they were incapable of killing every Christian. Helen would say God was not going to allow that to happen. Helen would argue that God would make certain His people triumphed. Helen would say....

"It just doesn't make any sense," he said, quietly. What about the ones he vaporized? Did he say anything about them? Is he planning to...."

"He didn't vaporize anyone, Thorold," said Helen. "They were raptured. God called them home."

Thorold looked at her angrily. He respected her beliefs but this was not the moment he wanted to hear them. Talk of Heaven was nonsense and he wished she'd just....

"Your family is in Heaven, Thorold. Your wife, your daughters. You don't want to hear that and I'm sorry to keep harping on the fact, but truth is truth.

You've got to…."

There was a loud beeping sound, some static, and then Len Parker's voice filled the room. "Hello, Special Agent Stone."

Frightened, Thorold instinctively drew his weapon, searching the room for the man he knew was his primary enemy.

"It's the police monitor, Thorold," said Willy, quietly. "I fixed it so we would hear any calls Parker made on his private frequency. I'm sure he knows we have one and that we monitor it. It can't be traced and he's not just outside this building."

Thorold's heart was racing as he holstered his gun and listened to Parker's voice saying, "Special Agent Thorold Stone. I know you're out there listening from somewhere. I just thought you might be interested in some special guests I have visiting me here in my office."

There was a slight change in the sound, one that Willy caught but the others did not notice. There was something happening that was not quite normal, though he could not tell just what. He also realized that the situation was too emotionally charged for him to say anything.

"Please don't hurt us anymore," said the woman's voice. "We don't know anything. I haven't seen him in months."

Willy looked at Thorold and realized it was Wendy's voice. He also knew that something was not quite right. He had heard Thorold's story about the day of the disappearance. He had witnessed others disappear in the same manner. Wherever they had gone, whatever had happened to them, none of them was going to be alive and talking from the office of Overlord Len Parker.

"Wendy...?" whispered Thorold.

There was the sound of a little girl in pain, her voice rising in a wail of agony. Thorold's fists clenched. His face was a mix of terror and hate. He was a man trained for physical violence. He wanted to smash Parker, to grab his wife and daughters and carry them to safety no matter who he hurt to free them.

"Mommy, why doesn't Daddy come and save us?" came the voice of one of his daughters.

Parker's voice was heard again, angry, menacing. "All of you shut up! Unless you want to spend some more time in the chamber."

The room was silent. Everyone stood near the monitor, listening intently.

"Stone," said Parker. "You have one choice and one choice only, so you had better listen to me very carefully. I want to see you here at the O.N.E. headquarters by two A.M., with the CD. Have you got that? Two A.M. If you're not here, on your hands and knees begging for their lives at one second past two...then they'll be the first ones to find out what the Day of Wonders is all about."

As Helen listened to the words, she silently gave a prayer of thanks to God. She knew in her heart that this was a trick, that whatever Parker was doing to recreate the voices for Stone, he did not have Wendy and his children. They had been raptured. They were safe, at peace, where no evil could touch them.

This so-called Messiah was being shown to be

275

an impotent evil, someone who needed a man like Parker to demand that Thorold show up and beg for their safety. He needed the CD. He was being threatened by an electronic device he desperately needed and could not locate. Perhaps he was more powerful than the golden calf Aaron had helped the people make when they feared for the loss of Moses while gathered at the foot of Mt. Sinai, but he was not someone who could stand before Jesus. Yet how could she say anything? How could she help Thorold, a man whose heart had been touched with a pain she could not even imagine?

▲

Len Parker stood in his office, delighted with the powers the Messiah had given him. He pushed the broadcast button of his radio microphone and made one last plea, his normally deep baritone the perfect imitation of Wendy's soprano voice. "Please, don't hurt my daughters. They didn't do anything. Please, you…." And then he released the button, ending the broadcast.

Smiling happily, Len returned to his desk, across from which one of the Special Agents for the O.N.E. had been sitting, marveling in the Overlord's performance.

"Like I said, a sporting match," gloated Parker. "And I think it would be fair to say, 'Advantage, me!'"

Still safe in their hiding place, Willy returned to working on the computers, trying to unravel the last pieces of the Day of Wonders CD. There was a desperation to his actions now, a determination to learn the truth, to help his new found friends.

Thorold had begun pacing like a caged animal, trying to think rationally, calmly, and to maintain control when all he wanted to do was explode. "I can't wait for Willy to crack this thing, Helen," he said. "I just can't. You heard what he said. He's got Wendy and the kids in there and they're going to be the first ones through....No, I've got no choice."

Thorold paused, then turned angrily towards Helen, looking her in the face and saying, "So much for your Heaven theory!"

"Please Thorold, you've got to listen to me. It's a trick."

"She's right," said Ronny. "I've been down there. If they had been there, they would have been murdered long ago."

"You said yourself that they disappeared in your presence, just like all the others," added Helen. "They couldn't be with Parker. It has to be a trick."

"I agree!" Thorold said, angrily. "About the trick I mean. I know he's just using them to get me to go there.

"I don't know how he took them in the first place. I don't know how many others he's got from the day they all disappeared. I do know that I don't have any choice. He's made very clear that I've got to stop the Day of Wonders before he kills my family."

"He's right, Helen," said Willy, looking up from his work. "He doesn't seem to have any choice. Besides, I think I may have a plan. The mainframe computer at the O.N.E. building is the main hub for the entire

O.N.E. computer system. Nothing can happen without it being involved, and that means that whatever is done to it, it will affect every other computer they use. If we could upload a virus to the main file server, it could theoretically infect every computer on the network."

"Meaning what?" asked Ronny.

"Meaning that if it works, when the world puts on the goggles tomorrow afternoon, they won't see any more in there than Cindy sees in her glasses."

Thorold was uncertain what to do. He realized that if he tried to break into the O.N.E. building by himself, he would be overpowered or killed before he got near Len Parker, much less his family. Willy's work might be the only way to take on Parker and save his family.

"But what about that line of code? You broke almost everything and all you saw was white. You said that the last line of code might be the key to whatever was going to happen. Have you been able to break it as yet?" asked Thorold.

"No, but I think I know how to do it. I've programmed the computer to work on it since it will go much faster than I ever could. However, I have to admit that I'm fairly certain that's not the answer."

Thorold was startled. "What do you mean? I thought you were counting on that to…."

"Remember when we were walking on the beach together in my house?"

"Yes."

"Remember that sea shell?"

"I'll never forget it," said Thorold. He looked

over at Helen and Ronny and said, "We were using Willy's virtual reality thing. It's a long story, but basically he wanted to show me how real these goggles can make things. He picked up a shell on the beach where we were walking, then cut my arm with it. It didn't hurt but it bled enough so that I thought I might have to have stitches. Yet when he had me take off my glasses, my arm was fine. Nothing had ever happened to it, even though it did. Or I thought it did. It was that real."

"Creating that single shell, making it look the way it did, making it able to be picked up in the virtual world, took almost four thousand lines of computer code. So whatever their plan is for the Day of Wonders, it's not on that disk, " Willy pointed out.

"So what you're saying is that at noon tomorrow, the whole world is going to put on those glasses and find themselves in the middle of who knows what?" asked Thorold.

"My family doesn't have that long, remember? Let's stop wasting time talking about 'if' and start talking about 'how,'" said Thorold. "The only 'Plan B' I can think of is to take as many weapons as I can find and go in there, taking out anyone who gets in my way. The trouble with that is that somebody's going to kill me before I can find my family. That's why I wish one of you could come up with a workable 'Plan A.'"

"I think I have one, Thorold," said Willy. "You'll have to go into the building, but the cleaning staff mostly works third shift. I can get into the security computer and have you authorized to be in the building at midnight. You'll be a janitor and they probably won't look at you twice when the computer says you're authorized."

The uniform Thorold Stone needed to blend in with the third shift workforce was fortunately quite simple. Helen Hannah, her hair deliberately disheveled and partially covered with a scarf, her face devoid of make-up, her shoulders slightly hunched, had driven to one of the inner-city variety stores and bought a pair of workman's coveralls, a work shirt, and a baseball cap in the size Thorold needed. There was no established uniform for the crew, the dress code allowing anything clean, neat, and functional. She also bought a pair of inexpensive magnifying reading glasses and a neck strap so he could have them hang against his chest, ready to be used as a quick disguise if necessary. She originally thought about knocking out the lenses and having him wear them that way, but if the light were wrong, the lack of a reflection would be noticed. This way he looked eccentric, something not expected of an O.N.E. agent on the run.

When Helen reached the outside of the building where she and the others had been hiding, she removed the clothing from their packaging, then beat the uniform against the wall and the ground. She wanted it just dirty enough so that it would not look totally new.

"Should I be carrying tools or something?" Thorold asked after he had finished changing into the new clothes.

"Just yourself," said Ron. "There are stations throughout the building where the supplies needed for cleaning and maintenance are kept. Some people move around the building. Others are assigned a set area with a specified number of rooms. It can vary with what went on earlier in the day or what is planned for the next day. But the stations allow the workers to have access to whatever they need, including special compounds for cleaning delicate equipment.

"Most of the security guards look down on the men and women who clean the place. They never really notice them or try to talk with them. They won't know if you're new or have been there for weeks if you act natural."

"Are you sure you're going to be able to find the VR lab once you're inside?" asked Helen.

"As long as these blueprints Willy pulled down are complete."

"They should be, Thorold. I got everything. I have the original plans from when the place was first built. And I have the plans for each modification that changed maintenance or tenants access. There are no hidden rooms or new areas. I checked each set of plans against all the previous ones to be certain. I've marked the pathways from the different entrances so you can see where to go from any place in the building. You'll also see how to get out in an emergency."

"Then I just have to worry about the alarm systems," said Thorold.

"There are two systems in use," said Willy. "The first is a monitoring alarm. There are hidden cameras throughout the building and monitors in the security station. They're on full time visual from midnight to six p.m. or so. Then they're put on audio alert for the rest of the hours. The guards are expected to check the monitors to see that authorized personnel are where they should be."

"That won't be a problem, Thorold," said Ronny. "There are so many people going in and out of offices during the day that no one pays much attention. And for the third shift, it's only the cleaning crew. No one else is in the building except authorized security personnel so they don't care. Security's tight on the first two shifts. Civilians are going in and out of the place all the time. The guards have to be alert to someone straying down a restricted hall or opening a door to a room that's off limits. That's when the monitors are checked. That's when alarms going off are checked. Third shift has only carefully cleared personnel, and because they're cleaning or performing maintenance, it's normal for them to be anywhere. The interior alarm checks are usually ignored."

"And the second system?"

"That's where you can be dead meat," said Willy. "There are certain sections of the building where there are alarms separate from the main security. These are bound to be tied in to critical areas of the VR lab. Fortunately they saved money by linking all this with the larger security system which has points for deactivation you can reach. I've marked these on the map and I've got instructions for you concerning each one."

"Then it should be a piece of cake," said Thorold.

"Not really," said Willy. "There's a limited time you can work on the controls before the system senses the person is unfamiliar with them and sets off a separate alarm. And even when it's deactivated, there's a risk.

There's a routine feedback to the monitor every few minutes. I don't know if there's some sort of meter or lights or what, but if someone's watching, they'll know it's not working. They should be lax on the third shift, but you never know. There won't be any time to waste getting in, and there won't be much time to work before you have to get out.

"I've reduced the plans to smaller sheets of paper, numbering them to make following them easier. I've also created a secure channel on this radio I want you to carry. It's traceable, but not with any of the equipment they're using. I've chosen a frequency no one's going to scan. Just make certain you keep the transceiver under your shirt and slip the earpiece off before you go in the building."

"Where's the microphone?"

"It's an induction unit. You can talk and hear through the same earpiece."

"Is this another of the inventions we have the Messiah to thank for?" asked Thorold, staring at the unit.

"Actually it's old technology that electonics stores used to sell for bicycle riders to use to keep in contact. It never went over very big because most people like holding something in their hands. That way they can sit in the driver's seat, talk on the telephone, and lose control of their cars at the same time. Of course, I'll admit I beefed it up a bit. This thing originally was used with low powered CB radios that you can overhear on a portable telephone.

"I'll keep the monitor on loud at all times. Anytime you need me, just talk."

Thorold stared at Willy, realizing the enormity of the risk. Then he thought of how Wendy and his children had sounded. He inhaled deeply, exhaled slowly, smiled and said, "Well, time's a wastin'."

Helen took Thorold's hand in both of hers and said, "Godspeed, Thorold."

"I'm not much for sentimentality, Thorold," said Willy. "But I will say this to you. If you come to a fork in the road…take it."

Thorold smiled as he walked out the door, looked around, then got into his car and drove off, hoping he would not attract attention as he approached the building. Helen waved, then turned to Willy and said, "Everything's a joke to you, isn't it?"

"I'd rather make jokes than spend all my time thinking about the fact that the world as we know it is going to end."

▲

Len Parker no longer worried about Thorold Stone. There were only a few more hours until the Day of Wonders was upon them. The CD was missing, but as near as he could tell, the security code had worked flawlessly. There had been setbacks. There had been the problems with the Haters. But no one had been able to accomplish anything that could create a major difficulty. If he found Thorold Stone he would kill him, slowly, painfully, until Stone was begging to have him end it all. And if he didn't…in a few hours it would not matter.

For now, it was time to prepare. The others had taken the chosen one from her holding cell. He had been told that the women were already performing the ritual cleansing. Soon it would be time to prepare the circle, to draw the sacred symbols, then to bind her within and drain her life essence for the ceremony. It would be a glorious night.

▲

"You okay, Willy?" asked Cindy, her hands on his shoulders as he sat by the computer equipment he had assembled so carefully. On one monitor was the graphic of the CD that proved he had penetrated the security system of all but the final line of coding. His work had been almost flawless, preventing the security system in the mainframe from recognizing the breach. Yet there was still that one line of code.

"I don't know what else I can do. There's just nothing in there, yet there has to be something in there.

"You know, Cindy, if everyone wasn't counting on me, I'd just switch to computer Solitaire and play cards until the end time."

Willy moved his fingers rapidly on the keyboard. The image on the screen twisted and turned, spinning left and right, but ultimately stopping where it always had. "It's just one line of code. One line. It can't say very much."

"Then why have they gone to all this trouble to keep you out?"

Willy leaned his head back against Cindy's shoulder. She was right and he knew it. The line was a key that would not only unlock the secrets, it might also change the rest of the program just enough to do whatever it was supposed to do. As much as he didn't want to admit it, that one line might mean everything when it came to understanding what was in store for the world. He looked down at his watch, then said, "I'd better call Thorold."

Willy gently removed Cindy's hands, backed up and rolled over to a broadcast unit set for the frequency on Thorold's radio. Before calling him, he reached over and turned on a computer, inserting a copy of the program he had used when preparing Thorold's documents. Then he accessed the security center's computer, using a split screen to run their system while crosschecking it against the security clearance he had created for Thorold.

Cindy found the chair and sat down, feeling for the goggles connected to the machine holding the CD. She held them for a moment, then removed her sunglasses and put the goggles on her head. All she saw was darkness, the same vision she had without them. Willy had seen white. She saw black. Either way, it was an abyss of nothingness.

"I'm about three minutes out," said Thorold's voice. The speaker magnified the sound and Willy could hear the sounds of traffic as Thorold drove into the city. "How are you doing there."

Willy ran his finger down the computer screen, checking all he had done. "No problem. I'm just crosschecking to make sure that whoever you are isn't going to be on duty tonight."

Willy found the name "David Nidd," then read the background and scheduling. The man was similar in age to Thorold but was definitely not working. He quickly switched to access Thorold's file, found the fingerprint used for cross match identification, and stored it in the memory. Then he returned to Nidd's file, erasing the fingerprint that would be checked against the janitor's when he reported for work. Finally Willy replaced Nidd's fingerprint with Thorold's. The finger scan would match perfectly.

"Okay, your name is David Nidd and you're working the night shift. The fingerprint scan will 'prove' who you are and there won't be any trouble. Just remember your name.

"And good luck, pal. I've altered the switch on the transceiver so you can turn off the send portion and not risk having it work while you're on the inside. Any radio broadcast waves going out in that building are going to be detected. I'll be able to transmit to you, so keep the receiver portion on and wear the earpiece when you're alone in the room. But don't transmit anything, even if you think there's an emergency."

"Anything else, Willy?"

"That's it, Thorold."

"Okay. I'm almost there. I'm going to stop the car long enough to turn off the transmitter and hide the receiver under my clothes. You sure about the fingerprint check?"

"Absolutely. It will register David Nidd, not Thorold Stone."

"I'm counting on you, buddy," said Stone,

stopping the car long enough to fix the equipment.

▲

"You are blessed to be part of this night," said one of the robed figures approaching the cell of Linda Evans, a dark haired brunette who had turned 28 years old at the end of January that year. She was a new Christian who had always maintained high moral standards despite her lack of religious faith prior to the rapture. She had never had sex, not even with her fiancé, also a new Christian, who had been killed shortly after his arrest weeks earlier, yet whom she was told was still alive. You don't have to be religious to have moral integrity, she had told him before they attended their first clandestine meeting of Haters to begin their study of the Word. And she loved him for respecting her beliefs before they both realized the spiritual basis for what they were doing. Now she could only pray that they would be reunited in Heaven.

The robes were like monk's clothing, though the hoods were larger, covering their heads and, with the intense overhead light, casting their faces in shadows. They spoke quietly, gently. Their coming to her was a joyous moment for them and they delighted in being in the presence of one so honored. They understood that she might not perceive what was to follow as they did and they tried to be gentle. When they had finished, when she had passed over to the other side, she would know the joy of existence in the world that had falsely been labeled damnation.

"You are cursed to be involved with this night,"

Linda said. She stood at the back of her cell, as though her leaning against the wall might somehow save her from the fate she was about to endure. "Jesus loves you, even now. Why not open your hearts to Him? It's never too late."

"Do you not realize the glory the Messiah has arranged for you? Why do you persist in blasphemy?"

"It is never blasphemy to praise the Lord, our God," Linda responded.

"And where is this Jesus when you need him? I don't see him breaking down the walls of the holding cells. I don't see him staying our hands with lightning bolts. He's nothing but dust, rotted flesh that became as one with the earth 2,000 years ago, if He lived at all. He was too weak to come down from the cross. And now...."

"You have no idea, do you? I don't want this time of suffering, but it is my turn to carry the cross for love of our Father."

One of the hooded figures looked at the other and said, "Overlord Parker was right. There is a fire in her damnable heart. She is truly the one for tonight."

"I am not going with you," said Linda.

"But you must," said one of the figures, a woman with a lilting voice that belied what she was about to do. "You have been chosen. We must bathe you and dress you and prepare you for the ceremony."

Linda's heart was racing, her skin cold, clammy. She felt lightheaded, wanting to run yet knowing there was nowhere to go. "I am not going with you, you living demons from Hell. In Jesus' name, get out."

"There is no need to make this harder than it is," said the other robed figure, a man with a deep, resonant voice. He sounded like a college professor she once thought was the finest teacher in her school. There was a friendliness to him that might have been comforting had it not been for the rope he carried in his hands.

"We only wish to prepare you. It is our honor."

"Dear Lord, if this is your will for me, give me the strength to endure it," Linda prayed silently. "Into your hands I commend my soul."

Suddenly the women took Linda's wrist, then moved swiftly in some sort of martial arts take down movement. Linda felt herself being pulled off balance, her ankle swept out from under her by the woman's foot, and she was on the ground, her arm behind her. The woman dropped to her knee and grabbed the other wrist while the man looped the rope about her, securely tying her hands behind her back.

"It would have been easier to drug her," said the man, fighting Linda's ultimately ineffectual struggles.

"The blood must be pure, untainted by chemicals," said the woman.

Linda was terrified. She did not know the meaning of what she had just heard, but she understood that she was not going to get away alive. As the woman took her arm and started to help her to her feet, Linda pushed against them, running for the cell door despite her wrists being tethered behind her back.

The man grabbed for her as she screamed in terror. She managed to scream one more time before he could pull her to him, his right arm around her waist, his left hand clamped so tightly over her mouth that her lips were pressed viciously into her teeth. She kicked at him as he lifted her off the ground.

"Get her ankles," said the man.

"She's kicking me, too," said the woman. "I wish we could just break her neck here and now and be done with it."

"Well, we can't," he said, holding Linda until the woman used a second rope to tightly tie her ankles together. "She must be cleansed before we take her blood, and the blood must be fresh for the ceremony."

As the woman took a large scarf from inside her robe, the man released Linda's mouth. She opened it wide to scream once again as the robed woman jammed the thick folds of the scarf between Linda's teeth. She wrapped it tight around her head, then looped it around once more, covering her gagged mouth and tying it all at the back of her head. As helpless as she was, Linda bucked against her captors, trying desperately to free herself.

The man released Linda, letting her drop painfully to the floor. Then he stooped down, took her under her arms, and placed her over his shoulder. He rose, carrying her and followed the woman down the hall to the preparation chamber.

▲

Thorold parked his car amidst other vehicles in the O.N.E. lot. Here and there other workers were entering the building. They were all dressed similarly, and though here and there friends greeted each other, walking inside together, for the most part the people entered alone. "Not a very social bunch," thought Thorold, realizing how lucky he was. He studied the material Willy had given him, locating the elevators, the supply storage closets, the staircases, and his objective. Then he pocketed the schematics of the alarm system and the notes Willy had given him. Taking a deep breath, then exhaling slowly, he whispered, "It's showtime."

Thorold matched his pace to the others. They all walked slowly, their shoulders slightly hunched, as though they hated the late night shift yet needed the extra pay such hours brought them. No one talked. There was no joking or sharing of gossip. Each seemed lost in his or her own little world, a fact that enabled him to blend with the others.

Trying not to show his nervousness, Thorold walked up to the security desk. The man on duty looked at him closely, something Thorold had not been prepared to experience. He wasn't sure whether to smile or look bored, as though he suffered this indignity every night.

Suddenly the guard reached into a drawer of the desk. Instinctively Thorold started to move towards his holster, then remembered that his holster and gun were hidden under the front seat of his car. Janitors never carried weapons, and though Ronny said there were no detectors at the entrance for night workers, he could not take a chance.

"Put your thumb on the machine," said the guard, holding out a fingerprint detector. "You know the drill."

Thorold didn't, hoping the way he touched the unit's sensor was the appropriate one. "Anybody ever borrow someone else's fingerprints to get inside?" he asked, hoping to distract him if he made a mistake. "Like adding lines to the bar codes on food packages in supermarkets."

"Not likely," said the guard. "But my wife tried something like that. She's a checker in a supermarket. Went in to work with a library book she had to return after her shift was over. They were slow so she scanned the library's bar code with the supermarket's scanner to see what would happen. Locked up the whole system. They had to reboot. Would've lost her job if the store manager hadn't admitted he was curious enough that he might have tried it under the same circumstances."

The guard paused, looked at the screen, then said, "Have a nice night, Mr. Nidd."

Thorold went to one of the storage closets nearest the elevator, opened it, and removed a spray cleaner and some rags. He put the spray bottle in one pocket of his coveralls and stuffed the rags in the other. Then he went to the elevators, pushing the button to go up.

The elevator dropped slowly, as Thorold watched it go from eight to seven to six, all the way down to the entrance level. The place was almost deserted, so Thorold was startled when the door opened and Len Parker, speaking on a cell phone, stepped out of the car.

Feigning boredom, Thorold took the spray cleaner from his pocket and sprayed the mirror just outside the elevator car. Ignoring Parker other than to step out of his way, he took one of the cleaning cloths and began polishing the glass.

Parker looked at him with complete disinterest,

then continued on his way. As he moved down the hall towards the lobby, Thorold heard him say, "I'll be back in an hour or so. And I don't want to be disturbed."

Before the elevator doors could close, Thorold stepped inside and pressed an upper floor button. Through the closing door he saw Parker glance back, then shake his head and continue on his way.

The floor on which Thorold got off was a low security area of the building. The workers were mostly clerks handling routine international communications. This meant that a handful were on the late shift, checking messages from half a world away. There would also be a security guard patrolling the halls, though at that hour, he would not be overly concerned about problems.

Thorold walked past two men who had just emerged from the restroom, neither paying him any attention. As Willy had told him to, he walked over to where a drinking fountain was located, then looked up at the ceiling. According to the plans, the false tiles concealed crawl spaces to allow for repairs and maintenance throughout the building. There were key areas for access, the framework for the removable ceiling tiles being reinforced to hold the weight of repair personnel.

Thorold leaned over to take a drink of water, listening to hear if anyone was around. There was nothing but silence.

Moving quickly, he stepped on the fountain, boosting himself up to where he could move aside one of the large tiles. Then he grabbed hold of the support frame and pulled himself up into the crawl space. He had to hold himself on the frame, being careful not to shift or break the tiles as he slipped the one he had shifted back into space.

As Thorold braced himself, trying to get balanced and comfortable before the next stage in the assault on the computer, he listened to the sound of someone moving rapidly down the hall. He glanced down, realizing that the tile had not been perfectly returned to the framework. Before he could make the last adjustment that would keep it from being noticeable, a man wearing the same security uniform as Ronny came into view. He looked all about, as though concerned something was wrong but not certain what it might be. Satisfied, he moved on down the hall. Thorold shifted the tile and plunged himself into darkness.

Thorold took a pen-sized flashlight from his pocket, and lit the passageway. He had to determine where he was in relation to his objective, and in which direction he needed to move.

▲

They had cut the clothes from Linda's body rather than go to the trouble of freeing her and renewing the struggle. She had been washed with scalding water, anointed with special oils, then strapped to a surgical table placed over a large pentagram drawn on the floor. As she bucked and struggled, trying desperately to scream, to free herself, the woman lowered the head of the table where a container had been placed under a drainage hole. Then, so swiftly that she did not at first feel the pain, the man used a razor sharp, jewel encrusted ceremonial dagger to slash Linda's carotid artery.

Willy Holmes looked at his watch. It was fifteen minutes after midnight. Thorold was either safely in the building, making his way to the computer center, dead, or in jail. Either way, there was no further support he could offer. Leaving the radio volume turned high, he shut down the computer he had been using to access the security system. He would not bother fixing the fingerprint identification changes he had made. Within a few hours it would not matter. Nothing would matter. Either they would stop the Day of Wonders or life as they had known it would be changed in ways where identification systems probably would not matter.

Suddenly there was a beeping sound. "Willy!" shouted Cindy. "Something's happening with the computer you've been using to try and decode that line in the CD."

Willy wheeled over to the monitor and saw that the screen showed a jackhammer on its side, the workman resting against a tree, the on-screen disk in pieces. "Yes!" he shouted. "We're in!"

"What's going on?" asked Cindy.

"That line of code. The last program I used to break it worked. It's cracked. We can finally see what all the fuss was about."

"No. You can see what the fuss is all about. I'll just hear about it."

Willy smiled sadly, touching Cindy's face. Then he hurried over to the VR equipment and grabbed the goggles. Excitedly he put them over his eyes.

"What is it? What do you see?"

"Nothing!" said Willy dejectedly. His shoulders sagging. As before there was nothing but an incredible whiteness. Everything was an overwhelmingly bright sameness. "It's what happened bef...Wait a minute..."

Just as he was about to remove his glasses, Willy spotted something in the distance. It glistened in the bright light, like sunlight reflecting from polished metal. He began walking in the direction of the object, his eyes widening with horror as he moved close enough to see what it was.

In front of him, perhaps ten feet high and made from surgical steel, was what he recognized as a guillotine, the infamous French device created for the swift beheading of enemies of the people. This was not some artifact, though. This was new, with all modern materials.

Fascinated, he walked slowly to the guillotine, studying it from all angles. Then he ran his hand down the side of the smooth blade, reaching under and touching the highly honed edge. To his surprise, he pulled back in pain, his finger bleeding.

"What the...?" he said, startled by the pain, an experience that once would have been impossible. He reached up and raised his goggles from his eyes, shocked to see that the blood was real. The virtual reality blade had truly cut his finger.

"Oh, God..." Willy whispered.

"What is it?" asked Cindy. "What happened?"

"Oh, my God, I can't believe it! This is impossible!"

"What? What is it, Willy? I can't see, remember?

What is happening? What's wrong?"

"My finger. Look at my finger."

"Willy, stop with the jokes."

"Cindy, I'm...Helen! Oh, jeez. Helen!"

Willy spun his chair, brushing past Cindy and rolling rapidly across the room. "Helen! Look at my finger, Helen."

"It's bleeding, Willy, but I don't think a paper cut is particularly earth shaking. I'll get you a Band-Aid if you think it won't stop bleeding with a little pressure."

"A paper cut, Willy? A paper cut? You mean I've fallen in love with a baby?" laughed Cindy, incredulous. She started to move in the direction of the sound, her face bemused by what she was hearing.

"No. You don't understand. I cut my finger in Virtual Reality. I cut it, I felt the pain, and I bled. This is impossible. Anything you do in VR you can't feel and it certainly can't carry over into your life without the goggles, the sensors, and the expensive equipment."

"Willy, relax," said Cindy. "You probably cut it on something on the table and it's just chance that it occurred when the goggles were on."

"Cindy's right," said Helen, walking back to Willy's work area. She studied the table, the keyboard, the various instruments, looking for signs of blood on something with a sharp edge.

There was silence for a moment, then Helen said, "Cindy. There's nothing here. Whatever happened, it didn't happen at this table."

Willy had wrapped a handkerchief around his finger and was holding it tight to try and stop the bleeding. The wound, though deep, was not serious. It was bloody, though, and it was obvious that whatever had caused it was in the virtual world.

"This can't happen in VR. This is impossible. I don't care what's in that line of code. This...."

▲

The altar was set in a clearing in the woods. It had been their gathering place before, but always in ritual preparation. Friday night at midnight the thirteen had assembled, drawing the sacred circle, the sacred signs. Celebrating the mass with the upside down cross, the words spoken backwards, a joyous "Hail, Natas!" punctuating the night air.

Now their faith was being rewarded. They were to commence the most sacred ritual of all, the ceremony demanded by the Holy One, the culmination of all they had worked for, all they had believed.

It was a time of exultation. They had prepared the sacrifice in the manner required. The doctor had attested to her purity before her cleansed body had been offered to his honor. The blood had been drained to fill the ornamental pitcher, the golden chalice cup unwrapped from its velvet shroud. Candles had been set in the appropriate pattern on the raised platform, then each lit in turn while chanting praise to Franco Macalusso.

Len Parker, his robe the most elaborate of the thirteen, kneeled in prayer before the altar. His garment was purple and scarlet with gold trim. Precious gems were sewn into the fabric in symbolic patterns dating back to the time of Sanhein and the pagan worship of the dead.

Rising, Parker pushed his hood from his head, then raised the ornamental pitcher, pouring the blood into the golden cup. Setting down the pitcher, he lifted the cup to his lips and drained it. Then, lowering it to his chest level, he held it out in front of him, turning smoothly in an arc of 180 degrees. As he did, pointing in turn to each of twelve hooded figures lined one on each side of a stone walkway; the others lit the torches they were holding. Then, when the fire of the torches illuminated the walkway, Parker intoned: "Speak to the world as you spoke to Eve."

"Let the Day of Wonders begin!" said the twelve in unison.

"When she plucked the apple from the tree," said Parker.

"Let the Day of Wonders begin," they chorused.

"Let each man see his heart's desire."

"Let the Day of Wonders begin."

"And believe our path will take him higher."

"Let the Day of Wonders begin."

"The real wonders are pride and greed."

"Let the Day of Wonders begin."

One of the hooded figures began striking a bell while another walked over to a large upside down cross that had been soaked in kerosene. As the sound of the tolling spread through the clearing, the second hooded figure used his torch to ignite the cross.

"And those shall be our apple tree," Parker continued.

"Let the Day of Wonders begin."

▲

George Hilliard opened one eye and looked at his anxious dog. The animal was whimpering, whining, and turning in circles.

"I just walked you at eleven," said George, groggily looking at the clock at the side of his bed. Without his glasses, he had no idea what the dial read. Still, he knew he had not slept very long. "It's only been a couple of hours. Go back to sleep like a good dog, Max."

The animal whined again, then barked sharply.

"You've been doing this to me every night, Max. I know you're an old man, now, but so am I. The least you could do is try to hold it through the night." Despite his frustration, George rose, putting on a shirt, pants, and shoes, and stumbled about until he found his glasses. Putting them on, he and the dog made their way to the front hall where he found the leash.

"A man needs a good night's sleep, Max."

The dog wagged his tail, still moving about, anxious to go out.

The two friends began walking down the street. Here and there a light was on in one of the homes, the sound of a television set or stereo system faintly floating on the night breeze. For the most part, though, the homes were dark, silent. No cars moved along the streets. No other pedestrians were out for a late night stroll.

"Are you finished yet, Max?" asked the man. In response, the dog tugged on his leash, anxious to go farther.

"You want a real walk?" asked George, incredulous. "Well, I guess if we've gone this far I might as well let you have your head. Maybe you'll get tired enough to sleep through the rest of the night. Big day soon, you know. That's what all the papers say. That's what the Messiah keeps talking about. If giving you some rest lets us both get some rest, I guess...."

Man and dog entered a park they regularly visited during the daylight hours when children were at play on the swings, slides, and jungle gym, old people sat talking with young mothers, and health enthusiasts jogged along the trails. Usually Max could find a squirrel or rabbit to chase. He was too old to move fast enough to do much other than scare one of the creatures, but this pleasure was not to be tonight. None of the creatures were out and about, not that George could see. "Even the rabbits have to sleep some time, Max," George said. "Now do you think we can go back home?"

The dog looked up at the man, his expression one that almost seemed to indicate he understood what was being said. Reluctantly he turned to leave, then stopped abruptly, a low growl coming from his throat.

"What is it, Max?" asked the man. "A cat lurking in the trees?"

As if in response, the dog began to whine, pulling the man in the direction of whatever he had sniffed on the wind. Uncertain what the animal had found. George relaxed the leash and followed Max to a clump of bushes. There, dumped amidst fallen tree limbs, piles of leaves, and other debris that only partially covered it, was the body of a young woman. She was sprawled as though carelessly tossed aside.

"Miss..." said George, frightened. "Miss..."

She was dead. He knew she was dead. Naked and dead. Yet what if he was wrong? What if his fears might be jeopardizing the only chance there would be to save her?

Reluctantly, George gently nudged the body with his foot. There was no response. He kneeled down, trying to see in the dim moonlight that worked its way through the thick, leafy covering of the tree limbs overhead. That was when he realized her wrists were tied behind her back, her feet were bound at the ankles, her mouth was gagged, and her throat had been slashed at the side.

Standing abruptly, George gasped for air. His stomach was queasy as he pulled on the leash, moving his dog back from the corpse. Then he turned, vomiting intensely. Over and over again his stomach heaved and retched until he felt lightheaded, barely able to breathe, a foul taste in his mouth, his shoes stained.

"Phone..." whispered George, pulling Max back towards home. "Got to find...phone...."

▲

It was just midnight according to the clock in the building where Helen Hannah and the other "Haters" had been hiding. Helen and Willy were talking intensely, unaware of the passage of time or of what was appearing on the computer screen that monitored the system Willy had managed to decode. Only Cindy was still by the machine, and she could not see the words appear.

"Welcome to the Day of Wonders. For God doth know that on that day your eyes shall be opened, and ye shall be as gods."

Cindy listened to the sounds from the other room as Willy said, "Do you realize what this could mean, Helen? Everything that happens in there is for real! When the world faces that guillotine tomorrow, they're really going to die in there."

"Unless Thorold can get that virus uploaded first."

Cindy felt the surface of Willy's worktable, found the goggles, and stroked them with her hand. Then, overwhelmed by curiosity to see what Willy had accomplished with his skills, she took off her sunglasses, put the goggles on her head, and adjusted them over her eyes.

There was darkness, just as before. Disappointed, Cindy reached up and then heard a voice stating, "Welcome to the Day of Wonders."

Suddenly there was a bright flash. In the VR world, which had seemingly engulfed Cindy, she realized she was seeing. What she could not know was that she now had two beautiful blue eyes where before there had only been an albino coloring.

"I can see...something," she whispered in amazement as she looked at the same all white world in which Willy had walked when he tried the glasses. There was the same enveloping whiteness, the same white mist. Yet even white was something she had not experienced since she went blind. This was more than she ever thought possible.

Cindy sensed the presence before she saw the figure coming to her. Franco Macalusso, wearing a flowing white robe bleached to a purity that was dazzling even in this white space, walked over to her, smiled, and said, "Hello, Cindy."

She wanted to say something like, "You're the most beautiful man I've ever seen," but she was certain the humor would escape the man whose voice she knew to be that of the Messiah. Instead, she just stared, open-mouthed and thrilled by the first person, the first anything, she could remember seeing.

"You're a little early, Cindy, but I'm glad you could be the first." Macalusso's voice was gentle, soothing, like a thick blanket in which to wrap yourself for warmth on a bitterly cold night.

"I...I...I know your voice. Y...You're the Messiah."

"Yes, I am, so don't look so frightened. There's nothing to be afraid of. On the contrary, you're about to be the first person to experience the power of the Day of Wonders."

"My...my eyes. I have...eyes. I can see. I can see!" Her voice rose excitedly as she realized what was happening. There was a smile on her face, a look of amazed delight.

"That's right, Cindy. You have beautiful blue eyes, perfect for that lovely face of yours. And now there's a whole world waiting for you, a world of blue skies and beautiful sunsets. This is a world beyond your wildest dreams, beyond the hopes I know you have carried in your heart of hearts.

"This is my gift to you, Cindy. You can see in here, but you will also see out there as well. Your eyes are not some trick of electronics. They are real. When you remove the goggles you will see with the clarity you are experiencing in here."

Cindy looked at the man, uncertain what to believe. She knew the headset was like what Willy had described as a game. She knew that for Willy, the headset had meant he could walk, even if only inside his mind. But she had been blind, truly blind. There was no way her mind could create the illusion of sight. She had no memory of what sight was like. All she had known was the dark she had experienced until she put on the goggles provided for the Day of Wonders. "My eyes," she whispered. "They're real? It's all I've ever wanted."

"And that's why it's so. On this special day, you and all of my people will achieve what is in your innermost being."

"But the last time I put on the goggles...I couldn't see then. I couldn't...."

"Midnight has passed," said Macalusso. "It's the Day of Wonders now. The time for illusions is over. Everything you see is real. I am real. And all you have to do is believe, Cindy. Believe in me. Trust in me. I am the one who brings you your most precious desire. Believe and all you have ever hoped for will be yours."

"I do believe, oh blessed one," she said, tears streaming down her face. For an instant she touched her cheek, wiping away the tear, then looked at the wetness glistening on her finger. She had never seen a tear before, never seen her fingers. "Oh, dear Messiah, I do believe.

Please, just tell me what to do and I will do it. You have given me a new life and I will do anything for you."

Macalusso's voice changed slightly. It was lower, harder edged, and almost angry. Yet Cindy ignored the tension, knowing whatever had caused the difference had nothing to do with her. "Renounce Jesus, Cindy. Tell Him that He has no place in your life now. Let Him know that you have tasted the fruit of knowledge and that you've seen the truth."

"I…I don't understand."

"What has Jesus ever done for you? You were blind and He let you stumble in the darkness like one eternally damned. You were blind and I gave you sight. Renounce Jesus, then agree to take my mark and pledge your eternal allegiance to me, the one, true god!"

Cindy looked at him for a moment, then smiled delightedly, holding out her hand, saying, "I do!"

Franco Macalusso smiled back, covering the back of her hand with his own. She felt a warmth pass between them. The back of her hand felt hot for a moment. Then he released her and she could see on her flesh a mark, the number 666.

▲

CHAPTER II

▲

The Mark And The Savior

▲

▲

▲

▲

Thorold Stone had begun to adjust to the crawl space in which he had been studying the maze of pipes, frame work, conduits, and the like that formed what seemed almost like the cardiovascular system of a modern building. He had eased one of the maps Willy had given him from his pocket, then checked it against the instructions. He found the location of the VR lab, circling it on the paper so he could see it at a glance. Then he found the location of the main alarm console, circling that as well.

Finally, keeping the flashlight between his teeth so his hands would be free to help him with his balance, he began moving along the framework. To his surprise, movement was remarkably easy. The inner workings had been designed to be a variation of a catwalk, cramped yet with enough room to move about and make whatever repairs might be required of such a building as the years passed.

Moving as quickly and quietly as he could, Thorold finally found the steel box marked Armstrong Security that Willy said would house the controls. The latch on it was a simple one, easy to open, because no one thought any unauthorized personnel would ever approach the casing.

Thorold carefully opened the box, staring at a variety of microchips and wires on an elaborate circuit board. "They're color coded, Thorold," Willy had told him. "The repair guys need as much guidance as you mortals. If you identify the colors and clip them in the proper order, everything will be fine."

Thorold had made careful notes of the procedures necessary, then read them back to Willy. "To disable the motion detectors, find the color coded wires, then locate the green wire and cut it first. Then take the red wire and cut it. Do not reverse the sequence. Any variation will set off the alarm."

Thorold took the flashlight from his mouth and carefully shined it on the wires. He identified the green one, a blue one, a black one, and a white one. There was no red one!

Frightened of failure after coming this far,

Thorold willed himself to be calm. He cut the green wire as he had been told. Then he looked at the others. He eliminated the white wire from consideration by guesswork, based on nothing, then looked at the blue and the black. Again acting on instinct, he decided that the black wire had to be the second one. Holding his breath, he lifted the wire cutters, made certain nothing else was in the path of the pincers, then cut the black wire.

▲

The cell phone rang in the hideout, the sound seeming to explode in the empty room. It was only when she jumped at the noise that Helen realized how tense they all were.

"Ronny?" asked Helen, answering the phone.

"If it's anyone else, Helen, we've got more problems than we know," he said on the other end of the call.

"Thank God you got my message. Ronny, Willy's cracked the code. We can get in to the Day of Wonders before anyone else. I think you better get back here right away. Can you do it?"

"No one's going to question my leaving. I'll be there in a few minutes."

Helen turned off the phone, then turned and looked at Willy. His hand was shaking as he sat trying to light a cigarette. Near him was an ashtray filled with partially smoked butts. He had been chain smoking for the last hour, something Helen could no longer tolerate. "Do you really need those, Willy?"

"Of course not. It's my proof of manhood, though. Anyone can quit smoking once they start. It takes a real man to stay the course and have to deal with lung cancer."

Helen shook her head sadly. They both realized their lives might not last much longer, yet Helen felt that was no reason to do something you knew was destructive to the health God had given you. Trying to argue with Willy was impossible, though. He turned anything he didn't want to face into a joke. Reluctantly she watched as he inhaled the smoke deeply, then changed the subject, saying, "It just doesn't make any sense, Helen."

"What doesn't make sense, Willy?"

"I put the CD on the reader and broke the code to make the thing work a few hours early. We've got nothing more than a machine with a device that stores images. That's what the CD is. But whatever we're dealing with here is not technology. It's something more."

Helen was startled by his words. "What's wrong?" asked Willy, seeing the odd look on his sister's face.

"Images? Is that what you said?"

"That's right. We're just dealing with a bunch of images electronically stored on...."

"That's it, Willy," Helen interrupted, excitedly. "Images."

"That's what? What are you trying to say?"

"The Bible, Willy. Look...." Helen began frantically searching amidst piles of paper, VCR cases, and other materials. Finally she found what she was seeking, taking the Bible and rapidly moving through the pages, seeking a section she had studied in the past without full comprehension.

"Don't tell me you're like our grandmother, now, reading the Bible, then taking passages out of context to explain everything in life," rebuked Willy.

"Shut up and listen, Willy. She didn't tell us false prophecy and lies. This book does have the answers, and you'll know it when you listen to this."

Starting to read, Helen said, "And he had power to give life unto the image of the beast, that the image of the beast should both speak, and cause that as many as would not worship the image of the beast should be killed. And he causeth all, both small and great, rich and poor, free and bond, to receive a mark in their right hand or in their foreheads and that no man might buy or sell save he that had the mark or the name of the beast or the number of his name."

As Helen read, Goss returned to the hideout after risking a short walk outside to get some air. He listened, then began speaking from memory as Helen paused. "Let him that hath understanding count the number of the beast. For it is the number of a man, and his number is six hundred three score and six."

Goss paused, then said, "What is it, Helen? Why were you quoting Revelation?"

"The images. Willy said that the CD was nothing but images, and that's when I realized what we were dealing with."

Willy was shocked by the reading, but still could

not bring himself to be caught up in ideas he had rejected all his life. "Oooooh, 'six hundred three score and six.' 666. You know, my home address is 668. That must mean I'm the neighbor of the Beast. I wonder if I should show more respect, maybe bake a cake to take as a peace offering. What kind would be appropriate, Helen? Devil's food?"

"Willy, would you please shut up! You really don't understand the seriousness of what we're facing here. This is not a joke."

"Aw, come on, Helen. Get a grip on yourself. This is real life, not a horror movie."

"I'm afraid it's about to become one."

"Later, Helen," said Willy, turning his chair and wheeling back into the room where Cindy had been using the equipment. "We don't have time for this right now."

▲

"What a terrible thing to happen on the Day of Wonders," said one of the police officers. He was standing in the woods, staring down at Linda's corpse. He and his partner had been the first to respond to the call. They had found the body, secured the area, and called in the homicide detectives.

"Probably another Hater murder," said his partner.

Portable floodlights had been set up in the area to illuminate the body and the surrounding terrain. The ground was soft enough so that it appeared at least two people had carried the corpse and dumped it. There was no sign of blood, no sign of a struggle, so the forensic experts assumed she had been killed elsewhere, then brought to the spot for dumping.

"Ritual killing, if you ask me," said one of the detectives. "Didn't know that was part of Christianity. More the kind of thing we used to see with Satan worshippers in the old days. Or maybe that's what we thought. Who knew what was really in these Christians' hearts before the Messiah came."

"Slap in the face to the Messiah, if you ask me," said the coroner's investigator as he carefully prepared the corpse for transport and autopsy. "One last Christian horror, like a two year old trying to spit in the eye of a giant to show his bravery."

"I'm just sorry everyone can't be happy for the blessings we're about to receive."

▲

Cindy was smiling as Willy entered. Her sunglasses were back in place, her right hand hidden from his view.

"You really are handsome, Willy," she said, quietly.

"That's what everyone without eyes tells me," said Willy, rolling over to the computer system.

"No, I'm serious," she said. "I knew you had a beautiful heart. I just didn't know you were so good looking."

"Please, Cindy, not now. There will be time to faun and flatter later. You've got to understand how incredible what I've just found is." He glanced down at his finger, the blood clotted but the skin bearing the slit from the cut he sustained on the guillotine blade. "I've got a cut from a guillotine blade."

Cindy looked quizzically at him. "A what?"

"A guillotine. It was the way the French chopped off heads during their revolution. But that doesn't matter. The point is that I touched the blade when I was wearing the goggles. I touched it in a virtual reality world and I'm bleeding here, now."

"So you cut yourself on something you're working with while using the goggles. You just assumed...."

"No, Cindy. This is the cut I got in VR. This is the same cut, the same problem, and it had nothing to do with anything that happened in the real world. They've invented a machine that will let you experience in the real world what you experience when the goggles are on. They've joined both worlds. They've...." Willy's voice rose in excitement.

"Look, I don't know how it works," Willy continued. "But unless we can stop it, then Parker's plan to kill all of the Christians may well become a reality. I don't know what gives with the Messiah, but that maniac of an Overlord now has the power of life and death over anyone who disagrees with him. I just hope Thorold can...."

"I have something to tell you, Willy."

Willy rolled over to the computer where he had tapped into the records for the O.N.E. building where Thorold was working to disable the security system. He brought one of the blueprints onto the screen and once again traced the paths of the interior crawl spaces, hoping his instructions had been accurate.

"Can it wait, Cindy? I just want to see if I can figure out where Thorold is. I don't want to radio him unless I'm sure there's no one else around him. Part of the building will still have a skeleton night crew communicating with parts of Europe and Asia."

"It's important," she said, interrupting.

"Okay. Just a second."

"It's really important," she whined. "Really, really important."

"What?" he asked, annoyed.

"Those white cowboy boots look silly on you. You can color coordinate the tops all you want, but if you're going to go to the shoot-out at the OK Corral, you're going to be stepping in…well, you know horses. No gunslinger in his right mind would wear white boots."

For a moment Willy didn't understand what Cindy meant or the importance of her statement. "Is that all you can talk about? The way I'm dressed?" he asked, annoyed. "I thought you said it was import…."

Willy wheeled around and stared at Cindy, his mouth opening in surprise. As he stared, she lifted off the dark glasses, revealing a pair of bright, healthy blue eyes.

"Cindy… How…?"

▲

They had planned for the assault. It was the only logical move a desperate man could make.

It was true that Thorold Stone might have come

into the building with guns blazing. He was upset over the loss of his family, a family they were certain he believed was still alive instead of being among the disappeared. He was also not the type of man to seek a spiritual reason for the loss. He would cling to whatever hope he could find, even the hope provided by the Overlord's telephone call.

Thorold was not stupid, though. He would come to them subtly. That was when they had assigned a team of Special Agents with training similar to Thorold's to look at plans of the building to see how he would get inside.

No one had seen Thorold enter the building. No one saw or heard him as he made his assault. What he did not know was that portable sensors had been hidden in the crawl space. They were able to track him from the moment he entered.

"Sir, everything is working perfectly according to plan. Stone is here and he's doing exactly what we expected him to do," said Agent Janet Lavina, one of those monitoring Thorold's progress. She had been told to report to the Overlord as soon as Thorold entered the overhead repair system.

"And is everything in place?" Parker asked, looking up from his desk and smiling.

"Yes, sir. Ready and waiting. The tracking system shows he's going to drop right into the VR lab."

"Excellent," he said.

Helen Hannah could not say that Willy's behavior was peculiar, not with all the eccentricities he had developed over the years as coping mechanisms to handle his disability. They had all been so tense, working under such pressure, the only relief seeming to be his growing closeness with Cindy. Perhaps he had closed the door to the room where he was working because he wanted to concentrate more. Perhaps he had closed it to be alone with Cindy. Whatever the case, Willy's dog, Elvis, was becoming restless without him and Helen was concerned about the passage of time. She walked to the door, the dog by her side, and turned the handle. To her surprise, it was locked.

"Willy! What's happening...." she called, just as the lock was turned and the door opened.

Willy, smiling, rolled into the room. As he entered, Elvis emitted a low growl, baring his teeth. Then he barked, harshly warning the man to stay back.

"What's the matter with you, Elvis?" asked Helen. "It's just Willy."

The dog remained tense as Helen gently stroked his head. She looked past her brother to see if something was wrong, something that had caught the dog's attention in ways she had missed. She could see nothing.

"I've been thinking, Sis," said Willy. "If Thorold can't get that virus uploaded, then we're going to need to warn everyone. And right now, you're the only one who knows where the other hideouts are."

Helen stared at her brother, confused. There was something different about him, a hardness he had not had before. And the issue of the hideouts.... If the Day of Wonders was allowed to pass, they would all have to deal with this time of trial in their own ways. To come together all at once would mean the death of them all. Willy knew that, so why was he…?

"A halo only has to fall a few inches to become a noose," Willy said.

"Thank you for the encouragement, Willy. I realize you don't agree with my thinking, but you're getting a little…I don't know. Is the stress getting to you?"

"I think you should tell me where the other hideouts are," said Willy. "In case something happens to you. I'll need to warn the other Christians."

"Willy, we've survived this long with the system we put in place. I love you with all my heart, but you're a part of this by default. God brought Thorold to your doorstep and then moved your heart to bring him to us. But you've never been comfortable with what we have done to be true to our beliefs. Even now you are convinced that the so-called Messiah knows nothing about the actions taken by Len Parker and the others. You think they're acting in his name without him being aware. If something happens to me, it happens. We've spent a lot of time living together in hiding, and we've all agreed how to handle any matters that might arise.

"I can't tell you where the other hideouts are, Willy. You know I can't."

"It's okay, Helen," said Willy. He looked down at his dog and patted his lap, trying to get Elvis to jump on him. Instead the dog backed away, pressing against Helen, growling as though to protect her from the man he had adored since he was a puppy. "I made a spiritual decision in there. After all your talk, I finally decided that I could not live my life on the edge. I had to commit."

"What? When? When did this happen?"

"Just now," said Willy. "I finally saw the truth."

Suddenly the conversation was interrupted by John Goss' angry voice. "Nice try, Willy," he said, angrily.

John entered the room, holding Cindy roughly. To Helen's amazement, Cindy was without her glasses, her blue eyes blazing brightly. She realized the woman was no longer blind, but what troubled her was the manner in which John was treating her.

"Show her your hand, Cindy," said John.

Cindy, smiling slyly, looked defiantly at Goss, then raised her hand and turned her wrist so that Helen could see the mark and the number 666 on her flesh. "She has been marked as Satan's own," said Goss, disgusted.

"Oh, God, no!" said Helen.

"Oh, God, yes!" said Willy, rising from his chair. "I told you Macalusso was for real. I told you he was filled with goodness. I told you that any problems you might have had with those around him had nothing to do with who he is."

Willy stepped forward, walking towards Helen. Elvis tensed, as though ready to spring, until she quickly grabbed his collar and held him back.

"The Messiah made us an offer we couldn't refuse."

Elvis began barking fiercely. Willy looked at Helen and said, "Tell that damned dog to shut up!" Then he walked back to the chair, brought out a gun, and pointed it toward Goss. "Let her go, choirboy!" he said coldly.

Goss released Cindy who ran over to Willy's side. He put his arm around her, leaning over to kiss her. For the first time Helen could see the mark and the number 666 also etched on Willy's hand.

Helen was in shock, tears streaming down her face. She could not think of what any of this might mean for her and the others in the hideout. All she could think about was what Willy had done to himself, not just now but for all eternity. He had willingly let himself bear the mark of the Beast. He had made a conscious choice, rebelling against a God he had never let himself come to know.

"No...No...." said Helen. "How could you, Willy? How could you? You've been involved with this project. You've seen the changes that were being done. You knew all that was taking place in advance. You could see exactly what was going to happen, how it had been corrupted from what you originally believed, and you fell for it anyway."

"I 'fell for it?' 'Fell for it?' You misguided fool!" Willy said, harshly. There was no gentleness left in his voice, no flippancy, no love for a sister with whom he once could disagree without hatred. It was as though, in gaining the one thing he had valued above all others, including his immortal soul, he had lost the very essence of what had made him unique. Even the dog that had loved him unconditionally now saw him as a stranger. "Thanks to Thorold and that CD, Cindy and I got a sneak preview of the power of the Day of Wonders. And in less than eight hours, when those goggles turn on, the whole world will finally know the truth. I just wish I could have seen it sooner."

"It's not the truth," said Helen. "It's a lie, Willy. It's the ultimate lie."

As Helen spoke, the initial shock wore off and she was left with overwhelming sadness, she regretted that she had not spent more time talking with both Cindy and Willy after she learned the truth about the Lord. Now it was too late to address the issue of why good people can have problems, of how the suffering we endure prepares us for the work that is yet to come. There was no joy in being unable to use your legs, yet because he was forced to be in the chair, Willy developed a brilliant mind with great electronic skills. He had compassion and a gentle heart so obvious that a blind Cindy "saw" it immediately. His own work in Virtual Reality, before it was corrupted by Macalusso, had the potential to be a blessing to those who otherwise might have to exist in physical isolation. She also remembered how, growing up, the doctors and nurses who treated Willy from time to time talked about how his spirit had been inspirational to them, giving them courage on the darkest days. Their grandmother had talked of God of her hopes of God working through his disability to reach others.

Cindy was younger, less experienced, but Helen knew that she, too, could have touched lives in ways that might not have happened had she not had to adjust to being blind in a sighted world.

To be the least among God's people was often

to be blessed with compassion, an understanding heart, and love for others that the high born and privileged had to learn, often at a great price. God did not hate Cindy, cursing her with blindness. He did not hate Willy, cursing him with useless legs. He was leading them on their special path, and now it was too late for them to see the truth.

John Goss watched his friend's suffering and knew that there was nothing to be done. "Save your breath, Helen," he said. "It's no use. His soul is gone. His conscience. Everything that was good in him. He's been made an empty vessel. He's not the Willy you knew anymore. Once they took the mark, there was no turning back. They'll never know what their lives could have been like. What they'll ultimately be, what the trade off will be for Cindy's seeing and Willy's walking....I shudder at the thought of what it will mean to spend eternity in their souls."

"That's right, Helen. You listen to old Johnny. You're preaching to the perverted," Willy mocked.

He and Cindy laughed at his joke. Helen found herself unable to stop the tears that streamed down her face.

Elvis began advancing on Willy, barking viciously. "Lie down!" shouted Willy, angrily.

Elvis ignored the command, moving as though undecided whether to try to herd Willy from the room or lunge for the gun in his hand. His fangs were bared.

"Lie down, I said!" said Willy, pointing the gun at the dog. He fired a single shot to the animal's head, killing him instantly.

Willy looked down at the corpse on the floor. Then, smiling, he quietly said, "Good dog."

Cindy laughed, enjoying the moment.

"Now, where were we? Oh, yes, you were about to tell me where the other haters' hideouts were," Willy said, turning his attention to Helen once again.

"No, Willy, I wasn't," said Helen. She was horrified by what she was witnessing, wanting to scream at the sight of the cold-blooded murder of what Willy had once considered a beloved friend. But she had to remain outwardly calm, to control her voice, and to carefully choose her words. "Not when I thought there was still hope for us all," she continued, "and certainly not now. I'd rather die."

"Are you sure?" he asked, raising the gun and pointing it at her chest. She looked at the weapon, at Willy, and said nothing.

"I should have done this a long time ago," he said.

"Do what you have to, Willy." She turned and started walking towards the door. Without hesitation, Willy aimed the weapon and started to pull the trigger as Cindy's eyes came alive with the joy of anticipating the death she would witness.

John Goss leaped at Willy, shouting, "Go, Helen." He grabbed Willy's arm, twisting the gun hand, pushing against him with his body, moving in front of the barrel. The bullet exploded outward, striking John as Helen ran out the door and down the stairs.

Willy pushed the heavily bleeding Goss away from him, then started running after Helen. Willy focused only on the door through which Helen had escaped, not on the glass that Thorold had knocked on the floor the night before. He slipped on the glass and lost his footing, hitting the ground hard. His gun hurtled from his hand out onto the stairwell where it clattered down the steps. Helen, startled by the sound, looked back, saw the gun, grabbed it, and then continued running.

"Helen!" came a sharp voice in the darkness. "Helen, what's going on?"

"Ronny? Thank God. Get back in the car. We don't have much time."

Willy struggled to his feet, kicking aside the glass. As he hurried down the steps, being careful to watch where he was moving, he heard a car's engine roar to life and the squealing of tires. Helen had gotten away from him...for the moment.

▲

Thorold shifted a ceiling tile, leaned over, and looked down into a windowless room. All was dark, too dark to see.

Thorold used his flashlight to check the floor directly below the tile he had removed. It was clear of obstacles so he held the light between his teeth, placed his radio receiver's ear piece inside his ear, then worked his body so he could lower himself to the floor.

Dropping carefully, he cursed as he scraped his arms against the ceiling frame for the tiles, landing otherwise without incident. Taking the light from his teeth, he carefully worked it around the room, looking for windows through which he could be seen. There were none.

The room was the electronics lab Willy had described to him. Some of the equipment was familiar. Most were advanced beyond anything Thorold had ever seen. What mattered, though was that there was nothing through which light could escape. He could turn on a light without it being seen from outside.

Willy had explained that the mainframe was the computer he needed. The problem was that Thorold had never used anything more sophisticated than a PC. With almost everything far in advance of his own equipment, it was hard to determine which was the unit that was his target for the virus disk Willy had provided.

Thorold began moving from computer to computer, studying the equipment, reading whatever identification it had, hoping something would give him a clue. Then, on a table isolated from the rest of the equipment, was a pair of virtual reality goggles exactly like the pair which had been delivered to Willy's home for the Day of Wonders. At least he was in the right area, he thought.

There was a crackling sound in his earpiece, then Willy's voice could be heard. The sound startled him, and for a moment he looked around the room before remembering that Willy planned to call him with any instructions he might need.

"Thorold...Thorold, I hope you can hear me. I wouldn't be doing this if it weren't absolutely necessary. Helen and I have learned more about the program. The virus won't work unless the program is running, and the way you can get it running is to put on the goggles.

"There should be a pair of goggles in the lab. Look around until you find them, then put them on. You'll have to stay in VR for a couple of minutes. After that, you can come out and upload the virus. Everything will work perfectly. And good luck, my friend."

Thorold walked over to the table, looking at the goggles. He picked them up, feeling all sides, looking for some sort of switch or other control. There wasn't any. Trusting Willy's judgement, he put them on. Suddenly he heard a voice saying, "Welcome to the Day of Wonders."

▲

The car stopped in a dark alley perhaps a mile from the O.N.E. Headquarters. "This is it," said Helen, stepping from the car. "Beat me up, Ronny."

"What…?"

"Beat me up, Ronny. You're about to arrest me. I'm not going to have my reputation sullied by going in without a struggle."

"Helen, are you nuts? I love you," said Ronny. "I can't do it."

"You have to, Ronny. You're a police officer in full O.N.E. uniform. You're trained to take me down if I struggle. So beat me up."

"Helen!"

"Okay, you coward," she laughed, mussing up her hair, tearing at her blouse, then laying on the ground and rolling around in the dirt. When she stood up, she took some dirt in her hands and smeared the front of his uniform.

"I'm bedraggled enough to look convincing," she said, checking herself in the side view mirror of Ronny's car. She turned her back to him, put her hands behind her, and said, "Handcuff me."

"Helen, if I put on handcuffs, you're going to be helpless. It's going to be a dangerous situation in there."

"If you don't put on the handcuffs, it's going to be more dangerous for both of us. How is it going to look to have me come in with my clothing ripped and smudged, my hair mussed, walking casually because you can now trust me to not try to escape? Put on the handcuffs, Ronny."

Reluctantly he did as Helen requested. Then he helped her back into the car and drove to the Headquarters. He unholstered his gun, holding it in his right hand, holding Helen's with his left. Then he entered the door that would take them to the holding area where Anna Davis had been tortured, her husband and daughter killed.

"Hey, Ron! Helen Hannah! Big time, baby. You got the one Parker's been missing for months. It's bonus time for you!" said the security guard at the entrance. "I'd give you a high five, but you've got your hands full. Nice going!"

Ron laughed. "This little thing? This is nothing. She practically arrested herself. I've got bigger fish to fry than this one."

The security guard shook his head and laughed. "Get lucky the first time out and you're so cocky, there's no living with you. Remind me never to go fishing with you. You're probably unbearable if something strikes your line first."

Ron laughed, leading Helen to the elevators.

▲

White. It was all white, just the way Willy had experienced it before the line of code was broken.

Gradually he adapted to the intensity of the light and gained more confidence. He began to move slowly, and then more swiftly as he gained a sure footing. Suddenly his food kicked against something. Reaching down, he felt a soft object. Picking it up, he realized it was a teddy bear, the battered brown bear that had been beloved by his daughters.

Thorold looked up, turned around, staring into the distance, and tried to see what he could find. He moved again, listening. Nothing.

Thorold changed direction, everything becoming clearer – sight, sound, and touch. He clutched the bear to his chest, walking rapidly as he thought he heard the faint sound of laughter. Then, up ahead, he saw a park swing set. Laughing and swinging happily were Wendy and the girls, Maggie and Molly.
"Wendy...Maggie...Molly..." Thorold shouted, running towards them, waving the teddy bear, tears running down his cheeks. "It's me. It's me, Daddy. I can't believe.... It's been so long, so long...."

The three looked over at the running figure, smiling, but neither stopping nor saying anything. Then, as he came closer, another figure appeared. It was Franco

Macalusso, the Messiah, dressed as he had been when Cindy encountered him.

"Hello, Thorold, my son. Welcome to the Day of Wonders. I've been waiting for you."

"Franco Macalusso…" Thorold stopped, staring. Then he looked over at his children. He realized that he was in a virtual world, yet it seemed much more than that. "How can this be? What is this place?"

"I guess you might say that it's a little bit like Heaven, Thorold. It's the Day of Wonders."

As Thorold stared in disbelief, Wendy and his daughters began their swinging more slowly. They looked at him, and the girls excitedly called out, "Daddy! We miss you, Daddy."

Wendy, her voice loving yet stern, said, "Don't abandon us again. You've got to open your mind this time. Listen to him. It's the only way."

Startled, Thorold started to argue with Wendy as he had in the past. He hadn't abandoned Wendy and the girls on the day they disappeared. They had all been together. One moment they were laughing and playing; the next moment they were gone. He had spent countless hours mourning their loss. He wasn't the one who had abandoned anyone.

And then Thorold remembered he was wearing goggles. He was in some sort of virtual world. He could not be certain of just what was happening.

"Look at their faces, son," said Macalusso. "Look at Wendy, at Maggie's and Molly. They're exactly as you remember them. That's because they are inside of you. Everything is inside of you. That's what I'm here to teach

332

you. That's what the Day of Wonders is all about."

Thorold was listening intensely. This was quite different from what Helen had been saying.

"The Day of Wonders is different for each person. For you it is about being reunited with your family. For others it is something different. Whatever their heart desires is what they can have. All you have to do is accept me and who I am. Once you do that, anything you can imagine can happen, anything you can believe can be yours. Not just in here. Not just with the goggles. Everywhere."

"What's the down side?" asked Thorold. "What if I don't? What if I don't accept you? What then? And what about the Christians? What happened to them? What happens to them now?"

Macalusso smiled like an indulgent grandparent lovingly talking with a petulant child. "Thorold, I'm here to offer you anything and everything you want. There's no limit. Do you understand? There is no limit to the fulfillment of your desires.

"You mentioned…. Haters. These Haters stand in the way of your dreams, Thorold. They stand in the way of the dreams of so many. They stand in the way of my plan for you and for the world."

Thorold looked over at his family again. They were no longer on the swings but standing together. Wendy smiled, holding Maggie's and Molly's hands. The little girls are happily anxious, as though waiting for a decision they know their father will make, a decision to go over and join them."

"You know, I was wrong about you," said

Thorold. "I'm embarrassed to say it now, but if you can believe it, I actually thought you were an alien."

Macalusso laughed. It was a gentle laugh, not derisive, as though sharing Thorold's amusement rather than mocking so foolish a belief. "I know. But now that you can see the truth, all you have to do is take my mark of allegiance. It's just like when you joined the police force, when you became a special agent for One Nation Earth. Only now, instead of thinking about a paycheck and retirement plan, you'll have everything you've ever dreamed about. You just have to extend your hand. You just have to give me your allegiance."

Thorold took one last look at Wendy and the children. He wanted to run to them, to hold them in his arms, to kiss their faces. But he remembered the seashell during his walk on the beach. He remembered all he had learned during his hours of talking with Helen. Whatever was happening, if they were real, his daughters would break free from their mother's hands and run to his side. Children, real children, had no restraints when they were excited. Maggie and Molly were not Maggie and Molly. Wendy was not Wendy. As much as he wanted to believe, as much as he wanted to run to them as he had started to do, Macalusso's presence changed everything. Instead of making Thorold grateful for reuniting him with his family, Macalusso's stepping between them convinced him that whatever was happening was a cruel deception. He wasn't certain how he knew. It was just some instinct, some....

"You can stand there and offer me anything you like," said Thorold. "But Helen was right. You don't

334

know the first thing about the love of a father for his child, or the love of God for His creation. I can not give allegiance to someone like you. I regret now that I was excited by the opportunity to work for the O.N.E. as I once thought it to be.

"Franco Macalusso, I choose to believe in a creator who would die for his creation, not one who would have them die for him. God gives life. God loves life. You love nothing but yourself."

"My son, you've got to...."

And then it became clear, the commitment Helen had said it was time to make, and the true identity of the stranger who would be a Messiah. "I'm not your son, Satan!" Thorold shouted. "You are a liar and the father of lies! I can't believe I didn't see it sooner. And whatever those...those things are over there....They aren't my family. I finally know the truth about where my family really is."

Macalusso's face hardened; his voice grew cold. "You say you've made your decision. Let's see if you're ready to pay the price because even your God can't save you now."

Thorold, smiling, said, "You know what? He already has."

As Thorold watched, Wendy and the children seemed to change. Their mouths opened and they screamed as though in great agony. Then their heads twisted into grotesque shapes. Their flesh seemed to melt away, and their bones became soft and malleable. Then their faces turned to hideous creatures, as ugly as hate, as ugly as greed, as ugly as lust, as ugly as gluttony.

Screeching, the three demons took to the air. A foul stench was left in their wake. They moved about Thorold, mocking him, before vanishing.

"You've made your decision, Thorold Stone. Now let's see if you are willing to pay the price."

Strong in his convictions, Thorold ignored Macalusso and reached up to take off the goggles.

▲

Overlord Parker could not contain himself any longer. He had to know what was happening with Thorold Stone. He knew the plan must have worked: it had to have worked. The Messiah would not be, nor could be stopped. Len Parker would have liked to destroy Agent Stone himself. That was not possible, but perhaps he could see the fate the Messiah had in store for Stone unless he was bearing the mark of the Beast.

Parker walked to the VR lab and unlocked the door. The lights were ablaze and Thorold was standing by the table, with the goggles on his head. His movements seemed odd.

There was no mark on either of Thorold's hands. That was obvious. And Thorold was struggling with something, his hands fighting to remove the goggles. But they were stopped just inches short of his goal, and his wrists trembled, as though he was using all his strength to fight something that had grabbed him. It was not what Parker had expected. He did not know what it meant.

There was nothing he could do, though. The Messiah was in charge. Whatever was to be done was taking place in the world only the goggles could let you experience. He would have to wait to learn the fate of Thorold Stone.

Quietly Parker shut and relocked the door. Then he returned to his office.

▲

There were two of them, uniformed O.N.E. guards, each bearing the mark of the beast and the bar code on his hand. Their faces seemed half human, half demon, as they moved, one on each side of Thorold, grabbing his wrists before he could take off his goggles.

Using his training, Thorold leaned into the guard on his right, then raised his left foot, and brought his knee towards his chest, then kicked out at the guard on his left. The blow was hard, landing just above the knee, yet the man did not flinch.

Reversing the action, Thorold leaned left and kicked right, again connecting solidly. Again the guard did not react.

The guard on the left moved behind Thorold, still holding his wrist. The guard put his hand on Thorold's shoulder, using Thorold's arm as a lever, pulling it back, and forcing Thorold forward to avoid having his shoulder dislocated from the pressure. At the same time, the other guard released his grip on Thorold's right wrist, stepped in front of him, and punched him twice, once in the stomach and once in the jaw.

The guard still holding Thorold released him, letting him drop to the ground. Thorold fought for air, as blood flowed from the corner of his mouth.

No longer able to physically resist, Thorold was hauled to his feet by the guards who began marching him through the mist until a new object came into view. It was the Guillotine on which Willy Holmes had cut his finger. The blade was up, ready to be dropped. Franco Macalusso stood by the lever, looking at Thorold with the same disgust as someone standing over the remains of a skunk freshly killed on a highway.

"So this is your game, is it?" asked Thorold. "Everything in here is for real. The whole world is going to come before you and be given the choice of worshipping you or dying. What a pathetically weak creature you are. You're all smoke and mirrors. You live on human weakness when God gives us strength. Worship you or die...."

"Oh, I don't have to make them worship me, Thorold. They'll want to worship me because I can offer them anything they want.

"Think about it. Whatever is in your heart of hearts. Do you covet your neighbor's wife? I will see that your lust is fulfilled beyond your wildest dreams. Do you want wealth that will let you buy anything or anyone you desire? I can deliver it. All your petty, self-centered desires that seem so important, I can give them to anyone who asks.

"Worship me? They'll praise my name from the moment they awaken in the morning. I'll be the last word they utter at night.

"It's like Eve in the Garden of Eden. They'll eat up what I offer in a second. And if they don't...You're right, Thorold Stone. If they don't, they'll die. Everything or nothing. Either way, I win."

Thorold was taken to the bench extending out from the guillotine. The two guards roughly pushed him on his back, positioning him so he was looking up at the Messiah, his neck exposed to the blade. They strapped his arms and legs so he could not move. To their surprise, he was calm, no longer struggling, accepting of his fate.

"I've seen who you really are because I've said 'no.' But what about the ones who say 'yes?' When do they find out whom they've said yes to?"

"They know," laughed Macalusso. "Do you think I seduce them through some hypnotic power. They know I'm the Anti-Christ. They make the choice. They're so blinded by their petty desires for instant pleasure, instant gratification, they happily renounce The One Who Came Before Me. I give them their hearts' desires and they give me their souls."

"And when do they learn what eternity is going to be like for them?"

"Tomorrow," said Macalusso. "They are the lost boys in Pinocchio. For twenty-four hours they will indulge in every self-centered fantasy they have ever had. They will think they are experiencing heaven on earth. There will be no restraints, no one telling them no. Whatever gives them pleasure, no matter how joyous or perverted, will be theirs. And then, twenty-four hours after taking my mark, they will know the truth.

"By then it will be too late, of course. Their souls will already be mine. And once you've taken my mark, there's no turning back.

"As for the rest of you, you'll all be dead. Either

way, a wonderful day, wouldn't you say?"

Thorold stared at Macalusso, then looked up at the blade. The lever was being pushed, and the heavy steel strained as it was about to be freed.

"Lord, I didn't honor you with my life," said Thorold. "But by your grace, may I do so in death."

Macalusso looked at Thorold with disdain. "Touching!" he said, releasing the switch and sending the blade hurtling towards Thorold's throat. The last thing he heard was an explosion before everything went black.

"Thorold! Thorold!"

It was Helen's voice.

"Thorold. Are you all right?"

Thorold opened his eyes to find himself back in the VR lab. Helen was kneeling beside him, holding the goggles she had just removed from his head. Standing nearby was Ron, with his gun in hand. When Thorold shifted his head, he realized that Ron had shot the computer to which his goggles had been attached. Wires in the unit were still sparking and sputtering.

"Helen! Thank God. It was real. It was real. Everything was really happening in there. You put on the goggles and it's like you've been drawn into a different dimension or something. Whatever happens with the goggles on is happening to you out here, only...."

"I know," she said, helping Thorold up to a sitting position, then rubbing her finger gently against his lip, and holding the finger so he could see the blood that was on it. She took a tissue and applied it to the cut. "I know. Ron and I got here in time to hear your decision, Thorold. It was the right one. I think you know that, too. I'm just so proud of you!"

"Where's Willy?" asked Thorold. "Now that we know what this is all about, we need him to...."

"He broke the code. He tried on the goggles. He and Cindy, both. They met Macalusso in there, too."

"My God, Helen. What happened? What was he offered?"

"His legs. Thorold, I never knew how intensely he felt about being in that wheelchair. I thought he had adjusted. I thought...."

"He chose his legs?" asked Thorold. "He chose his legs over his soul?"

"He wears the mark of the Beast, Thorold. And I keep thinking that...."

"Don't," Thorold said, harshly. He took Helen's arms and looked in her eyes. "Don't you dare feel responsible for the decision Willy made. You have no idea how seductive that world can be. You have no idea how appealing it is. All you have to do is pledge allegiance to the man who brought peace throughout the world and you can have anything you desire, any pleasure. What you don't know is that such pleasure is yours for only twenty-four hours. Then Satan—that's who he is, Helen, Macalusso's only a Messiah to the demons of Hell—does with you whatever he desires. You are his for eternity, and I suspect that those twenty-four hours of pleasure will no longer seem to be a gift.

"What about Cindy?"

"She chose her eyes."

"At least Willy's call makes sense to me now."

"What do you mean, Thorold? What call?" asked Ron.

"Willy radioed me…. It must have been after he made his decision. Anyway, he radioed me and told me to put those goggles on to activate the program before loading the virus. He knew what I'd find. He knew I'd give my soul to Macalusso or die."

"Is that what was happening, Thorold? Ron shot the machine right after hearing your prayer. Is that why you were lying on the floor?"

"There's this guillotine. I don't know if that's what's there for everyone, but it was what they were using on me. When I told Macalusso that I chose God, he had these…these creatures strap me down on the guillotine. Macalusso had just released the blade. A second slower and I would have been dead no matter what Ronny did to the computer."

"Either way you wouldn't have been able to upload the virus."

"We have to work fast," said Thorold. "With that uniform and your credentials, do you have full access to all parts of this building?"

"Everything but the executive floor and that's not a place where they keep this equipment."

"I'm not worried about the equipment. Everything that matters is in this lab. What I do know is that I arrested a bunch of very nice people who are locked up in here somewhere. They're going to be the first ones fed into this thing."

"There are only a few holding areas. I'll do my best to find them."

"I know you will, Ron," said Thorold. "I'm just sorry I let things go so long. Sometimes we have to cling to false hopes, I suppose. And I thought Cindy was the blind one....

"But enough self-pity. Get moving. We don't have much time, especially if they decide to have the Christians put on the goggles before the rest of the world gets to enjoy the Day of Wonders."

Ron went to the door, opening it slowly, checking to be certain no one was around, then hurrying out, closing it behind him. So long as he was wearing his uniform, he knew he was safe. He didn't want them to find Helen and Thorold moving about freely.

Thorold took a look at the equipment Ron had shot, then followed the wiring until he saw the machine to which everything seemed to be connected. It had to be the mainframe Willy had told him about.

Thorold took the disk from his pocket, then placed it in the drive mechanism. He found the keyboard and pressed "Enter."

For a few moments there was nothing except the whirring sound as the drive was activated. Then, on a nearby monitor screen he saw the words 'Uploading Wonder Buster."

Below the title of the program was a bar graph indicating the speed with which the program was being loaded. "1% loaded." "2% loaded." On and on it trudged, the time passing more quickly than desired.

"If we both wait to see this happen, we're going to be in trouble. I have to get out of here."

"How long is this going to take, Thorold? I want

to scream at it."

"Who knows? Willy didn't say and now we can't ask him. He was always talking about how involved programming can be, and this is a program to save the world."

"So what are we supposed to do?"

"Helen, you stay here. Keep a gun and guard this thing with your life. I'm not sure what I'm going to be able to do in the building, but I'll buy you as much time as I can."

Thorold grabbed a disk from the lab, placed it in his pocket, and hurried out the door as Helen returned to the screen. After what seemed to be an eternity of waiting the screen read "3% loaded."

Thorold moved rapidly down the hall, being careful to stop at every turn and exit, to carefully check if anyone was there. It was quiet, yet Thorold knew more was happening than he desired. Too much was coming to a head. The Christians had to be converted or murdered. The people of the world had to pledge their souls to Macalusso.

Suddenly Thorold heard voices coming from the stairwell. Agent Spencer and Willy Holmes were walking up the steps, apparently checking every floor. If they thought Thorold had found the VR lab....

Thorold still had his cell phone in his pocket, the one he had turned off so he would only be able to receive Willy's radio messages. Knowing he was risking his life, Thorold deliberately turned his back to the stairwell, facing away from the men as though he had not heard them. Then, pretending to be in contact with

Ron, he said, "I'm telling you, Ronny, I'm in here now. There's no VR lab on this floor. Willy's directions must have been all screwed up. I still have the disk. I've got to find the right floor, use the goggles, and then insert the disk. And I thought there'd be no problem...."

Agent Spencer relaxed as he listened to Thorold's words. He did not know that Overlord Parker had been to the lab, had seen Thorold wearing the goggles. He was convinced they were ahead of Stone. There was no reason to alert Parker to what was taking place because he had no way of knowing he was being misled.

"There isn't much more time, Ronny. If I don't find it and get this disk uploaded....'

"Perfect timing, Spencer said to Willy." As he started to draw his gun, Thorold pretended to hear the men for the first time. He turned, looking at them as they rapidly approached. He tried to make himself look surprised, then began running down the hall as though desperate not to be caught with the disk on him.

"Freeze, Stone!" shouted Spencer.

Thorold ignored him, doing whatever he could to slow the two men. There was a small alcove with a pop machine and trash can for recycling. Thorold grabbed the can, hurling it back towards the men. He took a fire extinguisher from the wall, pulled the pin, and "fired" the CO_2 gas, forcing them to stop and cover their faces. Then he threw it and kept on running.

"Give it up, Stone!" shouted Spencer. "Every exit is covered. There's no way out."

I don't want to get out, thought Stone. I just want to keep you away from Helen until the computer virus has been loaded.

Two shots were heard and Stone saw the bullets ricochet off the wall. With the running he was doing, Spencer was not steady enough to hit Thorold, though it would only take one lucky shot.

Thorold came to a second stairwell and ran inside. He flattened himself against the door, looking up and down. Knowing they would expect him to try to flee the building, Thorold moved swiftly up the stairs. He managed to get high enough to be invisible from the lower landing before Willy and Spencer entered the stairwell.

Willy and Spencer stopped, listening for footsteps, heavy breathing, anything that might give them a clue as to which way Thorold had gone. There was only silence.

"We'll have to go in different directions, Willy," said Agent Spencer. "I've got an extra gun. Take it and go up the steps. I'll go down to the lobby. One of us should be able to find him. There's no other way out."

Willy took the gun, checked to make certain it was fully loaded, and smiled. He happily began climbing the steps, hoping he would be the one to find Thorold Stone.

"Come on," whispered Helen. "Load faster. You're supposed to be state of the art. Show me what you can do." She was staring at the screen as it climbed slowly from 22% loaded to 23% loaded. "Why did you have to make it so complex, Willy?" she thought to herself.

Agent Spencer reached the bottom of the stairwell, then stood, listening, gun at the ready. There was no one.

He stepped quietly into the hall, looking in each direction, listening. If he went left, it would be towards the security guard. Now that he knew they were after him, Thorold was unlikely to go in that direction. Instead, he probably would seek to find a way to double back upstairs in search of the VR lab.

Spencer moved back towards the elevators, checking to see if any were in use. Satisfied that they weren't, he radioed to maintenance to shut them down during the search. Then he headed for the back stairs.

There was a rustling sound off to the left, and subdued voices. Spencer turned swiftly, gripping his gun in both hands, bending his knees slightly, taking the approved combat stance in which he had been trained. Then he saw them, Mrs. Davis and a small line of Haters being force-marched by one of the officers. No one was resisting. No one was out of line. The guard was firmly in control.

Another group of re-educated former Haters with all that Jesus nonsense knocked out of them, thought Spencer. They must be going somewhere for the Day of Wonders. If you ask me, I'd have killed them all and been done with it. The Messiah's a man of compassion, I guess.

"Keep walking," said the officer, guarding the prisoners. Then, turning to Agent Spencer, Ronny asked, "Any trouble, sir?"

"Nothing we can't handle. You take care of the prisoners."

Willy Holmes walked down the center of the hall, holding the gun in front of him. He was back in the OK Corral only this time it was real. This time when he shot, there would be real blood, and real death. He was thrilled. He could not wait to tell Cindy.

There was only one doorway in the hall. If Thorold had gone in that direction, it was the only place he could be hiding.

Willy moved slowly, carefully, trying to remember the mandatory training he had largely ignored because, when he was in his wheelchair, it did not apply to him. Keep your back to the wall. Show as low a profile as possible. Lead with your weapon....

Taking a deep breath, then letting himself relax, Willy pushed open the door, leaped inside the room, and swung his weapon from left to right. He was in the employee cafeteria, a room filled with tables, chairs, the food line, and the preparation area.

Willy began with the largest room, dropping low to see if Thorold was hiding under the tables. Then he moved to the serving line, trying to keep the steam table and register area between himself and Thorold if Thorold was hiding there. He would need protective cover if Thorold started shooting. Again, there was no one, nothing but silence.

Easing his way into the kitchen, Willy aimed his gun above the cabinets and counters, then swept slowly through the room. Storage areas were opened;

Willy was ready to shoot the moment that Thorold appeared. Still, there was nothing.

Confused, Willy took the radio and called Spencer. "Nothing up here. I could have sworn he was around here. He must have gone down. I guess you'll have the pleasure of killing him." He paused, then added, "I'm going to go to the VR lab to make sure he doesn't find it."

Inside the walk-in cooler, Thorold had hidden himself behind stacks of crates filled with pint containers of milk and fruit juice. The door was slightly ajar, enough so he could hear Willy on the radio.

It was obvious that the chase was over. Thorold had to confront Willy, whatever that might mean. If he reached the VR lab he would kill Helen and take the virus disk.

Thorold waited until Willy was off the radio. Then he eased himself between the stacks and threw himself against the door, opening it so fast that Willy turned and fired a shot into the wall. "A guy could freeze to death in there," said Thorold.

"Give me the disk, Thorold," said Willy.

"But Willy, don't you see that you're making a terrible mistake?"

"Give me the disk, Thorold."

How long would it take for the virus to be loaded? How long had it been? How long could he stall?

"Please, Willy, if you'll just listen to me. I've got new information, Willy. It should fascinate a guy like you with your interest in electronics and all. It's incredible. Really incredible. You're not going to believe what I've…"

Willy carefully aimed his gun at Thorold, then angrily said, "The disk!"

Thorold shrugged, then started to reach inside his pocket.

"Freeze! Hands up! You're not going to pull a gun on me. I'll kill you first."

Thorold held up his hands, trying to keep his voice calm, and steady, as he said, "The disk is in my pocket. I don't have a gun on me, Willy. If I did, I'd have tried to shoot you when I came out of the cooler."

Willy stepped forward, pressing the gun to Thorold's head. Then he slipped his hand in Thorold's pocket, removing the disk."

"So all your little believer friends are going to die, Thorold. All because you couldn't read a friggin map. Too bad you guys have more brawn than brain. Too bad you never…."

Willy stopped, his eyes widening. He realized the disk he was holding was not the one with the virus that he had given to Thorold.

"Where's Helen?"

"Haven't seen her, Willy. You remember how I left the hideout. Last time I saw her, she was with you and you were still in the chair."

Willy glared at Thorold as he pressed the send button on his radio.

Helen felt desperate as she sat on a chair, alternately watching the door to the lab and the computer screen. The virus was up to 92%, yet it had taken so long, she feared that someone would break in before it could finish loading.

On the first floor, Agent Spencer switched to the tactical frequency, alerting the security team to converge on the VR lab. Willy did not know if Helen was there with the virus disk, but if she was, they had to stop her at once.

Len Parker heard the call from Spencer and calmly walked to the lab. He opened the door and saw her sitting nervously. "Helen Hannah. The most hated woman on the planet."

The sight of Len Parker frightened Helen. She stood, making certain her body blocked the monitor. The virus had moved to 93% completion. She wished she had dimmed the screen instead of leaving it bright so she could check the progress. Maybe with a dimmed screen there would have been no problem. For the moment she knew only that she had to be certain Parker did not see what she had been doing.

"Somehow I don't think I'm the most hated woman on the planet," she responded. "My ratings at the network were never that good." Her heart was pounding as she fought to remain calm.

"I guess it's safe to say you're not here to worship the Messiah," said Parker.

"I'd rather die," said Helen, coldly.

"What a wonderful coincidence. That's exactly what I had in mind for you this fine morning. In fact, I've been looking forward to this opportunity." He drew his gun, smiling happily. He would have liked to torture Helen, but such pleasures would have to be foregone in the interest of time. It was the Day of Wonders, and in a few hours nothing would matter except what the Messiah had in mind for everyone.

"Sir! Not in here!" said Ronny.

Startled, Parker turned. When he saw the uniformed officer, he relaxed.

"You're right. This is the wrong place to kill her. Take her downstairs. Let her blood mingle with all the others."

Ronny walked over to Helen, noticing the monitor. Being careful to position himself and Helen in a way that would block it, he began searching her, running his hands down her body, feeling the fabric in case a weapon was hidden there. Then he slowly removed his handcuffs from his uniform belt and locked her hands behind her.

"What are you waiting for?" asked Parker, annoyed by the man's thoroughness. Who cared if she was hiding a weapon? He could not be hurt. This was the Day of Wonders, and already he had been triumphant over his enemies. As the Messiah promised, life would only get better for the faithful. Even if Helen had a weapon, it would be meaningless. "Take her downstairs."

Ronny did not move. He knew they needed to stall for time, though he had no idea how to do it.

"Is there a problem?" Parker asked, his voice becoming angry.

Before Ronny could speak, Agent Spencer rushed into the lab, gun drawn. Upon seeing the uniformed officer with Helen, he relaxed, lowered his gun, and smiled at Helen.

"Well, Helen Hannah. It looks like a perfect sweep tonight. Your knight in shining coveralls can't ride to your rescue and save the day. He was too stupid to find the right room. And now we have you, too...."

"Okay, gentlemen. This isn't the time to gloat. This is the Day of Wonders and we all have work to do," said Parker. "Get her downstairs in the execution chamber. It's about time that we...."

There were angry voices in the hall interrupting the Overlord. He turned and watched as Willy opened the door, holding the arm of a handcuffed Thorold Stone. With him were Agent Mel Walker and Cindy, both seeming to delight in the adventure they were experiencing. Cindy, especially, was joyous. She felt powerful with her new sight, her new friends. She was anxious to hurt those who had only delayed her experience, and the Christians certainly had done nothing for her. Of that she was certain.

"Him!" shouted Willy, wide eyed when he recognized Ronny. "He's one of them!"

Willy, overcome with anger, charged at Ronny who moved forward to meet the attack. Willy's upper body was unusually powerful from the years of having to propel himself in the wheelchair, but Ronny was better trained, better used to keeping his balance when fighting. Willy wanted to tear Ronny's throat out, to slash at his eyes with his fingers. Ronny just wanted to keep from being hurt while at the same time delaying anyone seeing the computer virus being worked in the machine.

Parker, fed up with all the delays, drew his gun

and aimed it at Helen. He would kill her on the spot rather than wait for her to be removed.

As Parker started to pull the trigger, Thorold dropped low, like an athlete about to do a broad jump. His hands were tightly cuffed behind him, but that did not matter. He aimed himself at Parker and leaped against the Overlord's body, knocking the gun hand just enough to send the bullet flying past Helen's ear, striking one of the lab's computer monitors. Off balance, Parker fell to the ground as Spencer grabbed Thorold around the arms. Thorold stomped on Spencer's feet, trying to free himself, but Spencer managed to wrestle him to the ground.

Parker rose to his feet, roughly grabbed Helen around her neck, and placed his gun barrel against her temple. "Give it up, turncoat!" he shouted at Ronny. "Give it up or I'll blow her head off right now!"

Ron glanced over as he fought, saw what was happening, and knew he had to stop. Perhaps they would be killed anyway, but he had to protect Helen, had to vie for time. He stepped back away from Willy who took advantage of the situation by punching Ron once more in the face. The blow threw Ron's head back. He wanted to retaliate but knew he dared do nothing. He just raised his hands, ignoring the gashed lip Willy's punch had caused.

"Now what is going on, Holmes?" asked Parker.

"They're trying to stop the Day of Wonders."

Breathing hard, Willy hurried to the computer. Agent Walker grabbed Ronny and roughly forced him into a far corner of the room where Helen and Thorold were standing. They were all disheveled, Thorold was depressed by his failure, and Helen quietly prayed as she observed what was taking place.

Willy checked the monitor. The virus was only at 95%. Unless it went to 100%, it would fail.

Knowing how slowly the program loaded, Willy, relieved, glanced at the equipment to make certain nothing had been changed since he last worked there. Then, certain he had the right keyboard, he quickly typed the code necessary to abort the virus. On the screen, the words "96% loaded" appeared.

"Has anyone changed this thing for security purposes?" he asked, frantically typing a different code.

"It's just as it was when you last worked on it," said Parker. "What's wrong."

Willy said nothing, typing frantically. The screen read "96% loaded"

Frantic, Willy removed the disk from the drive and broke it. Then he grabbed the connecting cord and ripped it out before retyping the string of commands that had to abort the system. "97% loaded."

Willy could not believe what he was seeing. With the disk removed and the code he typed in, there was no way that the virus could still be working. Horrified, he took his gun and shot the Central Processing Unit, the heart of the computer. Sparks flew and a flame erupted, then died. The unit was worthless.

"98% complete" read the screen.

"No!" shouted Willy. "This is impossible. This is impossible."

Len Parker stared in amazement, sweat forming on his forehead. All the preparation, all the work, and the Day of Wonders was being destroyed by....

"Impossible!" said Willy, tearing the monitor from the unit.

"With God, all things are possible," said Helen.

Ignoring her, Willy began ripping out all the wires attaching the CPU to the main computer. He threw the equipment across the room, then picked up the monitor. It was obviously disconnected from everything, wires dangling from the back. Yet as he looked in horror, the screen changed to "99% complete."

"No! No! This can't be. I designed the program myself. I know how it works."

"Ever hear of God's unlikely vessel, Willy?" asked Helen, quietly.

Willy stared as the screen read, "100% complete. Fully activated." In shock Willy whispered, "The virus was successful. The Day of Wonders program has been destroyed."

Helen, Thorold, and Ronny were jubilant. It no longer mattered to them what happened. Live or die, they had given the world one more chance to return to God.

Parker, irate, turned to the three Christians and said, "You may have stopped the Day of Wonders, Christians, but you can't stop prophecy. I won't let you interfere. I won't let you!" He raised his gun to execute them as they stood.

As if they were on a wind swept desert instead of inside a sealed electronics lab, a funnel cloud rose between the Christians and Parker. It reminded Thorold of dust devils he had seen in the Southwest when he and

Wendy had visited Tucson. Only this time the cloud seemed more intense, thicker. As he stared in amazement, he heard Helen whisper something about a voice out of the whirlwind.

Ignoring the funnel cloud, Parker fired his gun through it. But the bullet did not penetrate. It was caught as if in a revolving door, spinning around and coming back out in Willy's direction. Before Willy could cry out, he dropped to the ground. The bullet had gone through his heart.

Parker, enraged, tried to move to the side of the whirlwind. Instead, it became larger, stronger, seemingly thicker. It engulfed him, capturing Spencer and Walker in its vortex as Cindy pressed herself against the far wall, desperate to find safety. She stared at the whirlwind, raising her hands as though she could ward off its power. It was then that she saw the mark; then that she realized it was all she could see. All else had turned as black as when she was blind, the mark being the last thing she saw as she screamed. Then she was sucked into the swirling inferno that had trapped the others.

In shock, Helen, Ronny and Thorold ran to the door, slamming it behind them as they hurried down the hall.

"No! No! Get back here, Christians. Get back heeeeerrrrreeeee." Parker's voice rose in a cry of anguished pain as the three shut the door behind them, then continued down the hall, getting themselves as far from the VR lab as they could. When they reached the end, Ronny removed Thorold's handcuff key from the case Thorold carried on his belt. Then he used the key to free Thorold and the others.

The sounds in the lab grew louder and they could see someone trying to open the door. Realizing that whatever was happening inside the lab had to be contained there, they hurried back and braced themselves against the door. But their action was unnecessary. The door had become too strong for anyone to escape. They stepped back as they heard the winds inside grow to what sounded like hurricane force. The sound grew louder and louder, like a howling banshee. It was all they could do to keep the door from bursting out.

Suddenly an air vent flew from inside the room, through the archway of the door, smashing against the outside wall. Inside the room there were crashing sounds and cries of pain. The sound of the whirlwind was almost deafening, yet it could not drown out the anguished moans of those unfortunate enough to be living. Then, almost as quickly as it all began, there was silence. The pressure against the door had ended.

Thorold looked at Helen and Ronny. They knew what they had experienced, knew what they had heard. The question was what to do next.

Helen and Ronny stepped back away from the door as Thorold reached for the handle. He opened it slowly, the three of them moving inside as one.

"The room is empty," said Ronny.

"There's nothing here," said Helen, in shock. "No computers. No furniture. No people."

"It's as though it has never been used for anything," said Ronny.

"Not quite everything is gone," said Thorold,

spotting what he at first thought was a small scrap of paper in the corner where the mainframe had been. He walked over to pick it up and realized it was the photograph of Wendy, Maggie, and Molly he had been carrying with him. On one side were their happy faces. On the other were the words: "The truth has set us free."

▲

The One Nation Earth prison transport van, fully loaded with Haters, was parked in a darkened lot at the back of the headquarters building. Although Mrs. Davis and the others were not restrained in any way, there were no guards in the van. Instead, one of the former prisoners sat in the driver's seat. The motor was running.

Helen, Ronny, and Thorold ran out of the building and jumped into the van. "Move it!" shouted Ronny as the door closed and the driver accelerated onto the street.

Thorold, breathless yet exhilarated, walked back to Anna Davis and asked, "Remember me?"

"I'm glad the Lord has opened your eyes, son."

"I'm so sorry for all that you've been through, for your terrible losses. I didn't know. I thought you were...well, I thought that we all were doing...."

Holding on to the seat backs to keep her balance in the moving van, Anna Davis stood and walked over to Thorold, throwing her free arm around him, giving him a hug. "It's okay. You're forgiven. We all are." She stepped back, looking him in the eye, taking his hand and holding it tenderly.

"All our losses become tolerable if the end result is another soul saved. That's worth more than the whole world."

Smiling, Mrs. Davis looked past Thorold as though seeing something the others could not. The joy on her face and her uplifted spirit were contagious to all the others. As though led by some divine conductor, Mrs. Davis began singing, "Amazing Grace. How sweet the sound." The others joined in.

And as the van moved into the night, Thorold found himself, with tears streaming down his face, joining the rest, singing, "….that saved a wretch like me."

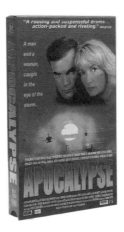